Bloodroot

Bloodroot

AARON ROY EVEN

Thomas Dunne Books / St. Martin's Press
New York

THOMAS DUNNE BOOKS.
An imprint of St. Martin's Press.

www.stmartins.com

Design and illustration by Clair Moritz

Library of Congress Cataloging-in-Publication Data

Even, Aaron Roy
Bloodroot / Aaron Roy Even.
p. cm.
"Thomas Dunne books."
ISBN 0-312-26561-1
1. Afro-American families—Fiction. 2. Brothers and sisters—Fiction. 3. Land tenure—Fiction. 4. Eviction—Fiction. 5. Virginia—Fiction. 6. Sheriffs—Fiction. 7. Murder—Fiction. I. Title.

PS3555.V323 B58 2000
813'.6—dc21 00-040226

First Edition: October 2000

10 9 8 7 6 5 4 3 2 1

For my parents,
Richard and Carol,
and for my dear one,
Monica

There I had sight of a gruesome prodigy
Beyond description: when the first stalk came torn
Out of the earth, and the root network burst,
Dark blood dripped down to soak and foul the soil.

—*The Aeneid*, Book III

The story goes that one member of the mob was a
12-year-old boy armed with a .22 caliber rifle.

—*The Crisis*, 1936

Bloodroot

1

1936

The good news arrived with her father one bitter snowstill evening in the first week of March: a position had opened with the county government, an honest position with modest salary and opportunity for advancement, and the chairman of the board agreed that she was the perfect candidate for the job. "Not a secretary," her father said, raising an emphatic finger, "an official representative, and they are specifically looking for a woman like you."

Past the window where he stood rubbing hands the snow was falling in windless silence through a vacuum of darkness. Fragments of the long winter, scraps of idle frustration and days without hope passed again through her mind, descending like the shed dust of a dismal road. And at the same time a school of phantoms assembled to grimace through the windowpane: gaunt-faced mothers and children and old men with their canes, a delegation of hungry and accusing eyes from all walks of life collecting from everywhere at once. One by one they pressed against the window and passed in an unbroken train back to the snow from which they emerged. She turned away to where her father knelt thrusting a poker in the fire. A cloud of sparks erupted and trailed off into falling ash. The house creaked ever slightly around them.

"I'll wear my blue dress," she said, "with a string of mama's pearls."

Her father said that sounded right. She looked terribly pretty in them.

"What do you think? Will they give me a chance?"

"You'd better believe they will."

She smiled. "I've worked hard for something like this."

"Just remember what we talked about. Keep your answers sharp but don't forget your manners."

"I won't."

"And mention your high marks in school, and volunteering for the WPA . . ."

It was all so simple and decided, the parts fit together so seamlessly and logically. At the interview her father's friend was charming as he explained the nature of the job and inscribed pallid whorls of smoke in the air with a negligent wave of his cigarette. An interesting job, he told her vaguely, with the cool, contented look of a man who has established himself in the world. And a difficult one, in many respects. The man before her, their former representative, he'd had a rough time of it. Just plain lacked a sense of tact and diplomacy. Would rush straight into things bullheadedly and end up leaving matters in a worse state than he'd found them. And he gave her to understand that these attributes—tact, diplomacy, or "charm," as he put it—were precisely what he needed most and what he saw clearly embodied in her like a seal upon a precious stone. He smiled at the metaphor. As for the work itself, she would be representing a new development project for the county board of supervisors, and that meant answering any questions the public might have, promoting the project among community groups, in the newspapers, serving as a spokesman for the board, and in a few special cases, negotiating terms for the sale of private lands. "Understand," he said, leaning forward and spreading his thick hands out over his desk, "that's thousands, tens of thousands in revenue. Heck of a lot of jobs. A real shot in the arm. A company from Pennsylvania—but you'll read all about it tonight. The word to remember is 'turpentine.' "

She accepted without hesitation.

The snow had let up a little but it was still bitterly cold outside and the sky a uniform gray, a stamped iron lid on the spine of the Blue Ridge Mountains. Stepping out onto the courthouse square, she felt flushed and impervious to cold. Her breath bloomed out before her, faded like words in a dream. She clutched the bundle of documents given her by the chairman and smiled in anticipation. At the corner where she waited for her father's car she began to rifle through the contents, but before she could begin to decipher them a gust of wind made her grasp the pages wildly, pressing them against her chest. She looked up and down the street at the glassy eyes of slush quietly winking in their asphalt beds; along the ledges and cornices of the government building icicles drooped like rows of stalactite growths elongated over the winter's methodical crawl. She returned the documents carefully to their folder and held them tight in her hands. Near and far there seemed nothing but that inverted plain of clouds stretching away to all horizons.

At home she drank a toast with her father. They sat across from one another in the kitchen as the sun sank behind snow-blurred hills, looking as if confused by the cheap white wine in their champagne glasses. Who could afford champagne these days? Even her father agreed. He was not a wasteful man. He drank exactly as he lived, in all ways guided by an instinctual economy and a belief in the simple fact of suffering, the necessity of self-denial. His eyes behind rounded spectacles were the calm blue tint of the mountains and his hair was slowly falling out, leaving a bald spot on top of his skull. She remembered brushing his hair as a child and how she imagined him a cat changing from brown to reddish in the sun. How he stretched like a lazy calico in his armchair and dozed with the fitful daydreams of evening in which time seemed lapsed in a blues tempo of darkening sun, darkening sky.

"It's almost too good to be true."

"What did I tell you? To the future . . ."

She felt a little flushed from the wine. "I thought there would be nothing, no work this year. I was afraid I'd be knitting sweaters."

"Well, things are never as bleak as they look."

"Such a lucky break," she laughed.

"You're not my daughter for nothing," he said.

Later that night at the foot of her bed she knelt and unfastened the pendant image of Mary her mother had worn round her neck—a tear-shaped copper disc the size of a penny hung from a delicate silver chain. The room was cast in a pale shade of moonlight. The only sounds were those of trees creaking beyond the window and her nightgown rustling as she shifted on her knees. But soon as she began to pray a strange thing happened: she faltered, lost her place, and had to start over again. Reciting her Hail Mary, she squinted and clutched at the pendant as if it might guide her words but only found herself concentrating very hard on nothing at all. She stopped. Opened her eyes. Again she began the recitation, but felt immediately an overpowering sense of silence stretched above her like open sky, the vast indifference of a turned ear. She composed herself and smiled self-critically, thinking that something was wrong with her. In a moment she would be ready, would try again, would feel the familiar comforting sense of acknowledgment however subtle and remote from physical life.

She lit a desk lamp and took the documents from their folder and went over the year-long history of soured relations that she was supposed to help set right. A poor land survey, shoddy record-keeping, and contrary statements of fact—but the main issue was a feud between the former representative and Negro caretakers of a valuable estate acquired under the terms of the Pennsylvania contract. Acquired in name but not yet purchased.

The Negroes were stubbornly refusing to sell their share. Soon she was so absorbed that she completely forgot her failed attempts at prayer and read on into the thickening night. When the clock struck twelve she was still sitting up hunched over the documents, trying to connect certain details to gaps in the narrative she sensed were either missing or obscured.

The hour passed into lethargy. An icicle moon appeared, eclipsed by breaking clouds.

"I wonder if they misunderstood," she said aloud, in a tired whisper.

The tip of a tree limb dabbed the crusted windowpane.

"Or the county man might have been too pushy, or somehow provoked them." She rose from her chair and turned off the lamp but only lay awake in her bed, dreaming the days to come. They seemed very distant and pliable like memories of a future self branching into various memories, various possible selves: but in each possibility there was the strain of a single-minded will bound and accountable to the origin like a root under earth.

Outside the snow continued to fall. All night it gusted and trickled, muffling the house, the stable, the rolling yard, in a field of unbroken white.

A drab ring of lukewarm coffee settled at the bottom of her cup. Through the fogged oval window of the diner, the courthouse and the government office building appeared in bleary double image, beaded with droplets of melting ice. Sitting at the table beside her, a woman in a long shapeless smocklike rag of an overcoat muttered strangely over her plate of food and scraped her shoe heels now and again in mysterious exasperation. Elsa glanced at her wristwatch. Her father was running late, he would be another half hour at least. She flipped the pages of the *Daily Progress*, killing time. Only one article caught her eye, conspicuous for its tone of irony, its worldly yawn in the face of another Nazi revision:

Berlin, March 9—(AP)—Christ's Sermon on the Mount has been adapted to a modern German view by the Reichsbishop Ludwig Mueller. The new official version reads: "If thy comrade smite thee in the face in his wrath, it is not always right to smite him back. It is more manly to preserve a superior calm. Mayhap thy comrade will repent."

She shut the newspaper and stood; a chuckle lodged in her throat like a crust of dry bread. You might as well have a look around, she told herself. But she only stood there considering the front-page headline—*Ex-Governor Pollard Claims the Pilgrims Landed in Virginia.* Was there a prize for absurdity today? She had spent the better part of her first day at work attempting to divine her duties, but all she could come up with were a few letters to answer, some notes to type up. The hours had passed in rummaging through the same documents the chairman had given her previously. She now had a store of odd facts committed to memory: a distilling plant with an average thirty- to forty-barrel capacity could handle a yield of about five thousand acres. Crude turpentine in various stages was known as "run," "chip," and "scrape."

Meantime the woman in the overcoat observed Elsa suspiciously, muttering softly as if hoping to catch her in some malfeasance. After a minute Elsa opened her briefcase and folded the newspaper away. As she paid her bill to the cook, the woman suddenly blurted out: "Well done, that's what I said. So how come I see blood?" Elsa glanced across the diner, then back to the cook who stared malignly and hopelessly into the open cash register. She thanked him and stepped outside.

In the street remnants of the snow lay shoveled in mounds of distorted gray slush. Nobody was out. A lone gust of wind blew down the street driving leaves that turned curling and skittering on the air. She saw a few dark silhouettes in the shop windows and a couple of boys running along the sidewalk with scarves trailing from their necks. Stopping before the courthouse stairs, she looked up into the sudden clarity of sky. For a long time she stood looking round the snowbright square with her leather briefcase dangling from her mittened hand. In the center of the square, astride the war monument's limestone pedestal, a nameless Confederate soldier regarded the town with a badly weathered snarl. The faded brick buildings, Baptist church, and hardware store all were aligned in a familiar and comforting arrangement of shapes. On the opposite end the post office still needed painting and the grocery displayed its wooden crates of potatoes and dried Indian corn.

But instead of going straightaway to find her father, she decided to walk down the street to see the old corrugated iron bridge that spanned the river. As a girl she had thrilled to leap from the rail into the purling water while the other children screamed. This and so many other memories complicated and clouded her vision. The town was built on the slope of a hill, and clumps of mostly poor, sulking houses trailed away from the center along streets separated by social code and custom. Yet she was jarred by the unshakable impression of a smallness and uniformity she had never noticed before. Stepping beneath the railroad overpass was like crossing the threshold of a town in miniature. She continued along the sidewalk and on toward the picture theater, which appeared deserted in the waning afternoon hours, before the evening's matinee would attract a crowd of patrons gathered eagerly round the ticket booth, ogling the various tempting posters with their images of lovelorn heroines and pistols firing in the dark, maudlin passions in exotic, distant settings, the promise of some forbidden desire.

She switched her briefcase from one hand to the other. Her breath as she walked came out in a vanishing steam, like the haze rising from melting snow, and her heels caught here and there on uneven bricks jutting from the sidewalk. She continued downhill, passing dime stores run by aging widows and the occasional, usually depressed private office of some rogue businessman or professional doctor or lawyer, the highly educated castoffs of well-to-do families. On the front doors their nameplates were carved out of wood or else painted in calligraphic lettering: Madison, Popham, Pope. For each name inscribed she knew the family history and current state of the children, whether prosperous or scandalized. Through the windows she could just make out the corners of handsome desks and bookshelves lined with volumes, or the casual tilting head, turned away from her, emitting a perpetual stream of smoke from the end of a fashionable cigarette.

Beyond their insular walls the town faded into folds and pockets of the hillside where tawdry houses cramped together, sometimes springing up overnight and vanishing as quick, then to field and orchard and farm. And farther out along the riverbank the Negro neighborhoods: a world unknown.

In the pale evening sun a neck of the river curved away between sloping embankments and the shallows glimmered over hubs of rounded sandstone. The water's depths showed black and placid, stirred only by an occasional gas bubble or paddle of a fishing skiff. She turned down an intersecting sidewalk and descended the road to the iron bridge. The warehouses and squatter shacks lining the banks now extended over the entire course like campgrounds on the side of a highway and she could see a group of men in blue jackets heaping scrap metal from a junk lot onto a flatbed truck and farther on a ferry inching toward the opposite shore, leaving its sludge of gray-black ash sluicing in the sky. As she went on the sidewalk narrowed to the point where it nearly merged with the road and she had to be careful when heedless traffic whooshed by, cars and trucks crossing the bridge to connect with the north-south state road, racing to places obscured by billboards reading O-BOY BREAD WITH VITAMIN D and LUCKIES ARE LESS ACID. Between the vertical posts of the bridge were little enclaves where she could stand and watch the drifting water, and she stopped there and put her briefcase down against the grate, leaning out with her elbows on the rail. She remembered standing in this very spot on the day she was accepted to the academy and she remembered thinking: this will be the bridge I cross to get away from here. A cold wind swept down the hillside. It whipped her hair wildly about her face and she raised her hands to shield her eyes.

Once the river had brought white explorers up from the coastland by way of the Chesapeake and James to territory inhabited by Creek, Shawnee, Catawba, and Delaware, which they called Shenandoah or Daughter of the Stars. The explorers came under orders from a London company named Virginia and in canoes and by foot they fanned over the foothills toward the rolling mountains, scraping and searching for the means to sustain themselves so they might see their homes again and justify claims of profitability in pounds of tobacco or tales of elusive mineral veins. As Elsa looked down from the bridge she could imagine them slipping upriver or huddling in forts established by profiteers, some of them betrayed, hacked or shot, some slowly starved, and many, many never accounted for in what scarce records she had found in the library archives. No visible traces remained. They left no mark on the hillsides, built nothing that could last, and perhaps revealed their imprint only where they had caused something to vanish along with themselves. And that same calm stretch of water still traced its way down from the mountains, shallowing in winter and swelling in spring, wheeling in slow rotation where the current lagged. At the edge of the channel a tire bobbed uselessly, coated in algae and motor oil.

Watch your step, young lady."

"It's all right. I'm wearing rubber shoes."

"Over here—river's jumped the bank again." Montgomery leaned against the bumper of his squad car, straddling a pool of muddy water in the road. He had been kind enough to drive her the two miles out of town, wanting himself to "keep things moving along." And though she could not quite see it from where they stood, she was aware of the estate just up the road, of the visit she would have to make there soon. "It's your typical crazy March," he said. The air was yet thick with the weight and smell of rain. "How's your old man these days?"

"Fine, thanks."

"Your old man, he's all right with me. Let me tell you something: once I had a little investment—nothing at all, really—that I'd put aside for the day when they go and elect someone younger for the job."

"Someone else the sheriff of Zion?"

"One day it'll happen."

"Age, youth, isn't all the difference it's built up to be."

"Maybe not. But let's just say that youth has a way of advertising and recommending itself, whereas a man who's worked in a job for a number of years has a way of becoming like a piece of furniture, a sitting chair to decorate an office. And when something happens to make people want to change that office, well, what do you suppose is the simplest way to do that?"

"I'm not going to give you the satisfaction of a response."

"Get a new chair," the sheriff said with a laugh. "Your father, he understood what I mean, which is how come I end up owing him a favor. He kept me dry when the damn market broke. All that money lost, just swept away. I don't imagine I'll ever have a chance to pay him in kind."

She remembered those days, though she was only a schoolgirl at the time. Her mother had been preparing her for confirmation, reading stories from a simplified children's Bible that Elsa swallowed with rapt serious-mindedness. The stock market was just another of the unexplained adult preoccupations her father dismissed with a vague shrug. But her mother had thought he would never sleep for all the telephone ringing and midnight knocking on doors.

"You're a lucky girl." The sheriff walked to the edge of the road and peered down the sloping ditch in the direction of the river. A swollen pond of orange-brown drainage had overrun the embankment and washed out the yard and in the center of the pond it was lapping up the stilted sides of the house and welling almost into the doorway. A ways ahead of them a stringy white woman and three squirming children leaned passively against the moving truck, safe and dry on the road. The bed of the truck was stacked with furniture wrapped in towels and sheets, with chicken boxes holding pots and pans and other necessary implements. The husband was wading back and forth between house and truck, pulling their belongings behind him in a little boat. "Should of condemned that place a long time ago," the sheriff quipped.

Elsa stood beside him and watched. The husband was just setting out from the house with a chest of drawers floating sideways on the boat. His withered legs slopped through the dark water which in places rose to his knees and in places to his waist. Here and there a rootless tree arched over, drooping limbs, while its inverted reflection crabbed along the water's surface. The husband waded on through the muck with a fierce scowl on his face, dragging his load by a ragged rope.

"Know what this place is gonna be?"

"Outbuildings," Elsa said.

"Outbuildings?"

"Warehouses, storage sheds." She pointed down the road. "The boilers and generators down there. At least that's what the diagrams say."

"Well, that company better be keen on levees."

"They'll fix it up. Better than these folks, anyway."

"Should of sworn out a warrant against them," the sheriff said. He had a resigned, fatalistic expression, a quality of stubborn inaction as if he were a kind of element or sediment, something intrinsic and inalterable like a stratum of the earth itself. "I never understood people that build their house longside of a riverbank. It takes an uncommon dullness of mind. You might figure the first time it runs over, well, give it another try. But Christ's sake it happens every year. You think they might catch on, save themselves the hassle. But they can't figure it out: that's how come they so poor."

"Perhaps they just wanted a chance to sell."

The sheriff shrugged. "You'd think they been evicted."

"Well, they signed the papers. If they want to go back—"

"They don't want to go back. Sullen is all, like a pack of crows."

From her perch on the rust-red wheel well of the truck the woman looked up suddenly with weary trepidation, as if she knew what they were talking about. On each of her knees an infant child was balanced and a scraggly boy squatted in the dirt at her feet.

"Maybe I'll go have a word with her," Elsa said.

"Suit yourself."

"You going back to the car?"

"I know a waste of breath when I see one."

Elsa walked slowly down the road. As she came near the woman, the stranger, and realized how close they were in age if not circumstance, she felt the first prickings of self-consciousness and set her face against them as an actress preparing to take the stage puts aside her private terror and assumes the mask of her character. The woman straightened and looked instinctively for her husband—still sloshing up the incline where the gravel drive should have been—then looked back at Elsa in near-panic as if a gun were being pointed directly at her forehead. Meantime the infants squirmed about her knees as if trying to wriggle free.

"Mrs . . . Watts," Elsa said.

The woman nodded, her eyes turned down. The straw hair closed over her face like a curtain and she waited with studied patience and passivity, an unyielding retreat inside the cavity of her own skull and skin.

"How's everything?"

The woman nodded again: "Fine."

"And the children?"

"Fine."

"Are they excited to move into a brand-new house?"

"Yes'm."

Elsa trained a smile on the squirming children and they stared back with a frank, goggle-eyed curiosity.

"Terrible about the weather," she said.

"Yes'm."

"I hear it's flooding all the way in Ohio, even."

The woman glanced up at her for a fraction of a moment with feigned interest and then looked away to where her husband was wrestling to free the boat from a snag. He had to let the boat drift backward on its own momentum and then reposition the chest of drawers and work carefully around the obstacle.

"It'll be nice living on higher ground," Elsa said.

"I 'xpect so."

"So everything's all right."

"Quit, honey," the woman said. The little boy was jutting his head back and forth between his mother's scrawny knees as if they were prison bars.

"My name's Elsa," she said, bending low. "What's yours?"

"You the gov'ment lady?" the boy said.

The smile Elsa was fixing on him quivered and slowly reformed.

"I guess you could say that."

"Know what my daddy says?"

"Hush—" the woman hissed, her knees locking him in a vise. His face grew suddenly distorted and piteous in fear of her tone of voice. And then sharply to Elsa: "Don't pay him any mind. He wants a whipping."

The husband was dragging himself and the boat out of shallowing water. He rasped out something unintelligible, unrecognizable.

"I'd better let you help him," Elsa said.

"Yes'm," the woman said, though she remained seated, the children bobbing and writhing about her knees.

"If you need anything—have any questions—"

"Yes'm."

"Well, goodbye then."

"Afternoon."

On the way back to town the hydroelectric plant went dead. Lights winked out inside the government building and when they arrived the sewers were overflowing into the streets and her office ceiling began to spiderweb and drip. She spent six days at home with the road washed out, waiting for repairs. There was nothing whatever for her to do.

2

Wednesday, the first of April. A cold, brumal hill and a path sogged with mud, winding long, blood-colored channels through the slickening clay. The streamlets trickling, joining and forking, hissing down the gradual slope leading to the cemetery gate. Stands of centuries-old chestnuts and oaks drooping their new leaves over the headstones, shuddering; the graves stood the deluge with impunity. She stood shivering at the doorstep and fumbling with her umbrella. She wore her rubber shoes and carried her briefcase, worried about her youthful inexperience and conspicuous white skin. Would they even listen to her? And if so for manners' sake, would they wait behind unblinking stares and laugh when she had gone? At the bottom of the hill her driver was dozing peacefully in the car with his feet resting on the dash. She knocked. Listened to the wind rake and die in the sedge. It was a well-constructed cottage with a stone base and lean-to porch, but she could hear everything inside: a chair scraping back and the creak of familiar weight on the floorboards. A mumbled word—what was it? Then silence, suspicious and self-aware, until the door hinge squeaked raucously and she summoned up a smile from God knows where.

Inside the cottage was damp and warm, pleasantly kept, a smell of sidemeat and fresh-ground coffee. On a square pine table a coal oil lamp hissed softly to itself; the flame in its glass shell spun a luminous carousel over the walls and ceiling. The woodstove was hot and crackling. For a moment she was completely distracted by awkward greetings and the creeping threat of a sneeze. "Excuse me—" she began, and released violently, drew breath and sneezed again, and came careening back into self-consciousness, shameful of her first impression yet full of the simple power of her presence.

She closed her umbrella and set it upside down against the door.

"Bless you, miss," the Negro said, at once stepping back and making a stunted gesture toward the woodstove. "You need something for that cough."

"Oh, don't trouble yourself."

"It's no trouble at all. A little coffee?"

His voice was a pipe smoker's, edged with what was perhaps the tail end of a winter cold. He was short, thick, around fifty years old. What hair was left to him formed a faint gray band above the ears. His shoulders and hands had been shaped by a skilled labor—most likely logging or carpentry—and he lumbered in his movements with the awkward grace of a man balancing on stones.

"Kind of a wet morning for a visit," he said.

"Yes," she said, "and cold. Too cold for spring, don't you think?"

He brought her a faintly steaming cup of coffee—it must have been left over from his breakfast—and she sipped at it leanly, with a touch of reserve.

"It ain't spring yet. She's coming late this year."

"I'm afraid you're right."

He looked at her incuriously. "Come to pay your respects?"

"Pardon?"

"Just let me root out an umbrella. I can show you where the whole family's laid resting name by name if you please."

"Oh no," she said. "If your name's Wesley, I'm here to speak with you."

He cut his glance down and away, as if distracted by something on the floor. Was he thinking how to get rid of her? There was a danger, after all. It lay there, unspoken. No white boss here; the whole order was thrown out of whack. Or perhaps he simply mistook her for one of the numerous well-to-do town ladies representing a social cause or offering charity to the less fortunate. A few polite "Yes ma'ams," and she would go. But when he raised his eyes he only nodded without expression and moved behind the table where the lamp unspooled its dim netting of light.

"I ought to tell you who I am," she said.

"Hold on," he said, as if he'd already guessed. "Let me call my sister."

"I wouldn't want to disturb her."

"Well, try explaining how she was left out of a business meeting."

Elsa smiled in such a way as he could have interpreted kindness or condescension. "Really, it's more an informative visit than anything . . ."

Wesley had turned toward the back of the room, ignoring her for the moment, but he paused and asked her to please sit down. He motioned toward a wicker chair pulled askew from the table's edge before lumbering stiffly on, stepping carefully on his right heel as though it gave him trouble. She straightened the chair and set her coffee on the table and sat. Her briefcase was leaning against her leg and spreading a molasses-colored stain over the hardwood floor. Abstractedly she lifted it to her lap, then set it down again. He had vanished into the next room but she was aware of his careful movements, the creaking beneath his heavy feet, a whispered word she couldn't catch. In front of her the lamp hissed and fluttered, the oil running low.

When he appeared again his face had an erased, hollow look. He sat across from her and knitted his hands into a tight fist. He looked unsettled, edgy, as though required suddenly to improvise on a stage where something has gone dreadfully wrong. "She ain't here," he mumbled, "must have gone to run some chore—"

"In all this weather?"

"She gets ideas I don't pretend to understand."

"Well, I'm sure she'll turn up soon."

"I suppose so," he said, "but she catches cold too easy, and I'll be up all night fixing tea and honey."

"My name's Elsa Childs."

He nodded respectfully.

"I'm with the county's board of supervisors, and we've been knocking doors down this way to explain a development proposal under consideration. Usually this sort of thing might take a while, even years, to get going. But this is a special circumstance. And so here I am, knocking doors like a Bible salesman, and I'm pleased to say the response has been overwhelmingly good."

"What proposal? You mean that turpentine plant?"

"You may have heard something of it already."

"Sure I have. The last man all but talked us into the ground but I figured it was all squared away—he said we could do what we pleased, for all he cared."

"That man is no longer employed by the county."

"Fired?"

"I'm afraid so."

Wesley nodded. "To tell the truth, miss, he got what he deserved. Twice I had to help him off the premises, he was so boozed up. I even caught him napping in the main house. No idea how he got himself in there but I know for a fact how he left."

Elsa smiled sadly. "The board realizes there was a problem and that's why I'm here. We're sorry if he caused you any trouble."

"And of course nothing he said made any sense, because who would want to buy an old place like this—" He gestured vaguely. "And without consulting the family? I actually thought he might of come to the wrong house."

"Perhaps we should simply disregard whatever he told you and start from scratch."

"Well, now," Wesley said, "I am confused."

"Naturally," she said. And she patiently explained what the proposal came down to: there was a chance to have a modern naval stores plant constructed right along the river—turpentine, pine oil, everything they used to make the hard way, with catch-cups and small stills. It was all going to be done at a rate and quality they couldn't have imagined before. "And I can tell you what the chairman believes, we can't lose the opportunity."

Wesley was staring ahead as if waiting intently for something to emerge out of thin air. "I've stripped pines since I was a boy, and there's many round here could say the same. But I think I'm too old—"

"I've got nothing to do with employment," she said.

He then gave her a quizzical look that asked what the hell she was bothering him for, but when she mentioned the words "potential zoning conflict" within the context of a sentence so long-winded and circumspect that even she lost track of where it had begun, his face went blank again and revealed nothing of what he understood. She retreated upon pleasantries.

"It's a lovely old estate. I saw the cemetery as I came up the hill. Do you know how old it is?"

"Excuse me—"

"How old is the estate?"

"Built in eighteen and forty-something . . ." He trailed off.

"You know who the original owners were?"

"Peers family."

"But they no longer live here."

He raised his eyebrows. The prospect of talking family history seemed to put him more at ease. "Well, if you mean do they no longer reside here, that wouldn't be true. They're resting out there on that hill where you passed by. On the other hand, if you mean do the Peers family, their descendants, do they own this estate?"

"Yes, that's it," she said.

"Mr. Peers had a sister when he died, the only close relation that I know of. But he didn't like her husband at all. A congressman from Maryland, 'jackass congressman' what Mr. Peers liked to say—" He paused and let out a low, nervous chuckle. "They never spent more than a few minutes in each other's company. Christmas, funerals, that sort of thing. I believe the estate went to Mrs. Peers, and passed down through her family."

"I see," she said. "And what became of them?"

"Packed and moved to Florida, excepting the old lady. She went to rest right here, longside her husband, and that's just the way she wanted it."

"Leaving you and your sister to look after things."

He ground his hands together like broken gears.

"Is something wrong?" she said.

He frowned as if preoccupied. "I'm awful sorry, Miss Childs. But I can't decide where my sister could have got to, and listen to the wind pick up."

In fact the wind had died that moment but the rain was falling thickly, in tantrum fits. Past the window, snarls of thunder broke and crumbled, echoing over the distance, while the rainheads steadily advanced upon the hill.

He looked expectantly toward the door.

"Excuse me," Elsa said, standing. "We can talk some other time. Maybe later in the week?"

"That'd be just fine," he muttered.

"Pleased to meet you," she said, "and I appreciate the coffee."

He was already turned, fishing for his coat and hat among a narrow closetful of shirts, trousers, sweaters, Sunday dresses, all hanging from an orderly series of pegs and hooks arranged over a pair of black shoes, a few ragged workboots, and leaning stock-down at each of the shadowed corners, a gun inconspicuous as a walking cane. "What?" he said.

"The coffee."

"Oh. It's no trouble, miss."

She was standing beside the table wondering if there was something more she ought to say. Whether to speak of the board's plans for the estate (the main house would be converted to an office, the stretch of land along the riverbank a loading dock) and the price the county would be offering for this little corner, their cottage, or whether that would be in some way unseemly, better not to rush, get the feel of the terrain before she went too fast. She had her briefcase and umbrella in hand; long drips of rain wormed from the ends onto the tops of her rubber shoes.

"Careful as you go down," he said, showing her through the door, and later she would interpret this as a warning.

Her days quickly settled into an established pattern: the routine of work. It was a kind of scripted existence, an unchanging relationship between expectation and fulfillment in which she moved easily, even thoughtlessly at times. It began each morning when the sun flooded her open shades around six o'clock. Even when it was cloudy, when a soft rain bowed the long grasses of the fields, she woke at the same hour with the same nagging tug of uncertainty, a residue of dreams she couldn't remember. She would drag herself out of bed, a little groggily at first, but soon enough she whipped herself into a state of determined readiness. She bathed and dressed before her mirror, her carefully chosen suits walking the line between acknowledging and masking her youth. Then she went downstairs to fix breakfast.

First she made the coffee, filling the back chamber of the percolator with water, opening the pentagonal lid and spooning in grounds that smelled faintly of burnt chocolate. Then she set the percolator on the stovetop and lit the gas burner with a match. About this time she would hear footsteps padding gently above her and know that her father was awake and getting dressed. Through the open window the repetitive high chatter of the birds sounded like an orchestra of damaged clarinets. Next she went about frying his eggs—sunnyside up, the yolk broken—and toasting the bread which they ate smothered in peach or blackberry preserves. When her father came down to the kitchen they exchanged good-mornings and the usual pleasantries about the day. If he was in a good enough mood he might come waltzing over to kiss her cheek; if soured, he would settle into the newspaper with his cup of coffee and make biting remarks about politics.

When they were finished eating she cleaned the dishes while he went out to get the car engine warmed up. He was the kind of person who took every available precaution with his car, though he would happily run a horse near to death. It was as if the years had taught him faith in the essential durability of flesh and bone in contrast to the fragile and vulnerable nature of machines. After ten or fifteen minutes of perfunctory noisemaking on the gravel drive, he would finally permit them to get in the car and drive off toward town.

It was only a little over a mile to town and in the days of her childhood she would not have thought twice about walking that distance, but now it seemed tiring even to consider it. Occasionally, if her father was feeling ill or was not going to his office at the regular hour, she would put on a pair of old shoes and make the familiar journey on foot. But rarely was the established pattern interrupted: most days he dropped her off in front of the government building and continued down the avenue toward his bank, where he parked in his usual spot against the curb.

She was on stage from the moment she entered the office door, smiling, wishing good-mornings, accepting hellos and polite inquiries about her health. From the start the junior men had appeared to regard her with the benign toleration accorded a crazy cousin or aunt, while some of the secretaries took a surprisingly harder line. Chief among her secret enemies was the receptionist, Lynn Ann. Ten or more years her elder, impeccably well mannered, even slightly pretty in an efficient, no-nonsense sort of way, she nursed a grudge that left Elsa bewildered, with an inexplicable sense of having somehow given offense. Yet she had searched all her actions, every spoken word since her first day. She'd done nothing wrong that she knew of. "Hello, Lynn Ann," Elsa said each morning. The woman merely adjusted her lips in a line that was not quite a smile and chirped "Hi there" back at her with a flat friendly inflection. Her face adopted that same flat friendly look which impeded any attempt to read her private feelings. "How are you today?" she asked. "Fine," Elsa said, "and you?" She drew her lips into that line that was not quite a smile: "Busy, busy." This was about the extent of their conversation. When Elsa arrived at her office on the second floor, she often encountered Lynn Ann's primary form of revenge: the daily mail was nowhere to be seen. She would have to trudge back downstairs and ask for it. By this time Lynn Ann would be busily accepting compliments from one of the junior men, who were endlessly and spinelessly flattering her looks, or else absorbed in some task requiring every modicum of her concentration, so that she made Elsa feel the full weight of her interruption.

Settled at last at her desk, she would begin answering the day's hailstorm of letters; the chairman insisted on prompt replies to all correspondence. Such menial tasks seemed to take up the bulk of her time, so that often she scarcely had enough hours in the day to consider the more important aspects of her job. In her mind the letters to various local newspapers, businesses, churches, lodges, country clubs, all merged into a single letter she was forever bent at typing. Her only break from the tedium came when she answered the numerous personal inquiries from anyone and everyone with an interest, no matter how remote or dubious, in the plant proposal.

"For example, one of the secretaries—a trite little thing, she reeks of cheap perfume—she comes over this morning and sticks her head in my door. There's someone asking for me downstairs, she says, and can she send him on up? Well, I had no appointments, but I figured I could at least take the time to see what it was about. So a few minutes later, up comes this drab skinny man with a long gray moustache, about fifty years old, with a straw hat locked in his hands. So I stand up and invite him in, I go around and shake his hand and sit him on down and find out his name is Shiflett and he's here about this piece of land he owns by the river. At first I think it must be one of the lots we've purchased. But I don't recall his name from anywhere, so I say, 'Has anyone from the county explained this plant proposal to you?' He looks at me respectfully and quietly, just turning the straw hat slightly in his hands, like it was a kind of windup clock, and says, 'Well, no ma'am.' So I go about my regular speech setting forth the reasons for the proposal and its many benefits to the community, listing the names of prominent boosters and what they've had to say on the subject, and I go into detail about how the county is fairly compensating those families with property affected by the land sale. It isn't a short speech, either. It takes about half an hour. And all that time he's just sitting there respectful and quiet, turning that straw hat in his hands, with his moustache hanging down over his mouth like one of those parlor photographs of Civil War soldiers. Finally, when I'm just about out of breath, I ask him: 'Do you have any questions, Mr. Shiflett?' And you know what he says?"

"What did he say?" Her father was already chuckling in anticipation, a soft half-choked sputtering sound. She looked across the verandah where he sat in a straight-backed chair sipping a glass of bourbon. It was early evening and the sky was poised between light and dark as if undecided how to proceed.

"He says, 'I'm just here about a property line is all. Because this neighbor's mule keeps crossing over and trampling my gardenias . . .' "

Her father burst out in a full-throated laugh.

"All right, it's funny," Elsa said, rocking slightly on the swing where she sat cross-legged in a sundress and sweater. In the yard sudden clusters of pale green leaves hung fringelike from the bushes and hackberry trees. "But what gets me is knowing this secretary, she knew beforehand, and it was all just some kind of practical joke, something to waste my time—not to mention his—Shiflett's . . ."

Her father leaned and stretched back his arms, extending from rolled-up and rumpled shirtsleeves. His jacket hung from the chairback and he had taken off his tie and thrown it onto the tray where his bottle of bourbon stood at hand. "Well, that's just the kind of typical nonsense you've got to learn to put up with. You take my bank. Think it gets any better as you climb higher up, when you're the manager or even director? Believe me, it just gets worse."

"But who would play a trick like that on you?" She pulled her sweater tight against the yet-creeping chill.

Her father let out a brief cynical grunt. "Elsa, for every step you take in life, there's someone looking to trip you up. Right now, these other ladies, they're probably jealous. Maybe a little bit frightened."

Elsa brushed at the top of her foot where a bug had landed. Her father waved his hand listlessly through the air and continued:

"See, you're a troublemaker, even if you don't realize it yet. Likely this woman, this receptionist, has been a kind of office matriarch for years, a combination two parts mother and one part unattainable girlfriend for these junior men who go about flattering her with their attentions and hoping to keep on her good side so as to get their mail delivered on time. Now you come along, competing with her—"

"That's ridiculous," Elsa said, "we don't even have the same job."

"The way she sees it, outstripping her even, by dint of your education and family connections—that figures into it as well. You said yourself that soon as you walk through the door these fellows are wishing you good morning, asking after your health. So she's dying to set things back the way they were, back when the only health they asked after was hers. Or, at the very least, to demonstrate where your influence ends, and what price you'll pay for interfering—"

"That's just crazy."

"Interfering by crossing onto her territory, whether purposeful or not, like that mule Shiflett was complaining about." He set his glass of bourbon on the tray and inspected the yard with contented and melancholic eyes. Crickets were droning faintly in the garden and a strong smell of damp pollen hung in the air.

"If that's true," Elsa said, "then these people, they are just—"

"Petty, trifling, vindictive, and weak," her father said. He sat back and laughed. "You may as well get used to it," he said, "that's my advice."

Elsa looked out where the darkening shapes of trees cringed and swayed. She wondered if he was right, and if so, how long she would be marked as a troublemaker, a problem. Abruptly the telephone rang. Her father got up and went inside to answer it. Elsa recalled the feeling she'd had earlier that day—it was not the first time—that a buzz of critical whispers was circling her. She couldn't understand why, or guess what they were saying, because she moved in a ripple of silence that spread at her every step. Rooms that she entered went suddenly quiet, and voices lowered in the hall as they passed her doorway. It sounded self-conscious, maybe even paranoid. After all, the chairman had assured her that she was doing an excellent job. What could they be whispering about? When her father returned from the telephone he calmly sat and resumed sipping his bourbon. He had a good-natured scowl on his face, the look of a man who has grown used to having his patience tested.

"I feel like Moses said in the desert."

"What do you mean?"

"In the desert, the wilderness. All the Israelites are complaining about this and that . . . and on top of everything one day they get a craving for meat. They keep on whining, 'At least we had meat back in Egypt.' "

"I don't know," she said.

Suddenly her father's face lit up with the fire of a street-corner preacher and he raised his hands, the shot glass glinting like an offering: "So Moses says to God, 'If this is the way it's going to be, just kill me now!' " His choked laugh tumbled off the verandah into the open yard. "I tell you," he said, "I tell you what . . ."

"Who was that on the phone?" Elsa said.

As quickly as it had come over him, the spell broke; he waved his hand in vague dismissal. "Oh, they don't know when to quit."

"You think that's what it is. Because I'm your daughter?"

"What?"

"That business with Shiflett. The others . . ."

He looked at her in surprise. "Elsa, it cuts both ways. If anyone thought that was the case he'd be asking you to the picture show." Slowly he stood and lifted his jacket off the chair-back, fixing her with a worn and humorous look. He pointed drowzily toward a far corner of the yard. "Remember when that stable back there was full of horses?"

"Sure I do. Old Ebony."

"You were terrified of that horse."

"Who wouldn't be? She bucked."

Her father laughed. "She was a pussycat. She ate sugar cubes off your mother's palm." He removed his glasses and wiped them on his jacket pocket. "It's getting dark out here. Why don't we go inside and make something for dinner?"

I don't know what I expected. Alone in her room with the lamplight thrown limpidly over her desk, she thought, *There's no way he would know, nothing in his experience that would tell him otherwise.* Her papers fanning out of a crisp tan folder lay there with a neglected, forlorn air like scraps of trash. While she looked down at the perplexing disarray, she remembered how her father had come out of the university near to first in his class (whose own father had received his only education in the U.S. Army) and proceeded straightaway and without incident into a series of respectable and lucrative jobs with insurance companies in Norfolk and Richmond, before settling finally at the bank in Zion. A town whose attraction for him had consisted mainly in the vision of a graceful young woman with chestnut hair who emerged from the bank's glass doors on a Friday morning in June wearing a yellow sundress and hat and holding a white leather pocketbook with a copper clasp in her hands. She had barely noticed him, grazing him with her eyes sun-squinted and solitary while he held the door and nodded with customary businesslike courtesy. He was still nodding a minute later in his dazzled mind; he spoke to her and she replied not coldly, seeming curious, even interested, so that swelled with courage he asked if she would lunch with him at . . . But she had long since walked away up the sidewalk in the direction of the town square. It was this image that stayed with him after the interview and subsequent meeting with the bank's directors and pursued him all the way back to Richmond, where his friends thought he was crazy to consider a position in some small town. But the image was speaking in a voice soft, sibilant, more powerful than theirs, causing him to begin packing his things, though he did not know yet where he was going to live. A purpose vaguely driving him west and north out of the flat riverbottom country where the James lumbered heavy and mud-logged toward the ocean.

He found a small four-room bungalow recently vacated on the edge of town and moved in without bothering to unpack his boxes, in the understanding that it was a temporary circumstance which could not be amended until he had gone farther toward his purpose. Because he would be incapable of choosing the right place before he knew the first thing about her, before *her* even took on a proper name. So he started his job and settled into learning the business, rising from his bed in the morning and putting on a shirt and tie, eating breakfast at a diner and proceeding straight to the office, where he was absorbed in a warm and reassuring abstrusity, returning at the end of the day rumpled and wearisome, eating at a cheap restaurant and reading a wrinkled newspaper left over from earlier in the day. He did not know how long it would go on like this. He understood that he had no right to question his fate, to imagine that it would ever be different. That the woman would ever come into the bank again. That he would be able to meet her, speak with her. That she would not turn out to be engaged (he did not remember a ring on the hand clutching that white leather pocketbook) or disinterested, foolish, a snob. He just continued on with his established routine, a little worried perhaps but hardly deterred, still in the full-blown flower of his confidence. A confidence built on the quasi-religious conviction that a man can control his own destiny, can shape the future through hard work and intelligence and perseverance. Or perhaps that was just the way he liked to tell the story. It was possible he'd lain awake at night, sweating, cursing himself with mechanical self-disgust, despising the nameless image that inhabited his sleepless hours, making plans to return to Richmond the following week. But that a certain cowardice held him: he could not yet face up to failure the way all men do and must. So the routine continued . . .

And that he should ever succeed in his purpose, much less be introduced to the woman-image (her name, Elsa's mother's name, was Evelyn May) within six months at a benefit for the Women's Christian Temperance Union and be engaged to her within a year now struck Elsa as absurd, almost sinister good fortune. The charming romantic anecdote told and retold over dinner tables throughout her childhood took on an aspect of disguised ruthlessness. And at the same time it showed a flippant disregard for the odds of chance, like a man staking everything on a hand of cards and drawing twenty-one. Elsa's aunt, visiting one Fourth of July, had said: "You know that story puts me in mind of the world's fastest racehorse. He got put by accident on the dog track and broke the record books." Her father had said: "Well, that's just the kind of thing you would say, isn't it?" To which she had replied: "Speaking from the dog's point of view, I'd say you ran a hell of a race." At the time Elsa had not understood the adult jibes. But now his story caused her, too, to flush with indignation. Somewhere a rule of essential fairness had been violated. She asked herself: why should some without cause have such fortune, while others go lonely?

She next saw Wesley unexpectedly in the center of town heading toward the railroad overpass with his hands crunched in his trouser pockets and a cap pulled aslant over his eyes. It was more than three weeks since their first meeting and Elsa felt the negligence acutely. But the chairman had kept her busy with a thousand smaller things, waving off her worry with casual unconcern. By now the weather had settled and warmed. The April day was such that the street glittered a thousand needlepoints of sun and the glare made him appear dark, huddled, depthless—a cardboard cut-out making its stiff deceptive way through the street, dragged perhaps by an invisible child. She followed. It was Saturday afternoon and the streets were crowded with cars, children, elderly grandparents strolling arm in arm. The dogwoods were in bloom, flowering pink and white along the main avenue. On the opposite sidewalk a fat clown with a wig and false nose was twisting balloons and making rapt, wide-eyed expressions of wonder and dismay for a tangle of noisy onlookers. She edged her way to a clearing, mindful of the good shoes she wore, the dress that fluttered at her calves. She had been waiting for her father to arrive but he was late as usual and so the sudden appearance of Wesley was convenient in many respects and already she was having pleasure imagining the empty space she had occupied at the table of an outdoor cafe and the confusion of her father in discovering himself alone.

She was on a clear track now and could see him well ahead, an ungainly shape pressing forward with constancy, not deferring to young toughs who hung about the storefronts like pale predatory birds, not challenging them either. It struck her in that moment how unremarkable he was and how gracefully and efficiently he employed it to his advantage.

She quickened to a jog. It occurred to her that she was not interested in confronting Wesley but only in following him. The thought came sudden and random as a formless shuffle of letters might for an instant spell out a single truthful word. In the afterglow of her realization a cool clarity overtook her. She turned up an intersecting street, harassed by a stray dog that snuffled curiously at the backs of her legs. She threatened it with a kick and it fell off briefly but soon was at her heels again like a long-lost companion. "Get!" she said, stomping her shoe; the dog gave an orphaned look and subsided to a prudent distance. When she looked up again Wesley had vanished. The sidewalk here was shaded from the sun by two- and three-story brickfronts and there were hardly any people out except a few gray-faced women presiding over rows of spring flowers and a gang of half-crazed children kicking an orange ball. "Stop it!"

one of the girls was screaming. "Stop! It's mine!" The child's face was smeared wet and glistening, and noticing Elsa her mouth closed in an imploring, seductive pout. "Did you see?" she whined. "They took my ball!"

"Nice girls always share," Elsa said.

"But it's mine!"

"Now listen, have you seen anyone walk by?"

The girl only made a sour face as though all the world had at last betrayed her. She wiped her small white blob of a nose, curled her lips in a sneer, and ran suddenly into the game and was absorbed by the general chaos.

Elsa's feet were hurting, she was beginning to breathe uncomfortably quick and shallow, but she kept up the hill at a hard pace. Rounding the crest, she immediately spotted the brim of Wesley's cap floating over a row of parked autos toward a shabby brick stoop lined with swollen trash bags and boxes of varicolored bottles. A sign she couldn't yet decipher hung swaying ever slightly from a black metal post. He was not far off—she could distinguish the silver flecks in his hair and the stiff-necked dignity of a starched shirt collar—and she slipped behind a curbside sapling where she pretended to rifle through her purse. He mounted the stoop slowly, his right leg dragging, and entered the door without knocking. All around her the street was silent and spinning with wind. She crept forward until the words OSCAR WEDGE, ATTORNEY, COME SEE ME were clearly visible and unmistakable, freshly painted in block letters on the signface.

That night in the kitchen she warmed milk for her father's insomnia. An investor had been with him in his study for nearly two hours, the house was a tomb, the steam from the copper saucepan traced slow, curling rings in the air. She lit a pair of candles on the table. Stared at her reflection in the windowpane. The milk was starting to bubble over and she turned it with a wooden spoon in the heedless and languid rhythm of a dream. Her thoughts crept randomly about. Overhead a dying electric bulb flickered through various shades of light and half-light.

After a time she heard her father and his visitor exchanging final congenial remarks and then footsteps padding in the hall and the door shutting fast behind. She lifted the pan of milk and measured it into a mug. Soon she heard him returning, his walk a slow, monotonous whisper that was almost no sound at all. His face when he entered the kitchen was sour and annoyed. His upper lip and both eyebrows were screwed in a sarcastic flair. "Stockholders," he said, "the bunch of crybabies. You've got to hold their hands every minute of the day. What do they expect from me?"

"Glimpses of the future."

"Let me look into my crystal ball . . ."

She handed him his milk. He sat slumped at the table and she rubbed his knotty shoulders while he drank. He started in with the latest round of troubles for his small and struggling bank, a drone that was endless, unchanging, inexorable: cotton was down, industry in a slump, and everyone a coat change from a pauper. Meanwhile she reviewed a trouble that was beginning in her mind. Wesley had been to see a lawyer and therefore was not wholly unaware of his property rights. It was a tangled matter, to be sure—conflicting claims and surveys and covenants, a quitclaim deed and a dead woman's will all colliding in what amounted to an intricate paper puzzle—but the chairman kept to his position that a black man could not withhold land on a technicality to the detriment of the entire county. And that seemed a matter of course.

"Lower," her father said, "Lord, it hurts to grow old."

The lumps in his back felt like beetles had worked their way inside.

"Dad, can I ask you a question?"

"Mmm."

"Have you heard of a man named Oscar Wedge?"
"Why? You got a crush on him?"
"I've never even met him."
"Uh-uh."
"He's a lawyer. He has an office in town."
"Never heard of him."
"Isn't that odd. Then he couldn't be very good at it."
"Not with a name like that."

It was almost nine o'clock and long since dark. The night was a palpable throb against the house, a heart beating softly in the darkness. She felt his back softening in her hands, the beetles scurrying at her touch, and had a flash of her mother walking in another part of the house. She smiled at the silly thought. Her mother had always been to bed by eight and was up at dawn clipping roses and geraniums.

"I'm falling asleep," her father said. "Those fools have worn me out."

"Why don't you go on to bed."
"Are you staying up?"
"No," she said, "not for long."
"Your hands feel tense."
"So does your back."
"Anything the matter?" he said.
"I was just wondering—"
"Mmm."
"Well, what do you think about this plant proposal?"
"We've got to keep up with the times . . ."

"But this nuisance of a company. They won't come if there are unions, they won't come if there are taxes. They won't come unless they get the right-sized lot, and no matter the trouble they put us to."

Her father sighed. "That's just the way it works, Elsa. You play host to your guest, like it or not. Ultimately he's your benefactor. Folks may kick a little at first, but they'll be standing in line for those jobs all the same." He paused to haul himself out of the chair and his voice took on a cool, bureaucratic tone. "You know, a young lady in your position. You ought to be more careful."

"What do you mean?" she laughed.

"Griping about the company. I hope you don't do that at work."

Elsa drew back her hands. "What a mood you're in tonight."

"It's nothing to laugh at. Political opinions—taxes, unions for God's sake. That kind of talk can get you in trouble. Elsa, you've got to be smart. Think about it. Are there any other women in your office, outside of secretaries?"

"No. Well, one."

"Who's that?"

"Betty Greene. She's a bookkeeper."

"Great. An old maid with a slide rule."

She went over to the sink and bit her lip in anger. Half the warm milk was left in his cup and she poured it out and scrubbed the cup clean and set it to dry. Then she put the candles out.

From the earliest days when he'd taught her stories from the children's Bible, encouraged piano lessons and school studies, even tossed the baseball underhanded in the backyard, by the elm tree, she'd felt this conflicted wavering on his part, this back-and-forth between pride and censure, encouragement and disillusion, though for a long time she failed to understand the reason behind his unease. In her mind she peeled him apart, separated him into twins. Twins whose arms and legs intertwined, each pushing and yanking in an opposite direction, each swiveled head rising to shout commands in the other's ear. With such a state of affairs convention tended to win out, dictating whether or not she ought to attend a dance or which academy best suited her interests. And she learned to accept this, though not without a shade of disdain. Yet every now and then one of the twins got the better of the fight and he would surprise her, nursing an independent streak or unexpectedly cracking down, insisting that she wear her hair in a traditional style and accompany some cousin to the picture show. In his more tyrannical moods he became especially keen on dull boys who were friends of the family, the kind she'd never volunteer to spend time with, boys with respectable parents and futures bought and paid for by previous generations, who looked on the world as a kind of playground invented purely for their pleasure, where no wish or desire or preference could go unfulfilled.

Thankfully, he never questioned her education; he wanted that much. And when she took school seriously, when she spent hours combing the library archives on rainy winter days, purely out of interest, without so much as an awareness of what she was looking for, he never complained. He only scolded her mildly now and then, calling her an expert in apocrypha. But always the doubt, the uneasiness, returned. She'd laugh to dispel him, but his concern was real. What if she grew old and never married? He wanted a grandson. How would he ever get one if she kept scaring off suitors with her knowledge of colonial history and her crazy talk about labor unions?

Once he asked her, "Do you want to end up a spinster?" It was a serious question, at the same time gentle and angry, and she hadn't known how to answer him. But it seemed to her that ever since the cancer devoured her mother from the inside out, leaving her a desiccated husk before the breath even left her lips, the twins had grown tired of contending in him, and he stopped asking or expecting answers to such questions. Now he tended to his business, avoided conflict, and wordlessly pleaded with her to follow suit.

Meantime the flower garden her mother had kept, in her absence, grew wild and overgrown. Tall, purplish weeds took root where the geraniums used to stand, opening crowns of bad-smelling berries to the delight of the crows. Rain and sun beat down on the soil and squirrels scratched and buried their secrets under the hardening crust. Over time the garden became so tangled and hopeless, so infested by woodchucks and rabbits, that it hardly seemed worth the effort to make it presentable again. And Elsa was certainly not interested in that kind of work, sweating and straining with a hoe and trowel. The one and only beauty the garden continued to possess was the moonvine her father planted around the stump of an old dogwood which cracked during a thunderstorm shortly after they buried his wife. Knowing almost nothing about gardening, he never really expected it to grow, much less encircle the stump as it had, until you could scarcely see a sign of the old tree for the large, drooping green leaves and pale blossoms that only opened after sunset. Once they counted twenty-six flowers arrayed on the vine and at midnight it was a miracle of blooming white, like a set of china teaplates laid on a serving tray. And even now, looking through the kitchen window, the half-dozen early blossoms palely slipped their sheaths, opening under the moon like crystal mouths gaping at the wide night world, in a stunned and changeless longing which only deepened and grew in the gathering dark.

3

"Well, I don't know where to begin," Wesley said.

"Should of never answered the door."

"We can't play dead in here like we was hiding from the law."

"So tell her we hold the deed."

"What's the good? A piece of paper."

"A legal deed," Cora said.

It was a damn nuisance, he thought, rummaging through the closet for a pair of work gloves while his sister hovered over him with both hands sharply rigged to her hipbone, like some deacon's wife offended by the scent of moral turpitude. Ever since coming back from the main house and informing him that the cellar was flooded, she'd been prodding, prying, and interrogating him for information about the woman from the county office.

"You know where my gloves have got to?"

"How would I know a thing like that?"

The other one, the one named Zellers, he'd started coming round the year before. He was a thin, nervous alcoholic with sunken eyes and it had been easy enough to lay back and wait for him to exasperate himself. And before him, real estate highwaymen representing various companies would drop by now and then expressing interest in the estate, wondering who the owners were and how they might be reached. But the old Peers widow had drawn her will in such a way that the Wesleys might continue living on the estate as caretakers so long as the family heirs remained out of reach. She had done this in part to punish her relations for, as she termed it, "quitting town and praying for my death." A tenderness for Cora, who entered the household as a nurse, had also moved her. Now every time a stranger came snooping around, asking questions, Cora laid into Wesley as if he were a prisoner of war.

"This lady, what did she look like?"

"Young," Wesley said.

"That's a fine description. Was she tall, short? Was she ugly?"

"Maybe in the toolshed."

Cora stared at him like he was crazy.

"My gloves," he said. "I've got to get over to Henry Atwell's place. Promised him last week I would help move a cabinet today."

"Atwell?" She used last names exclusively when speaking about their white neighbors. "What the hell did he ever do for you?"

"He's got that bad back."

"Look here. I've got a right to know what concerns me."

"I already told you what the county lady said. How does it matter what color her hair is or whether she's got blue eyes or green?"

He straightened and shot her a glare, throwing on his coat with a kind of threatful brusqueness. It was maddening, how she could make him feel the villain with only a few well-chosen words. He was just pulling on his cap when she called out, "Don't think I'm gonna pump out that cellar on my own."

"I know it. I'll be back soon."

Outside the rain had let up but the sky was still a ragged, stormy gray and the land a sopped expanse of puddles and slicks draining onto the road, which had become a uniform track of mud since the ditches overflowed. At either side lush stands of hardwood and scrub pine bent their limbs to the fields. Wesley moved along slowly, picking his way. He'd found the gloves lying on a makeshift sawhorse looking like worn-out leather scraps. Folding them in his pocket, he brought out his favorite pipe, lit and smoked it as he walked. Ahead of him and on both sides of the road springtime birds were darting, settling, whistling in communion while they plucked the berries from wild bushes and rooted insects from the grass. Yellowthroats, thrushes, warblers. If he believed the almanac it would be warm as August soon.

As he walked along he thought about their troubles and they seemed, like the muddy road, to stretch back a long, long way and continue before him as far as he could see. There was no real beginning or end to it, only places where you could rest awhile and others where you had better watch your step. But for all that he would never wish back those rough-and-tumble years before they settled on the estate, the moving from one place to another, the labor that changed according to the season and took him as far as West Virginia, Carolina, and Tennessee. Those were years for a young man, a man with strong hands and few responsibilities. To get stuck on a life like that, well, that was the same as catching your arm in a mill machine or at best hanging on but falling further into debt as your production declined. There was just an age where you had to get out if you could and no going back.

At a small wooden bridge he paused and looked into the roiling creek below. The water was a turbid brown, the color of bread pudding; it reminded him of the time he discovered a drowned dog washed up on a flooded creek bank. He was only a child at the time and so buried the dog with great ceremony and seriousness, choosing a spot in his grandmother's garden which she helped him open with a shovel. In order to lend the occasion a suitable atmosphere she had spoken some words in a language he didn't understand and often he'd wondered what she said, whether make-believe claptrap to humor him or something in a tongue from the past.

He crossed the bridge and continued about a mile down the road until he came to a badly rutted, zigzag drive that cut up to Atwell's place. Either Atwell or his wife had apparently forced a car through the muck, leaving a track of deep gashes in which Wesley toed his way, sparing his shoes. The house was set to the edge of a small rise with a field spreading out beyond in freshly turned geometrical rows. To the east a pale disk was visible through the screen of clouds, crossed by darting swallows and crows. He was just halfway up the drive when, as if springing to life from his thoughts, a black dog came rumbling down to meet him in a fit of barking and dribbling spittle. Wesley stopped, held out his hand palm-up. Sensing him, the dog reined herself at the last moment, paused and sniffed him and abruptly walked alongside, wagging her tail. "Good girl," Wesley said. He scratched the flat of her head and she growled softly as if irked by false expectations.

"That you, Wes?" said Atwell, emerging from his front door. A tall, thick-chested man with a look of having worn down over the years.

"None other," Wesley returned.

"Why, that's perfect timing. I just came in from the field and said to Mason I wonder if Wes'll remember to come by today."

"We ain't hit bad, only the cellar. How'd your crops hold up?"

"Soaked, but they didn't flood," he said with pride.

"Glad to hear it."

"Well, I don't want to keep your cellar waiting. Come round back and let me show you this cabinet. It's a beauty. Mason, get out here goddammit!"

They picked their way over the yard with the black dog yelping and trotting along and Atwell slapping at her head, spouting angry commands while the dog watched with eager anticipation.

When they arrived at the little workshed where Atwell had built and stored the cabinet, raising it on wood blocks to keep the bottom dry, a sloppy teenage boy appeared and fixed Wesley with a suspicious look. He wore a crimped Dodgers cap and a pair of oversized pants tucked into high, muddy boots.

"Wes, you know my son Mason."

"How you doing," Wesley said.

The boy looked him over and nodded slightly, squinching his eyes. His look seemed to ask: Just what do you figure you'll get out of this?

"Mason helped me put the moldings in place," Atwell said.

Wesley took the pipe from his mouth. "It's a heck of a job," he said, looking over the high-shelved cedar cabinet, the laquered double-door front.

"Took me damn near literally forever to finish it," said Atwell. "See that trim flushing the drawers, and how the sides are joined so they can't split?"

"I see it all right."

Atwell stood back and took a deep breath of satisfaction.

"You ever seen a cabinet like this before?"

"No, nothing quite the same."

"We gonna do this or what?" Mason said.

Atwell fixed him with a gloomy look. "Anytime you're ready you can take hold of the bottom—that's the *heavy* end."

When they had succeeded in hauling the cabinet indoors, straining and progressing slowly through the back entrance and down the cramped hallway as Atwell jumped excitedly here and about, clearing obstacles from their path and barking impatient instructions at Mason, they rested it gingerly against the living room wall opposite the fireplace. "Nice and easy," Atwell said, "how's it line up?" Wesley stood back to have a look when Atwell's wife appeared, rubbing hands on a checkered apron, to replace the boy who slunk away as if fleeing persecution.

"That looks wonderful," Mrs. Atwell said.

Atwell beamed. "You don't think it's leaning a little left?"

"Nah, straight as an arrow."

"Well, then."

"Why don't you come have something to eat?" she said to Wesley.

Wesley followed her into the kitchen where biscuits and maple syrup and coffee were laid out on a small fold-out table, while Atwell continued fooling with the cabinet. Standing by the sink, Mrs. Atwell asked after his sister and he reported that her health was fine and they exchanged pleasantries and remarks about the day. Finally Wesley got up to excuse himself. Overhearing from the next room, Atwell came in and thanked him again and walked him back outside, a bit awkwardly Wesley thought. It was strange to know that were they to meet under other circumstances, in town for instance, a curt nod would be all he might expect by way of recognition.

As they came around the side of the house Wesley was beginning to hear a kind of rumble from the road, a low-throated growl, and when they arrived full in front he looked down to see a flatbed truck piled high with furniture and wooden crates held fast by coils of tightly fastened rope. The truck was bulling its way over the road with much effort and spouting of smoke, slipping and righting itself as it barreled recklessly ahead.

"Who the hell's that?" Wesley said.

Atwell observed with cool disapproval. "That Short family, ones that lived by the river about a mile off a here."

"What's he doing? Moving?"

"Sold his place to the county. He made out pretty good, I hear."

Wesley watched as the truck rounded a bend of trees and pulled out of sight. "Must of made a pretty dollar to move in this kind of weather."

"Let me tell you, I'd sell in half a minute," Atwell said.

"You'll get the chance."

"Nah. We're too far from the river." Atwell paused and looked at him keenly. "You?"

"A man came by last year, but it never amounted to nothing."

Atwell continued watching him a moment, then sighed. "Guess we can't all draw the lottery ticket. But I tell you. I'd get a pretty little house in town, give up this farming racket, what with my back the way it is, and that boy . . ."

On the way home Wesley had another smoke and considered what he would say the next time the county woman came round. It was sure to be any day now and he still hadn't thought anything up. With Zellers it had been easy enough. The situation presented itself. But this new lady, she had that go-getter look. He'd been able to put her off once, taken advantage of her inexperience. But when she grew impatient and no longer cared about good manners, what then?

Cora loved the old estate, she worked and cared for it and more or less thought of it as her own. He had asked her once before, when Zellers first came nosing around: "But what if one of them nephews or cousins comes back to claim it anyway, what then?" She looked at him calmly and firmly, as if she were the presiding judge. "I'll just tell them to read what poor Mrs. Peers had to say on her deathbed in that will, all alone and with no family at her side, where she left us that quitclaim to the cottage. And if they're beyond shame, well, I can live with the family throwing us off, but not no damn gov'ment." The conversation ended there and Wesley devoted the rest of his efforts to derailing Zellers with offers of whiskey, helping him along toward his own worst tendencies. Lost in such thoughts, Wesley found himself confronted unexpectedly by a chair standing upright in the center of the road. It seemed to be waiting for him. For a moment he just stared at the small wood-backed chair, its legs a bit splattered with mud. Then he understood: it must have tumbled off the back of Short's truck and somehow landed square on its feet. He chuckled softly to himself, picked up the chair and set it by the roadside where Short was sure to see it.

When he arrived home he found Cora had gone against her word. She was already busy pumping water into the yard through a crude hose, and she glared at him when he approached, giving over the pump to him without so much as speaking. They worked in silence through the morning until the water was low enough to finish with a mop. Swishing in the muck, breathing the sour odor of the dank, draftless room, Wesley attempted to tell her about encountering Short's truck and finding that chair standing upright, as if waiting for him to sit and have a smoke, but she only looked at him darkly, without humor. By the time they finished, the afternoon was wearing on and Wesley thought he had better make himself scarce for a couple hours if they were to have at least a tolerable evening together. So after cleaning up and eating a handful of biscuits, he put on his coat and hat and walked in the direction of the river, thinking he would see what damage it had done.

He took a winding path through the trees, watching the groundwater ooze and swell at every step, little clay-colored bubbles that fizzed and burst around his shoes, emitting pungent fumes. A cool breeze was blowing off the river and he could hear the sluicing current long before it came into view. He followed the path until it leveled to meet the washed-out bank. Near the water's edge some burrowing creature, alarmed by his approach, rustled away through the underbrush. He stood and looked over the scene. He was surprised. The water had receded back within the normal bounds of the river, but everywhere toppled trees, whorled swaths, and depressions stamped the story of its travels on the earth. Ahead of him the main channel raced swiftly along, carrying the occasional broken branch or rubber tire. "Ah damn," he said, finding his right foot suddenly ankle-deep in mud. He limped along a while before finding a bunch of broad green leaves to use for a rag.

While he was drying off he became aware of a flash of movement downriver and a few isolated cracking sounds, as though logs were being split. He began wandering in that direction and soon made out what appeared to be a mound of wreckage piled against the shore. After rounding a vile-smelling slough, he drew closer through the trees and spied a man crawling on top of the wreckage like some giant crab, bent at a labor of twisting, yanking, and hammering. Now and then a soft cursing became audible between the blows and Wesley could see that the wreckage itself was the husk of an automobile which had apparently been swept along with the current. The man, an aging Negro fisherman, was going about the business of gutting it.

"Hey there," Wesley called. The old man stood abruptly still on the roof of the car, eyes hooded under the brim of a baseball cap.

"That you, Wes?"

"Sure it is."

"Why'd you come up like that? Try and give me the shakes?"

"I didn't mean to sneak up."

The old man raised his baseball cap and grinned.

"Sure you didn't. Come on out if you like."

The car was standing in about two feet of water and the old man had pulled a fishing skiff alongside, into which he was depositing scrap pieces of the engine. Wesley stood at the edge of the shore and laughed.

"River god made you a little present."

"And why not? Sixty years I been going to church."

"You been out in that boat of yours all day?"

"Sure," the old man said, twisting a piece of pipe with his wrench. The hood was already in his skiff and he had only to reach down from above like a graverobber.

"How's the current?"

"Running powerful."

"You ain't actually crossed it, have you?"

"Nah, just working down the bank. You crazy? I'd probably end up in the Atlantic Ocean. It's all I can do just to keep from turning in circles."

Wesley let him work awhile, watched as he took out the oil pan and distributor, crawled back over the roof and dropped them roughly in his skiff.

"Where you think it came from?" he finally said.

"Don't know and don't care."

"I wonder."

"I know where it's going, that's all."

"How much you get for them scraps?"

The old man shook his head. "These are good working parts. Ain't nothing scrap about them. They just went for a little ride."

Wesley lit his pipe and smoked and they traded comments about the weather, the automobile, the poor month of fishing. It was the worst in years, the man complained. Damned rain had kept him from the perch and now it would be another week or two before the water cleared and catfish began to bite. Right now they were just laying tight on the bottom, he said. He glared down through the clouded water as if he could see them there, flitting tails.

After half an hour the man had more or less filled his skiff with what he considered the choicest parts of the car. Rubbing his sore shoulder and complaining about "rusty joints," he unloosed the skiff from its tether and rowed in, allowing Wesley to fasten it to a sycamore tree while he hopped gingerly to shore. He was a hard, athletic old man with long sinewy limbs wrapped in a leathered skin. From his chin a whisk of knotted beard curled out, lending him a roguish air. "Know anything about cars?" the old man asked with a wink. Wesley shrugged and said, "A little bit." The old man plucked a crumpled pack of strawberry chewing gum from his pants pocket and began to gnaw on a stick while Wesley smoked. "Ever owned yourself a car?" he asked, and to Wesley's undecided look responded, "Me neither. But I dearly love them. I could get hooked, you know. Be one of them fellas that's always buying and trading up and all the rest of that business. Be reading the magazines. But then what's the trouble with the whole thing, I'd be looking over my shoulder wondering, What's Wes driving these days?"

Wesley laughed. "Maybe you better stick to your boat."

"I say the same thing myself," he said, leaning back against the sycamore tree and regarding Wesley with a look of self-conscious amusement. "And the truth is I ought to know, because I've made a pretty living these last few years taking cars like this, what the owner calls junk, though he's only saying that because he looked over his shoulder too, and selling them piece by piece back to the very same dealer he's buying the new ones from."

"I suppose you got to know something about engines."

"What's there to know? It ain't like you got to make it run. Unscrew this, take apart that. The dealer just wants the parts in good enough condition so he can make repairs cheap, without having to order the parts new."

Wesley smiled and told how he used to drive a Zephyr for the estate.

"A Zephyr? Oh, I could make a killing . . . Hey," the old man said suggestively, "it ain't still lying around?"

"Nah," Wesley said, remembering. "The widow sold it off." He leaned back against the grounded prow of the skiff, explaining how the widow's husband had enjoyed driving too much to let anyone else at the wheel, but how certain important occasions made it impossible to do without a driver. These were the kind of social and business gatherings that made everyone sick, because the widow would be nipping at her husband about his poor dress and his manners and he'd be growling back how she couldn't get along without hassling him to death and meantime Wesley sitting in that Zephyr in some scratchy suit waiting for them to dog it out and emerge, primped and simmering, for the evening. Then the long, tense, silent drive to wherever they were going and the inevitable instructions from Mr. Peers, slow down or take your next left, though Wesley never drove more than thirty miles an hour and knew the roads perfectly well. Soon he'd turn up some stately driveway and park in front of a big house, while they pulled themselves together, suddenly pleasant as you like. When they returned hours later it would be more of the same: little criticisms, angry stares, and that tension suspended between them like an electric current.

So after Mr. Peers had his heart attack and once the funeral was dispensed with and the house put in order, one of the very first things the widow did was call Wesley into her room and ask him to sell off "that damned car." He asked if she was sure that was a good idea, seeing how she would doubtless have need for it in the future. But she only responded, "Debts, debts!" So Wesley did what she asked, though he knew the estate was in good enough shape to pay its creditors. He had always figured she just couldn't stand the memory of that car, and the truth was, he didn't blame her.

"Ah well," the old man said. "Too bad for us."

They talked a while longer about those days, about the widow and her husband and how their deaths followed so quickly and strangely one upon the other. "Only there wasn't any love," Wesley said, "so don't go saying she died of a broken heart." But the old man spat his gum in the river and shrugged. " 'Course, you never know. What people seem to feel ain't always the case."

They considered this a minute in silence, abstractedly eyeing the eddies that circled and shimmered on the passing surface of the river. Mr. Peers had approached Wesley on the eve of his death in that shabby purple robe he used to wear around the house and said he had an urgent need to attend a stockholder's meeting in Richmond the next day. He asked if Wesley would mind terribly driving him early that morning? Wesley recalled thinking, *Mind terribly?* It was the sort of small kindness of phrasing that Mr. Peers usually held in contempt, which was the source of so many bitter arguments between himself and his wife. So the next day Wesley was up and they were on the road by seven o'clock. It was summer, bright and hot. They drove with the windows nearly shut and the wind just trickling in and they said almost nothing to each other the whole way.

For once Mr. Peers was unconcerned with giving directions; he sat in the back reading some kind of business report, with a slew of papers spread out on the seat beside him. When he did speak it was to make a pleased, sarcastic remark, such as "Serves them right." But to speak truthfully, Wesley was hardly paying attention. He was occupied in watching the country roll by, thinking about the weeds choking up the garden and the wasps' nest he would have to take down with a hoe. Death was nowhere on his mind that day. And though he remembered, or thought he did, Mr. Peers looking a little bit flushed or odd in some way as if he couldn't quite catch his breath, Wesley drove on and made it none of his business to ask.

Mr. Peers was the kind of white man you didn't like to fool with. Even when he was in a good humor, he could coil back suddenly and bite like a cottonmouth. It was best to leave him alone. You kept yourself separate. You lived in a world of your own duties and obligations, and when he showed up every now and again demanding this, that, or the other thing, it was like a soldier receiving written orders from a colonel he's never met.

"Yeah, I know how it is," the old man said, peeling another stick of gum from its wrapper, "only you're more like a conscript, a ditchdigger."

Wesley nodded and continued. So they drove into the city around eleven o'clock and were heading to one of the big hotels where this company was having its meeting, when Wesley noticed something funny in the mirror. He looked back and saw Mr. Peers give a kind of flinch as he gathered his papers together; his face went pale and for a moment his thick red eyebrows wrinkled like caterpillars crossing his forehead, and he sat back, just breathing a while, steady and hard. Then it seemed to pass. Wesley thought, *Ain't nothing I can do for him. If he's sick he'll have to say something.* But a minute later he was all himself again, drinking from a pewter flask and making sudden friendly remarks about how they were fixing to rout this stockholder proposal which he called absurd. Wesley nodded here and there, pretending like he was listening. But mainly he was looking over the city, which he hadn't seen in years. "Richmond ain't a bad place," he said, filling his pipe, "but there's some hard feelings there, I can tell you that."

When they arrived at the hotel the first thing Wesley saw was this overdressed doorman rushing forward to help Mr. Peers out of the car. He remembered the young man's eager, expectant look, as if he were waiting on the President. And Mr. Peers was pleased. Wesley recalled him turning and saying offhand, "The meeting won't start till noon and it'll take a couple of hours, in case you want to get something to eat." Wesley considered it a nice thought, though impractical. They were in a part of town where he wasn't sure to find a colored restaurant and Cora had packed him something in anticipation of that fact. It was safer to stay in the car than wander about, asking for trouble. He remembered parking the Zephyr in a hotel lot surrounded by pretty green hedges buzzing with bees, hemmed in by brick walkways that drifted off through a nearby park. He considered finding a shady bench to sit and pass the time before he caught sight of a strolling policeman and decided he would eat his lunch against the hood of the car.

And only a few minutes later noticing the black sedan pull up in a hurry before the hotel entrance and the man leap out carrying the black bag he ought to have recognized but didn't, it never crossed his mind, until he looked up half an hour later, a gnawed chicken leg in his mouth, and saw the policeman with two other whites in business suits standing outside the hotel. The white men pointed him out, their long fingers extended, walking directly toward him and speaking in low tones. He felt a sudden buzz as if he were slightly drunk. He thought quickly what he ought to say and only one thing came to mind: You're driving Mr. Peers from Zion—he's a company director at the shareholder meeting. So when the white men were close enough to hear him, with their matted-down hair and pale, sun-squinting eyes, he called out: "I'm driving Mr. Peers from

Zion—he's a company director at the shareholder meeting." The whites, all three of them, stopped in unison as if preempted. It was the policeman who finally spoke: "Then you're just the fella we're looking for," he said. "Put that chicken leg down and let's get moving." They led him into the hotel through the front entrance where a crowd was gathered whispering and wagging colored paper fans and then down a long carpeted hall to an anteroom where another policeman was waiting to question him.

The second policeman looked him over with interest. He was older and portly, with a look of cunning severity. "You must be the driver," he said, drawing out his words. A glassy blister wiggled on the corner of his lip like a bubble of spit.

And Wesley, hearing the stupid sound of it and not caring, wanting to sound stupid now, repeated: "I'm driving for Mr. Peers from Zion—he's a company director at the shareholder meeting."

"Not anymore he ain't."

Wesley looked around the room at his interrogator, the other policeman, and the two men in business suits, waiting for a prompt that never came.

"Anything you like to tell us?" the policeman said, looking straight through him with his little bludgeoning eyes.

"Mr. Peers all right?" Wesley asked.

"Funny, that's just what we'd like to know. Was Mr. Peers all right when you arrived this morning at . . . what time was it again?"

"Round eleven."

"Twelve minutes past eleven," the other policeman corrected, reading from a sheet of paper.

The interrogator nodded. He folded his arms. "Was Mr. Peers all right when you arrived this morning at twelve minutes past eleven?"

"He seemed fine to me," Wesley said, beginning to feel flushed in the warm, windowless room. He added: "Maybe a bit peaked . . ."

“Maybe a bit peaked is right, considering he barely got into the hotel lobby before he fell over dead.” He paused a moment to gauge Wesley’s reaction. “Didn’t nobody tell you what happened?”

“No sir.”

“So you didn’t know about him dyin’ so sudden.” He turned, addressing the other policeman with a blistered scowl. “Where’d you find this driver?”

“He was in the parking lot, eating lunch.”

“Oh yeah? What was he eating?”

“Looked to me like a chicken leg.”

He turned to Wesley again. “So you didn’t know about Mr. Peers dyin’ when you were hanging around the premises eating that chicken leg?”

“No sir.”

The interrogator considered this with a frown. “And the same time, you say he didn’t look well. You noticed he was . . . how would you describe it again?”

“Just a little worn out, maybe.”

“A little worn out.” He motioned to the other policeman, who wrote it down. Then he continued: “How long you worked for Mr. Peers?”

“Five, six years.”

“You live with him on his estate?”

“Yeah.”

“Yeah? What’s your full name?”

Wesley heard his flat, lifeless voice answering from a long way off.

“How old are you, William Wesley?”

Again, he could barely hear his own voice.

“And the widow’s name?” the interrogator said. “I’m talking about Mrs. Peers . . .”

But in the middle of the questioning the doctor appeared and motioned the policemen outside into the hall; it was the same man he’d seen leaping from the black sedan with the black bag in his hand. Wesley felt trapped, sinking. He toyed with the idea of running. And there was the horrible feeling chasing him that maybe he was guilty of something, that wondering and doing nothing might be a crime in itself. But when the policemen reappeared they no longer seemed to notice him at all. They stood off to one side passing papers back and forth and when the interrogator finally spoke to him it was to say, "You can take the car on home now."

"And let me assure you," Wesley told the fisherman, "I got out of there quick."

The old man sniggered and stretched, resting a wary eye on his skiff.

"I imagine that was the last time you went to Richmond."

"Never had occasion to return."

"So that doctor told them heart attack, eh?"

Wesley nodded.

"Changed you from suspect back to servant."

"Quicker than you could blink."

"Which reminds me, I should be clearing out before some fella comes looking for his car." Wesley said that was true and wished him well with his catch. Glancing up and down the riverbank, he said he might plan on some fishing himself once the weather cleared, but that would be the kind of fishing involving actual hooks and worms. The old man untied his skiff, flashing callused hands while he slyly grinned, and Wesley helped push him off, then watched as he sidled and snaked along the swollen bank, moving in and out among the shallows and hauling what appeared from a distance an iron jigsaw. When he was almost out of sight he turned in his skiff and called back in a high, playful voice: "Hey Wes!" Wesley raised an arm and waved. "What you want?" The old man hollered: "You ain't fooling me, Wes. Not for a minute. I know you killed that white man and I say, you better watch out!"

4

A warm and sun-drenched morning in May. Wind fanning off the mountains. Wildflowers blooming, bluebells, dandelions, bloodroots. Flecks of milkwhite, indigo, saffron, crowding between the headstones and along the border of scrub pines. A limpid sky stretching through treetips.

She unlatched the iron gate and closed it carefully when she had passed through. The path she walked was damp and wandering, attended at either side by flowers and headstones, the occasional sarcophagus. At the foot of an old chestnut she paused to read the names of the souls resting there. They were none she recognized. Farther on she saw the spare Doric façade of the old family house and wondered how she had missed it that first time in April, though she'd been distracted and the clouds had been low. Now it stood evident and well kept. Set discreetly at a distance. The path curved and the house fell momentarily from sight, rising again between banded oaks as she neared the Wesleys' cottage. He was standing in the yard in overalls and a simple undershirt, stooped above a galvanized water basin that stamped a flat moon-shaped depression onto the surrounding grass. He'd been watching her all the way.

She managed a casual wave and he raised his hand woodenly in response. Around him the leaf shadows quivered in drifting constellations.

"Mr. Wesley."

"Miss Childs." He regarded her without surprise. "How you been?"

"Fine, if the weather will hold. I'd have come sooner except for the rain."

He nodded, still averting his eyes as if she might find a weakness there.

"I've been wondering about your sister. I hope she didn't catch cold."

"No, she's all right."

"Is she home today?"

"She's working."

"Where?"

"In the main house." They turned briefly toward the white columnar front set deep in pools of shade. It looked clean and inhabited, the owners gone for an afternoon. "There's a snake loose inside. I tell her it eats the mice but she's after it all the same."

"Mr. Wesley, I wonder if we can talk."

"All right. We can sit on the porch if you like."

As they mounted the steps one of Elsa's fingers brushed a spiderweb under the railing and she drew it back with a secret shudder. Wesley sat in a rocking chair that appeared worn by years of patient service into the perfect human contour. Elsa sat beside him in a wicker. They did not look at one another but stared out into the yard as if speculating on the beauty of the cloudless day.

"I know what you're going to say."

"Really?" she said, amused.

"You're going to tell me the deal's fixed," he said.

"What deal?"

"It must be fixed or you wouldn't be here."

"Well. I don't think that's a fair choice of terms . . ."

"Then bargain, contract."

"There's been no contract, I can vouch for that."

"Obligation, then. There's at least an obligation, or nobody would take this serious enough to pack their belongings, to move like them folks that lived by the river moved and in the worst kind of weather, in a flood."

"I think we can settle on agreement," Elsa said.

He nodded. "Say what you came to say."

And she did. She told him everything in the calm and reasonable tone of an advisor. She told him about the plant proposal and the subsequent bidding and haggling, the final and politic agreement between local authorities and the Pennsylvania-based company. How they had tried their best to find a suitable lot which would not infringe upon tenants but had been unable to do so. How they had arranged for the relocation and reimbursement of all parties affected and how the other families had already accepted terms and doubtlessly gained from them. Finally, she told him that the county had a claim on his land. He looked at her then, coolly and evenly. "We'll see about that," he said. The candor of his speech appalled her. She assured him that she was telling the truth. She had prepared for this moment, turned it over in her mind during the previous weeks and decided on a resolute push, but now his reaction unnerved her. She said that anyway there was no court in which he could argue his case. He was silent then, morosely examining his shoes while in the yard before them a ring of delicate chickadees lighted to bathe in the water basin.

"I'm sorry," she said simply.

He rocked back and looked vaguely at the chittering birds.

"You can't just go digging up what's buried."

"If you're speaking of your graves, Mr. Wesley, let me put your mind to rest: exhumation is nowhere in the county's plans."

"I wonder what the family will think."

"Are you trying to scare me off?"

Wesley shifted in the chair, his voice lowered to a whisper: "It's their word over mine, of course. Whatever I think one way or the other . . . I don't imagine you would scare easy, Miss Childs, even if I wanted to try."

"Look. I'm only trying to help you."

He gave her a mocking look. "I never took a woman's help."

She felt the blood drain from her face and thought fleetingly of what a simple word or lack of a word in her downtown office could do to him. When she looked on him again it was with a chill she had not wanted to believe she could feel, what she had rejected in every conscious corner of her mind, what she loathed in others and only feared and disbelieved in herself.

"I know the law won't allow me much," she said. "I'm only a messenger. But right now I'm all the voice you have, Mr. Wesley, and that's nothing to laugh at."

His eyes glazed instantly, that same expressionless worry as on the first day they'd met, while in the yard before them the birds chittered and shot from the water basin into the trees. In the same moment she noticed a woman walking toward them over the shaded lawn. A small, slender black woman with a man's hat on her head. Elsa looked at Wesley and found him apparently unsurprised; he passed his eye over her as if she were some familiar aspect of the landscape, a tree stump or scarecrow. "My sister," he said. Elsa stood. The woman was walking with an easy stride and dangled a limp snake from one hand, jet-black and long as a rubber bicycle tube. "Don't be scared," the woman called, "he ain't got a lick left in him." Elsa began to waft a hand reassuringly but slowly she realized the words were for Wesley, whose face was turning a strange powdered gray. "Thought he was smart but the poison got him. Ain't he grand, though? A pretty black snake but he's sure enough dead."

Wesley began tracing lines with his fingernails onto his knees. "My sister Cora," he said to Elsa. "Miss Childs," he said to the floor.

"Please to meet you, miss."

"Likewise," Elsa said. "I was hoping you were well."

"Oh, I'm always well. The Lord has blessed me with wellness. Only the poor snake wish it weren't so." She held it up by the head and looked into its leaden eyes, then draped it over the wash basin so that it hung there half in the water and half in the grass. "You appreciate some tea, maybe?"

"I'm fine, thank you."

"Fetch a cup, William."

Elsa shifted uncomfortably against the porch railing. Wesley was already rising, automatic, and Elsa heard the ring of his Christian name and wondered that she had not known it before. Meantime his sister was gliding up the stairs with a serene and implacable ease—she was yet pretty, though her face showed the skeleton's edge—and Elsa watched in alarm as she removed Wesley's hat to fan herself and casually usurped his seat.

"We ain't had many visitors of late. Even when my mistress was alive, she was never what you might call a social person. After she died, the first year or so, a few came to pay respects at her stone. Now they keep away mostly."

"When was it she died?" Elsa said.

"Oh, just about sunrise of a day like this."

"I believe I saw the stone. It was nineteen—"

"Nineteen and thirty-one."

Elsa nodded. "Was she all alone?"

"Excepting me and William. But I suppose we're all of us alone in death."

"You must have been a comfort to her."

"Miss Childs, it was I held her hand when she saw the Lord."

Elsa nodded and sat again. From inside came the clatter of dishes on a stovetop and the sound of a kettle heating up.

"She left us a legal deed. Legal, a lawyer says."

"You mean Oscar Wedge."

"That's his name."

"Unfortunately, he's not what you might call an upstanding

member of the bar. I don't doubt but he'd say anything to get hold of your money."

Cora didn't flinch. Her gray eyes simply strayed, seemingly vacant, wandering from Elsa to the sunlit yard to crusts of flaking paint on the porch railing, which she scraped absentmindedly with her fingernail.

"No matter, since we decided it all beforehand."

"Decided what?"

"We ain't gonna sell."

Elsa tried holding her stare but it was like wrestling twin puffs of smoke. "That's a bad idea. Look, you may as well argue with the river. This plant needs a large area for operations and it needs access to the water. Your neighbors have already signed on handsomely. It doesn't make any sense."

"There was a young man nosing round the main house this morning, poking through the garden and looking in the windows. I damn near shot him for trespass." She fixed Elsa with a sharp, questioning glance. "He might of been a drifter, I guess. But then I never saw a drifter wear a striped tie and wingtips. Not that I'm saying anything about it one way or the other. It's just there's been an unnatural lot of drifters hanging around lately and, like I said before, we don't get a whole lot of visitors."

The screen door opened and Wesley came out with a steaming cup in each hand. Cora allowed her lips to curl. "It's good lemon tea," she said. Elsa took her cup in amazement. Wesley leaned back against the doorjamb.

"Do you realize what you're doing?" she said.

" 'Course we do."

"I'd like to hear it from him."

"That so?"

"Yes."

"Go on. Tell her, William."

Wesley shrugged and ran his shoe indifferently along the flat porch boards. "It's a nice piece of land here, the deed's in our name, we ain't bothering no one. Guess I don't like the idea of starting over someplace new."

"So what do you think happens if I go and tell the county that?"

"Maybe you don't got to tell them yet," he offered.

"You mean why don't I make something up?"

Wesley kept his eyes on the porch.

"Well. I don't know about that."

"I could say 'Sorry, sir. They were falling over themselves to sign the papers, but just that minute the pen ran out of ink.' "

Cora laughed, a weird trilling ululation. Her jawbone shuddered through a haze of tea steam.

"That's pretty good," Wesley said.

"But what's the point? The only thing you can bet on is you'll make a whole lot of important people mad as hell."

"Maybe so . . . But this lawyer, he says we got a case. If he can just have a couple of weeks, he says. I got no reason to distrust him."

Elsa placed her hands on her knees and rose briskly from the chair. "Thank you very much," she said, and indicated the teacup, leaving it unfinished on the railing. They watched her, both pairs of eyes like the eyes of cormorants poised among cattails, searching for a shadow in the pool. Or like the reckless eyes of gamblers staking their fortunes on a number. In her mind the sun was crossing the brick-and-tar buildingtops, angling down to the streets below, where fixed at the high end of the avenue the lawyer's fresh-painted sign strayed slightly from its frame, and she could read the lettering as if from miles away: OSCAR WEDGE, ATTORNEY, COME SEE ME.

She waited out a week in the grip of a queasy unease, a festering in some remote psychological backwater. Meantime the chairman harassed her with his urgencies and her father complained that he was ignored. At times she felt buried underwater, in a strange weighty state of slow motion as if the river had rushed in and numbed and overwhelmed her yet she had not died but had gone right on living. One night an odd thing happened. She dreamed that she was pregnant. Her belly wasn't swollen, she didn't feel anything special, but the whole town was turned dead against her and she traveled all night along unfamiliar roads, waking at last to the creeping noises of dawn.

She gathered her briefcase and umbrella and put on her walking shoes while watching the morning sky come apart at the seams, islands of dusky cumulus loose and drifting and rimmed with sudden light. She put back her hair with a clip and then covered it with a wide straw hat and left without waiting for her father. The road was bright and steaming, the air cool, she watched the neighbors' horses bluster vainly along the fenceline. She thought how nice it would be to drive herself into town, but their car was a brand-new Chevrolet and her father was a miser in this respect. There was no fighting him. The country here was broad level farmland cut section by section with silos aglint in the sunlight and cattle squat in shallow draws. A team of mules worked across the far end of a bean field and she wondered at the sheer monotony, the hypnotic boredom of it: like a seamstress stitching an endless quilt. Long and long after she had stopped expecting it a car came laboring from behind with the tires making crude sucking sounds in the wet road. She stopped still in the center of the lane, lifted her straw hat as though she could hardly bear the weight, flagging softly at the driver, a smile for a ride.

In town she took a booth at the diner and had a cup of coffee and skimmed the pages of the *Progress*. Signor Mussolini, speaking from the central balcony of the Palazzo Venezia, had announced to a cheering crowd "that the war in East Africa was finished and that Abyssinia was henceforth Italian." Her eye strayed from column to column: an unknown tonnage of mustard gas and asphyxiates . . . Ethiopians routed . . . the LZ 129 *Hindenburg* made the journey from Friedrichshafen to Lakehurst, New Jersey, in record time. After a while she put down the paper and went out.

The streets were crowding with businessmen heading to work, familiar glances from acquaintances and strangers alike. She returned them with a heady coolness. Rushing to and from the residences in which they cooked and cleaned, carrying bundles of laundry and groceries in their arms, the Negro women greeted one another with smiles. The county building was only a block away, but she found herself idling at a newspaper stand reviewing the same articles she'd read in the diner. She felt a loathing for the colorless walls of her office and for the little square window looking out on the back lot. The man next door was constantly banging her wall with the back of his chair and often she'd hear him on the telephone glutting with laughter over some remark or other. Other times he was so quiet that she wondered if he was sleeping at his desk. As she stood there brooding a colleague called good morning; she waved and set off in the opposite direction. It was almost nine o'clock and a fine skin of moisture was burning off the black tar rooftops. Errant clouds were subsumed, dissolved, without the faintest slighting of the sun.

In that part of town there was a druggist her mother had frequented and she was heading in that direction hoping for a medicine for her stomach when she noticed old man Leon sprawled beneath the barbershop awning, changeless, like some fixture of the street itself, his face scarred from recurrent bouts of pellagra. Beside him the barber's pole threw down its stripe like a red snake uncoiling. "Spare a dime?" he said. He was sitting on an upturned milk crate with the haggard look of a biblical beggar. Elsa fished a coin out of her pocketbook which he received with a boyish pleasure. "I got a new line: you want to hear it?"

"A line?"

"A hook, you know. For business. What's the greatest nation on earth?"

"I don't know."

"The greatest nation on earth."

"America?"

Shaking head.

"I don't know . . . what about Canada?"

Grin, gray eyes winking.

"*Do*nation."

"Leon. That's awful."

"I think you like it. You're gonna laugh."

Elsa reached into her pocketbook again. "Here, buy yourself some cigarettes."

When she crossed the next block her stomach began tightening like a fist. A train was approaching the overpass in a fury of rattling and whistling emissions and two men in blue jeans stood waiting at the far end with signals for the engineer. She could just make out the coal-black top of the engine as she turned to enter the store. A cowbell jangled as the door swung open. Behind the glass counter stood a broad bullish figure of a woman; morose, dictatorial, her arms thrust impatiently under her breasts, she looked up without surprise from the book she was reading and set it on the countertop with the pages facing down. " 'Morning," Elsa said. The woman nodded. On the shelves behind her stood rows of dark-tinted bottles with store-brand labels, familiar names and representations. Elixirs and tonics and gels, syrups and sodas. The standard repertoire of liquid agents. A tangle of spiderlike plants hung against the window, blocking sunlight from the room. She had to squint to see inside a low glass cabinet where the medicines continued, boxes of colored pills and apothecary jars with handwritten labels. The mystery had thrilled her as a child. Her mother would be deadly serious, solemn as a saint, leading her by the hand with the promise of black licorice. Whispering at length with the druggist. But she had died all the same and now Elsa came merely as a ritual, without hope or belief. The packages seemed absurd and alien with their ruddy colors and gaudy claims: Old Mohawk Indian Tonic *for stomach kidney and liver pains and for rheumatism gas and bloating.*

Elsa was still fumbling in her change purse when the woman said: "Haven't seen you in a while, dear."

"I was away at school."

The woman asked her what the trouble was.

"Stomach ache," she said.

"You've complained that way before."

"It's just a kind of queasiness . . ."

"Seen a doctor lately?"

"He said as much: nerves."

"That right?"

Elsa nodded. The druggist shrugged, a have-it-your-way expression on her face. She wrapped the bottle of Old Mohawk in a brown paper bag and handed it to Elsa. "Thanks," Elsa said, and turned to go. But halfway through the jangling door a young woman, entering the store in a cornflower sundress and summer shoes, broke into an exaggerated smile of surprise.

"Why, Elsa."

"Janet."

"I heard you were back in town. My goodness." She smiled through a whorl of brushed black hair like a pearl's velvet backdrop. She reached out and took Elsa's hands in her own slender grip. "Why haven't you dropped by? I've been dying to see you."

"I've just been so busy . . . I'm working for the board of supervisors."

"Oh, you must sit with me a minute."

"But I'm already running late."

"A minute, that's all." Her eyes coolly implacable, impossible to resist. "I don't suppose the board will pass any resolutions while you're gone. We'll do a little catching up. And you'll get to see Beauford, he's meeting me on the corner at half past nine . . ." Janet had been Elsa's closest friend for a long while, but they had grown apart in recent years. It was with mixed feelings that she'd received the news of Janet's engagement to Beauford Carr, a local boy, for she'd always liked him and thought him smart, while Janet seemed to grow increasingly foolish and flighty, like a chattering bird. In fact, since reading Janet's letter in her dormitory room, with its self-conscious dreaminess and romantic "Oh Elsa's," a soft dread had nagged within her at the thought of running into Janet. But it was done now and there was no way of getting out.

Elsa accompanied her to a small table by the window, where they could see the brick storefronts and manicured walkways lining the street. Beds of flowers were coming up among the patches of grass while new-planted saplings stood in violent blooms of translucent green. Elsa felt hurried, annoyed. Meantime Janet, grasping her arm, was chattering on about her wedding plans, describing with scientific precision the style of dress she was to wear and how the ceremony would proceed, who would be invited and who would not, and a host of other petty details down to the lace trim on the tablecloths. In all this account she scarcely mentioned Beauford, except to say, "Of course, he doesn't give a damn about the color. Naturally, he doesn't give a damn," which seemed to Elsa a calculated attempt to impress her. She couldn't help feeling vaguely sorry for Beauford; he would have to contend with her false offhand manner, her thirst for social supremacy, for the rest of his days.

"And you," Janet finally said, squeezing her elbow, "I want you to tell me all about the academy . . ." The store was empty this hour and their voices echoed in the quiet. The druggist had returned to her book. As if wanting to drown out their voices she flipped on the radio; it hummed softly in the background. Janet settled back in her chair, reclining like an empress (and looking nearly as beautiful, Elsa thought, with a twinge of jealousy), and began needling Elsa with an array of questions about her courses and professors and such, but mainly she seemed interested in the boys from the nearby military school. "And who was your favorite, Elsa? Who called on you? Who took you to the homecoming dance? There must be a homecoming dance, I suppose. Every school has one, or so they say. Of course, Beauford took me to his . . ." Occasionally she would lean over the table and mutter something nearly unintelligible, pinning Elsa with her dark eyes as if she were dissecting a butterfly. "The trouble with you," she said chidingly, "is you keep secrets."

"I don't mean to."

"Yes, you do."

Elsa smiled for lack of anything to say, but Janet only stared at her, waiting, with a look that clearly said: Don't think you're fooling anyone.

"There was one boy," Elsa said.

"There. It's like pulling teeth."

"But he wasn't from the military school."

"No?" Janet seemed disheartened.

"He was the son of one of my professors. He would visit sometimes, not often. We rode horses together. Once he took me to see a race."

"Did this boy have a name?"

Elsa told the story, but felt as though the blood were draining out of her veins: how his family had a tent at the race, under which they sat in fold-out chairs, the men drinking gin and checking their betting cards, the women assembling sandwiches and commenting on the strange names of the racehorses; how the sun beat down as the afternoon wore on, until the older men nodded off, and the women sat fanning themselves, and Elsa went off to circle the track with him, strolling, speaking with ease, in a kind of comfortable harmony she'd never felt before; how they saw a group of four horses whip by, neck to neck, with only three riders on top. When she was finished she felt ashamed, as if in some obscure way she'd betrayed him.

"But where is he now?"

"He's studying in England."

"Oh." Janet gazed off into a distance all her own. A minute passed while traffic rumbled past the window and the druggist coughed and fiddled with the radio antenna. "Do you want some licorice?" said Janet. She crossed the room and purchased a dozen sticks and came back giggling: "Remember when we were girls?" She placed the candy on the table. Then her eyes grew soft and sentimental. She sat and looked at Elsa with the air of a heroine from a Victorian novel. "You know who we miss?" she said. "Your dear mother."

Elsa felt her heart deflate.

"She would have known the right things to say . . ." Janet continued, faltering over her words, "how best to keep his heart, how to win him back from gloomy old England." It was true, her mother had always been expert with romantic advice.

"It's all right."

"Oh, Elsa."

"We weren't all that serious."

But Janet was following some private line of thought and wouldn't be put off the trail: "Do you remember how we used to visit your mother in bed, and read her the newspaper?"

Elsa nodded.

"Well, I wonder, is it all right if I ask you something? I remember every time we sat with her, she'd have these funny bottles of medicine like those under the counter over there." She motioned across the room and hushed her voice for fear of the druggist.

"Oh, Mama loved those patent medicines."

"Imagine. And she was educated."

"You never tried one?"

"Lord, no. Did she believe they helped?"

"Yes. I think so."

"Why do you suppose?"

Elsa paused. "I guess there's a certain way of thinking when you're really ill. It's a kind of terror that takes hold of you, growing day and night, without food or sleep, and of course that just makes things worse. But what you're convinced is that a cure exists and for some reason is being withheld. Next thing you begin to get suspicious of your doctor. Why can't he do anything to help you? He's supposed to be so well educated yet it seems like all he can do is say 'Rest up, rest up,' and wave your husband into the hall."

Janet looked at her perplexed.

"Well, I don't know exactly how to put it," Elsa said. "It's not the thing but the idea of the thing. Especially for the terrified. Is that the moon watching you through your window? Well, just someone try and prove that it isn't. And what goes for terror also goes for hopes, and for beliefs."

"I don't understand."

"See, the amazing thing is they worked, at least for a while. A tonic in the morning, some kind of pill before bed, and she was like a different woman. I don't know how that happened. But maybe they did what the doctor's drugs couldn't because she believed and for no other reason. Because naturally they're a sham."

"How strange," said Janet.

Elsa said that it was strange but she thought it made a kind of sense. After all, it was possible for entire communities to act the part of the patient, revealing their nightmares on the sickbed. How else to explain the madness of Salem, for instance? She thought that such fantasies only dressed themselves for the ball, so to speak, but eventually the clock would strike midnight.

Noticing Janet's pinched expression, she stopped. The druggist had looked up from her book to fix them with a look of disapproval.

"Well, it all sounds a bit extreme . . ." Janet wriggled under the squat woman's gaze. She appeared vaguely out of sorts, as if disturbed by something she couldn't put words to, or perhaps by her very inability to put words to her intuitive feelings. She seemed to struggle for a moment, then gave it up. "Pennies from Heaven" came on the radio and she hummed along, tapping painted nails on the arm of her chair. "Honey, is that Beauford outside?"

Elsa looked through the window, feeling farther than ever from Janet. Whenever she let her thoughts out in the open this tension and difficulty resulted and that was always the way it would be. "No, it's someone else."

"Too bad, he looks so handsome in his new suit."

"I really ought to go."

"Must you?"

"I'm late for work."

"Well, only if you'll promise to pay me a visit. Perhaps we can meet Beauford for dinner and you'll tease him the way you used to . . . remember?"

"Tease him?"

"She's always been a shameless flirt," said Janet, looking up at the druggist. The squat woman creased her lips, playing along.

"What nonsense."

"Don't deny it . . . you used to make eyes at him. When we were girls, I mean. You come out to dinner and we'll see what transpires."

Elsa smiled flatly. "All right."

"Promise?"

She slipped her pocketbook off the chair and nodded. More children's games, she thought. It would take all morning to remove the aftertaste of licorice from her mouth.

"Say hello to your father?"

"I will."

The debutante's name was Shirley Ann Price and the invitation came a month ago in the mail, but Elsa found it hard to believe. Who could afford a debutante ball? And even if it were possible, if a secret family treasure were buried somewhere in the basement and unearthed at this moment for the sole purpose of display, would anyone show? Scenes from Dickens novels flashed through her mind, throngs of hungry peasants carting them off to the guillotine, and she put the card away and promptly forgot it among other casualties of poor taste and limited time. But when her father appeared smiling in his silk tuxedo it all came crashing down on her: the date, the hour, the social miasma through which she must allow her father to escort her.

She dressed in a rose-colored formal gown, hose, heels, and evening gloves. She hung her mother's image of Mary defiantly from her neck and put her hair up in a French twist. Appraising herself in the full-length mirror she saw that she looked morbid and tired. Her eyes had a pinkish tinge and seemed to draw their sockets down, her skin was a shade too pale, and there were tremblings in her stomach that made her fear she would vomit butterflies.

They left for the country club in her father's Chevrolet. At sunset there had been a wash of faint gray cirrus and a change in wind; now it was full dark and no moon, a neutral starless sky. The road was narrow and wood-encroached with no way to see ahead of the curves and once they passed too close to a farmer driving an apple cart, whose mules loomed in the headlights like stone statues. Her father had to swerve to miss them. But soon he was chatting imperturbably about the beautiful girl who was to be honored tonight, her prospects and possibilities, and her earnest feeling for romantic poetry. She allowed him to yack on. Outside the window dark patches of farmland formlessly combined and separated, revealing the silver gleam of a pond surrounded by ink-black trees. When they arrived at the club entrance a line of cars was already winding its way up the drive. The gate they passed was large and iron-wrought, like a harp cut in half. Streamers and festival lights of various colors hung from lampposts and tree limbs and three Negro attendants in rented uniforms assisted with the parking. "Lovely," her father said. "Like a fairy-tale ball. And the young men will all have their hearts broken from the sight of you."

She smiled. "You have a father's eyes."

The broad double door of the club stood open and music was leaking out over the yard, dissolving even as voices and pipe smoke. She'd taken a few spoonfuls of Old Mohawk and felt light, warm, and relaxed, but gliding up the high front stairs she somehow caught a heel and nearly tripped over the threshold. Her father chuckled and offered his arm. He smelled of sweet tobacco. When they entered the dance hall a waltz had just ended and couples were disengaging and rushing for drinks and gossip. Many were family friends who must stop to say good evening, or else wave and grin in passing, or else pretend some disorientation or myopia. All of them obliged and accountable. She received a glass of champagne from an attendant's tray and quickly downed it. Her father was chatting loudly with a man from the bank and his prim immobile wife, whose voice was dull as a windless trombone. "Excuse me," Elsa said, and wandered toward the catering. The tables were swelling with fruits and cakes, chocolate flowers and finger sandwiches, animal shapes in ice. A military man gave way to her. He wore an officer's uniform and smoked feverishly while haranguing a group of young cadets about the need for preparation in the face of unknown enemies. She listened for a while as she drank a second glass of champagne and then one of the cadets came over and asked her to dance. The music was starting up again. She nodded, taking his hand, and the room began to whirl, drums buzzing, cymbals swinging, and he whispered to her as they danced, but she couldn't hear what he said. Finally, she asked him who it was they were preparing to fight. "It's hard to say for sure," he said. "Bolsheviks, I guess, you never know what's next." Overhead the chandeliers sparkled as they whirled. Soon his hand was creeping lower down her back and she allowed it, pressing into him.

What her father would say if he knew. The boy was handsome. He had pale olive eyes.

When the dance was over she went looking for friends, hoping that Janet wouldn't be there. But just then the debutante made her entrance, shy, deferential, against a mob of well-wishers pressing in like acolytes. The girl curtsied and took her grandfather's arm. Someone was trying to take a picture. His necktie had come loose and he was holding the large silver bulb like a club in one hand. Flare: the entire hall went bone-white from the tips of chandeliers to the bottoms of wine glasses. Elsa saw that she was drunk. Or rather saw the room tilt slantwise like a stricken ship and deduced from this the rest. She began searching for a chair, of a sudden deadly serious, and as she did the floor continued to sink away beneath her. Very unexpectedly, a tall, gaudy woman in an appalling formal dress blocked her way. She had dark watery eyes and alabastrine skin and she wore heavy streaks of makeup that made her face appear bruised. She seemed hard-pressed to keep her dress from falling into rags. "Excuse me—" Elsa started to say, but the woman only regarded her with indifference and, placing one long hand on her shoulder as if to steady her, shifted her weightlessly aside. Elsa turned to watch the woman go. She saw a ring glittering from the fourth finger of her left hand.

She managed to find a soft velvet chair and dropped into it. The room was slowly coming under control, but it was weak at the edges and shivered slightly like a merry-go-round that has abruptly come to a stop. She shut her eyes, floating in darkness. When she opened them again the debutante was waltzing with her grandfather while the orchestra chimed along in andante. Across the room at what seemed the end of a long tunnel the tall woman she'd never seen before whispered to a thick man with a white flower in his pocket. They looked too out of place, too awkward and posturing, their clothes out of style. All at once Elsa had a presentiment; in the same moment the man opened his mouth and licked his top row of teeth.

"Cheers," called the photographer, and his flashbulb fired again.

Elsa rose and made her way across the hall, feeling her bladder wince. She'd nearly reached the entrance when a man with flushed cock's jowls came pressing up against her. "Your old man," he said. "Well, he's lost for sure. I can't make him out."

"Have you seen him?"

"That's the trouble," he stammered. "There he is, there he isn't."

"I thought—somewhere over there—" She pointed, but he wouldn't take the bait.

"No, no. It's Sweeny, the bastard."

"I'm sorry, I don't know—" But the man was already rushing away, dissolving in the tangled mass of bodies. She saw her father's face appear for an instant floating like a balloon over the crowd and then she turned and found her way out and down the hallway, thinking of the flower-printed walls of the ladies' room.

Bloodroots. The toilet swirled and hissed and the lid felt cool and smooth. High heels clapped sharply outside the stall door. Voices giggled, hushed, conspiratorial. She opened her purse, uncapped the bottle of Old Mohawk and downed a mouthful, sitting and thinking of bloodroots sprouting from the walls, from the polished floorboards. Did they grow wild on the hill, she wondered, or did Wesley plant them? Why not let the graves go to rot? Why not plow the whole thing under and knock the house down? She tried to imagine their lives, and she would be old now and feeling it in her hands and her back, the floors scrubbed, the pines cut and stripped, the winters piled up, the illnesses, the debts paid and owed, but there was too much, she could only list what she knew, and that was hardly anything at all . . .

Soon there was a knock. She got up from the bowl and unlatched the door to find a woman of poor manners and doubtful social standing in line for the toilet. It seemed that anyone and everyone had been invited to the dance. "Finished?" the woman said, staring openly and hungrily in Elsa's face.

"Not quite," Elsa said. She shut the door and replaced the bottle of Old Mohawk in her purse, blew her nose, straightened her gloves, and looked at the wallpaper flowers. The lives of strangers weren't her business, in any case; she was just trying to do her job. Why should they make it any harder than it had to be? Why try to stand on crumbling ground? The woman knocked again, more urgently.

"Just a minute," Elsa said.

The woman rasped and rattled the latch: "If you don't hurry up in there I'll be ruined."

"All right, I'm through." But Elsa paused to fix a run in her hose with a trick dab of nail polish, set like a glass bead at either end of the nagging split. She dabbed once and again to be sure. Then she waited for it to dry.

"Please, it's a rented dress," the woman hissed.

I could tell that by the tailoring, Elsa thought.

Back in the dance hall the crowd had thinned and the orchestra was taking a break. Her father was nowhere in sight. She searched the patio and dining rooms run over with faces amazed, indifferent, and resentful, like a mob in the halls of a museum, and finally a long plush corridor marked MEMBERS LOUNGE at the end. The room was soundless and perfectly still. A pair of dozing children lay sprawled on voluptuous divans while a black nanny coolly watched over them, knitting as the evening wore on. Beyond them an exit was propped wide to let in the breeze. He's with Sweeny, she thought, his old fraternity brother, and is probably having a look at the stables. She was certain she'd seen them together and had a sudden vision of the two marauding bareback over the golf course like officers of the First Virginia Cavalry. Sweeny was an amateur jockey and a veterinarian and once had put his arm to the shoulder up a horse's anus trying to clear its intestines. He liked telling that story at dinner parties. He'd had to shoot the horse.

The stable was set at a short distance from the rear of the club near the golf shed and loading dock. The walls were made of white pine and the roof slanted to one side, oblong against the sky. As she walked the gravel path her shoes clicked and twisted beneath her and the noise of the hall fell away until it seemed a part of something unreal and insular, music in a wind-up box. Once she looked over her shoulder in the certainty that she was being followed, but nobody was there. She recalled the reluctant debutante she'd been in her day and the dress, the dance, the humiliating curtsy perfected before a mirror weeks in advance.

Coming to the stable door she imagined voices going quiet on the inside.

"Dad?" she said.

A swish and a nicker. She pushed open the door. A wet, warm odor breathed upon her and the horses turned their red eyes out of the dark. Again she heard the swish beneath their hooves.

"Hello?"

She took a step inside. A long empty aisle. A spare inner structure like an inverted rib cage. The horses adjusted ever slightly and incuriously to her presence. Ahead a stallion swung its long black nose over the rail of its stall and she went and brushed her fingers down the bone, coarse and dry as coal. It gave a blustering sigh in return. Farther on a rack of bridles hung faintly illuminated over shelves of tools and clutter; nothing else save the sound of scavenging mice and the corrupt odor of dung and sawdust rising off the floor. She turned back, hearing footsteps. Her stomach was throbbing, the straw crunched and slipped beneath her, and she saw the long, white hands stretch forward out of nowhere. The tall woman blocking the doorway asked her indifferently to hold on. She did, grasping the rail for balance. They stood watching one another. Neither spoke. Then the woman unclasped her purse and withdrew a small slip of paper. "Elza Childs?" she said. Elsa nodded and took the paper from her. It was a business card. "Mr. Wedge wants to see you," she said quietly. She had a nasal Yankee accent. Her hands drew back like phosphorescent crabs. "I won't keep you," she said. "He wants you to know he's a reasonable man."

A faint murmur sprouted up from the darkness, growing like a weed, becoming the lecherous incoherence of a man mumbling to himself on the floor of a stall. Elsa flushed. The woman looked past her and gave a wry, knowing smile. She reclasped her purse and leaned luridly forward.

"I won't keep you," she said again.

Elsa couldn't answer. She couldn't form a coherent thought. Then it seemed she had been standing there listening for a long time and had only dreamed the tall, gaudy woman because the doorway was clear and no one to be seen save herself and the silent, stoical horses. She heard them shifting and scuffing in their hay-strewn cells. She heard the drunk's voice rise sinuously toward the rafters, looping and clinging, echo upon echo, a senseless monotonous babble against the orchestra's distant lullaby, and next thing she was out and rushing down the frail gravel path connecting the safe and bright-lit country club to the swampy dark beyond.

5

The pair of faces emerged bit by bit through a faded sepia cloud, eyes first, staring straight ahead into the camera, while the noses, cheekbones, foreheads, lagged behind, receding into the haze of hair and Sunday hats that blurred with the shadows of the wall at their back. The subjects, man and woman, held themselves with a formal, serious stiffness. We are taking our portrait, they seemed to say, please don't interrupt. The man was wearing a dark brown or black suit of what could have been any material; the woman wore a flower-print dress with a high lace collar. To the unknowing, their stone-faced bearing made the relationship unclear. They might be cousins, husband and wife, or brother and sister. They looked about thirty years old.

"But you were 'thirty-one,' " Wesley said. "Older sister."

"I'd watch that 'older' business if I was you."

"I'm just trying to remember is all."

Cora pretended to ignore him, leaning down over the quilt she was mending. The patchwork squares were of all different colors, but mostly reds, oranges, and browns. "I've always had the edge on you," she said.

Wesley placed the photograph back on the mantel in its frame. Seeing them together as they were that day some twenty years before, it was hard to believe they'd been through rough times as well, times of anger and even estrangement. Each face seemed to cast a kind of subtle presence over the other.

"Yep, we look like a couple of serious hardcases."

Outside the open window a calm blue twilight darkened the outline of the hills. Crickets were droning in the bushes, holding their single recurring note while the birds disappeared and the sky grew crowded with stars. Wesley turned and put his hands on the sill, breathing in the night air.

"You know, I look back and think those were some crazy years."

"Mmm," Cora said, raising and lowering her needle in a quick, looping motion.

"Seemed like I was forever taking a train somewhere to find work, then coming back home, trying to get on my feet but in the end throwing all my hard-earned money at some pretty sloe-eyed girl who wouldn't of married me anyway, not for all the money in the world. Staying awhile with you, then with some friend or what I took for a friend at the time, till I'd have to go looking for work again, and the whole thing would start all over."

"Just young, is all."

"And you with your male friends, Lord."

Cora suppressed a secret smile.

"And then, I don't know what happened," Wesley said. "It just seemed to stop all at once, around the time you started nursing regular, and I quit turpentining for good. In fact, around the time we took this picture."

"Well, most everybody grows up, you give him a little time."

"Or grows old, maybe that's more like it."

"There you go with that word again."

Wesley grinned and moved away from the window. A pot of water was beginning to steam on the woodstove and he went over to make the tea. Meantime Cora continued mending her quilt, passing the hour with a quiet humming of some sorrowful tune. "Want honey and lemon?" Wesley asked. Cora nodded, then stiffened and screwed up her face. "What's that noise?" Wesley told her it was the heating water was all and she returned to her mending, but a moment later looked up distractedly again. "You sure about that? Listen over here, by the window." Wesley went over perfunctorily and stood beside the window with a mind to humoring her. But shortly he caught the rumble of a car engine down on the road, a low insectlike buzzing. The pop of a backfire and a muffled shout. "You hear that? Who the hell could that be?" Cora said. Wesley shook his head and said he didn't know. Finally he shrugged and said, "Well, they're making a lot of noise, whoever they are. But it sounds like they're going away." He walked back across the room and continued fixing the tea, aware that Cora was watching him with disapproval and trying hard to keep his thoughts to himself. His hands, sweating from the steam, quivered reflexively with anger and fear. For a minute it was silent. The pot of water quit its hissing and neither of them spoke. Then slowly, as he brought the cups in and laid them on the pine table, the sound of the engine rose again, as though it was coming back the other way.

"Dang it," Cora said, "if you don't go out there I will."

Wesley put down his cup and trudged over to the closet. He reached into the back corner and pulled out his shotgun, a Smith 12-gauge. Then he felt around until he found a box of number 7 shells. "Back in a minute," he said.

On the porch he broke and loaded the shotgun. The box of shells was a little old and damp and he wondered if they would even fire. But then he wasn't planning on shooting anyone, that was only for Cora's benefit. By this time the car had reached the bottom of the hill where it proceeded to race its engine and screech its tires as if celebrating some victorious football game. Wesley even thought he detected a couple of high-pitched voices hooting at the moon—or maybe at them? "Be careful, now,"

Cora said, calling through the open door. He stalked across the darkened yard, past occasional oaks and chestnuts, into the tight stands of hickory attending the cemetery. He followed the path downhill, passing old Peers relatives at rest in their graves. It occurred to him that trespassers might trace their quiet way up the selfsame path and he began to stare into the leafy gloom as if preparing any moment for a glimpse of advancing shadows. Suddenly he lurched, twisted, and felt the ground rushing up like a gust of wind; he dropped the gun as he tripped and landed hands spread out on the path. "Damn," he said, brushing himself off. Ahead of him the engine let out a throttled growl, echoing over the night.

At a high point on the edge of the woods, Wesley crouched and looked down on the road. He held the shotgun barrel-up between his knees.

Below him the car had finished a final turn and was heading away up the road, its headlights stretching ahead like long moonlit fingers. In the darkness he could see the slashing circular ruts it had left in the road. He crouched a while and listened and thought. If it were just some kids out for a joyride, raising a little hell, wouldn't they have spun out somewhere else? In front of a friend's house? Who knew there was anyone living up this inconspicuous path? He considered that the drive leading to the main house was a good quarter mile down the road and that anyone could walk right up without encountering so much as a bad-tempered dog. Coming out of the shelter of the trees, he passed through the cemetery gate, shutting it fast behind, and came out alone and worried onto the road. As he watched and listened, darkness and silence returned all around. The lights of the car blurred and vanished and the sound of the engine faded away. He began to hurry toward the main house drive.

A pair of bats shot over the trees, making wild, zigzag changes in direction. He watched them flutter away under a waning moon. Soon he came upon the drive's entrance and noticed ruts similarly gouged into the dirt, but only cursorily, as if for good measure. He scanned for signs of footprints but saw none. Still he decided to check the main house. A cool breeze was blowing from the river and the air smelled sharp and fresh as he walked. He recalled from his church-going days the complaint of Job, that the wicked prospered, grew powerful, and sent their children out to sing and dance upon the earth. He began to feel a nagging wish for his pipe, thinking: it's on the mantel next to that old photograph, and Cora pacing back and forth, and my tea getting cold. He broke the shotgun and carried it slung over his left arm, starting up the drive. When he arrived at the main house, standing awash in stark moonlight as if a part of another world, he made a slow, deliberate circle, checking the doors and lower windows and hearing nothing but the thrumming of crickets and the soft pad of his shoes in the grass. Finally he stood and looked over the rolling lawn leading back to their cottage. Nothing stirred. The trees leaned out from pools of shade like sentinels at their watch. Soon he began hearing Cora's voice, strained with annoyance and worry, calling: "William? William!" He hollered twice in return, knowing she wouldn't hear.

"Where the heck have you been?" she said, when the cottage's first porch board creaked under his foot.

"Thought I'd better check the house."

"Meantime I've been stuck here wondering."

"Well, it was nothing to get worked up about. Just some bunch of fools. They were already gone by the time I got down there," he said, scraping off his shoes and stepping through the doorway.

"No you don't," Cora said, when he opened the closet to return the shotgun to its resting place. "We don't know it's safe yet."

"Cora . . ." he said, but the look on her face silenced him. He removed the pair of shells and set the shotgun against a chair.

"Used to be nice and quiet round here. Would of thought this sort of business sounded crazy."

"I don't put nothing past them."

Wesley found his pipe and settled into a chair. "Who's *them*?"

"Ha, ha," Cora said. She crossed to the window and peered suspiciously out, looking like a long marsh bird. "Go ahead, have your little joke."

"All I'm saying is let's not get all wound up. Why don't you finish up with that quilt of yours?"

Cora threw him a dry, sharp look. "I think I'll go to bed," she said. Wesley could see that she was upset. It filled him with a kind of guilty dread, a sense of having been slack in his duty to her. He turned in his chair as she walked from the room. "I don't mind staying up awhile," he said.

He made himself a place on the porch, spreading out with his pipe, a lukewarm cup of tea, and the empty shotgun, which he propped against the doorjamb. He put his feet up on the railing and considered the deepening night, while in the cottage he could hear Cora making preparations for bed. Around him the sounds of the crickets swelled and pulsed, a continuous rippling song, like raindrops breaking the stillness of a pool. He closed his eyes for a while and listened and smoked until Cora settled into silence. An hour passed. His pipe went out. Soon he began to dream, hearing voices, senseless words. Then he opened his eyes. From a stand of nearby trees an eerie squawk rose and echoed over the cemetery, where he could just see the tips of headstones palely curved like thumbnail slivers under the trees.

With a start he recognized the widow's voice in his dream. That harsh, hoarse tone. The crisp ring of her demands: "Debts, debts!" He twisted in his chair, balancing his legs on the rail. He'd sold off that Zephyr all right, sold it to a dealer in town. After the burial was done, it was the very first thing the widow asked him to do. "Open a window," she coughed, "I'm choking in here! Now I want you to do me a favor, William. Take that damn car and sell it off as quick as you can. No, I don't care about the details. So long as they make you a fair offer, no less than six hundred. Just get rid of it quick." Cora moved briskly, efficiently, across the master bedroom, raising a window to let the humid air rush in, returning with a bottle of medicine poised slickly gleaming on a silver serving plate. Wesley remembered. It all came back. That long, enduring sickness and fits of temper and terror. As his eyes fell closed the voices rang in his ears again. Throats clean as flutes. He came awake, banging the cold ashes from his pipe. If only you could grasp memory in your hand, if you could compose and arrange it and keep it shelved like a photograph album.

Wesley felt his limbs grow heavy, as if he were handcuffed to the chair. Even his lips were too heavy to move. "Poor thing," he heard Cora sigh. "She's just wasting for loneliness is all. You could try and understand." But he never really cared to try and now, years later, it was nagging at him.

Wesley told himself: I paid what respect was due. If I held back from showing more than that, well, she was no relation of mine. And let me tell you, that widow was no kind of easy person to get along with either. Started the moment I arrived at the estate and it didn't end until the day she died. I knew I was in for it that very first day. Cora brought me in—she'd got her foot in the door nursing that sickly husband—and when she saw they needed help around the estate she told them all about me, how I was finished turpentining and looking for steady work, how I was good with tools and didn't drink too much and whatever else they wanted to hear . . . I believe "unmarried" was the word they were looking for and why they agreed to move us into the cottage so quick. But whatever it was, I won't complain. It was a good situation. I was past forty at the time and I was just glad to settle down somewhere nice.

So that first day, the moment we were introduced, that widow looked me over—of course, she wasn't a widow yet, just called her Mrs. Peers—and I could tell she wasn't too pleased by what she saw. Can't tell you why. Sometimes it just happens that way. She was a strict old-time white lady and she let you know it. She looked the part too, with her hair pulled back and her cool blue eyes. So right off she sets to questioning me about where I was born, did I ever go to school and how many grades, what jobs I had worked and how long, and which church I was a member of. Don't know why she cared about church because those people were godless, I can tell you that. Well, I stood there and answered her questions until I felt like I was in front of a judge, with Cora standing by and corroborating my testimony, saying "That's right, Your Honor."

And that's the way it was, from the first day forward. We never got on any better terms. The trouble was, she was just the kind of person where every now and then she would out of the blue pretend to get familiar with you, keeping you off balance, but before you could get too comfortable, bam! Left-handed undercut. It was a kind of testing she kept up, I don't know why.

At least that's how I remember it.

But the way Cora got along with her, understood and ministered to her, I'm just at a loss to explain it. I can still see them together, whispering, the widow lying back with her head propped up on lacy pillows, Cora sitting on the side of the bed, holding her hand. What they talked about so urgently I don't really know. I know my sister, though, and I've got my suspicions. "Poor thing," Cora used to say over my muttering. "She's just needing a little more faith is all." Faith in what, I wanted to shoot back, in her family? She ain't even seen them in God knows how many years. In her husband, who was thinking about stock prices on the day he died? But I kept my mouth shut.

I believe the sickness—if it really was a sickness—started less than a month following her husband's funeral. I'd been on the estate five, six years by then. Cora since '23. At first the widow said she was tired was all. Had plumb worn herself out. And that was easy enough to believe, what with the suddenness of it all, then the funeral preparations and the friends from town following one upon the next to pay their respects, and having to meet with her lawyer to settle the inheritance, and the long walks she took under that hot summer sun and not even wearing the hat that Cora had insisted she buy. She would walk up and down the garden, inspecting how the tomatoes were growing and the peppers and the squash. And she would lean over now and then to touch a green sprig or feathery vine and she'd get a funny look on her face. Her interest was only for looking and touching, though, because she'd lost her appetite. Cora came and complained to me: "I can't get her to eat a thing. And her a lady who always liked my cooking. What am I supposed to do?"

I said maybe we ought to call a doctor, find out what the trouble was, but I didn't really mean it. And Cora only waved her hands in kindly-cruel imitation of the widow, saying that doctors reminded her of death. The summer wore that way into autumn, with Cora prodding her, nagging over her, winning little victories, "All right, I'll eat the asparagus but nothing else," and all the while the widow growing more and more stubborn in her ways. Come October of that year, we both began to worry more serious. It seemed like she wasn't getting any better at all, but was just settling right into her sickness and taking her grand old time like you might test the water in a pond before wading in. One day I admitted to Cora that I didn't understand, because I hadn't thought she even liked her husband, much less would grieve over him so fierce and determined. "Typical," Cora said, "it shows what you know." But still I wondered if it weren't the loss of her family she grieved over most, for as much as she resented them and called them "Florida crocodiles," she would every now and then say to me how lovely it was with Cora and me, that you couldn't look for the one without finding the other as well.

Then again, that house just seemed built for sickness.

Soon the widow more or less settled into her bed, not getting up but a couple of times a day and even then not bothering about getting dressed, but just shuffling about in her robe and slippers with her hair all matted like straw. Her face was beginning to look drawn and pallid; you could see the cheekbones coming out sharp and her eyes growing big in their sockets. And about that time, one night like this, clear and cool but with the woodsmoke snap of autumn in the air, Cora announced to me over dinner that after three months of careful questioning and confiding she was ready to make a diagnosis. "Oh yeah?" I said, my mouth stuffed full of beans. Cora looked at me sternly. There was nothing wrong with the widow, at least not physically, she explained. And it wasn't a case of morbid grief either. But if we wanted to keep her from wasting away to nothing, Cora said: "Then we'd better move quick and call a minister to the house. Because the trouble's in her soul."

"Her soul?" I said, putting down my fork.

"That's right," Cora answered, with a tone of finality. "And I'm calling for a minister first thing tomorrow. So make sure the house looks proper."

I didn't bother to argue, it wouldn't have done any good. I remember that look of steady seriousness in Cora's eyes which had always been the mark of her faith. Never one to attend church every Sunday, to climb the social ladder, to make a show of herself, she nonetheless nursed a fierce, silent conviction about the work of God in the world. I'd always been the wayward one, the doubter. And besides, I told myself, it wouldn't be the first time death had caused a person to lose hope. I decided to stand back and wait and watch.

Cora left early the very next morning, putting on her best gloves and hat, walking away down the hill in a blaze of sunlit frost. By noon she returned with the minister of the First

Baptist Church. Wesley was in the foyer, polishing an oval mirror, when the long black car pulled up the drive and slowly came to rest in front of the house. He walked briskly to the kitchen and put the dust-browned cloth away in a drawer. From upstairs came the widow's voice, coarse with disuse, a bit cough-choked and worried:

"William? Who's there?"

He walked back to the bottom of the stairs. "I believe it's Cora," he said, looking up at the harried, bloodless face of a recluse.

"Oh," the widow said. She began to wander away from the rail, then suddenly she seemed to recollect herself. "But who's that with her? In the car?"

"I'll go and see, missus."

Wesley went directly to the door, aware of the widow drawing back toward her bedroom as if she intended to hide there. Through the narrow vertical panes of glass framing the door he watched the minister of First Baptist step from his car uncertainly and accompany Cora up the smooth brick walkway, their shapes distorted like shadows. He was a gaunt, middle-aged white man with gray eyes that seemed to ponder the gloomy, nethermost aspects of the divine mystery. He was not frail, but walked toward the house almost with an air of apology, as if acknowledging the superiority of its inhabitants. Wesley couldn't help screwing up his face in a wry smile. This ought to be interesting, he thought. Before they could spot him standing there he opened the door and stood back for the minister to enter. Perhaps a bit too ceremoniously, for Cora narrowed her eyes and fixed him with a frown.

"Afternoon," Wesley said. The minister nodded palely, crossing the threshold. He stood there a moment in an awkward daze, glancing around the foyer and down the hall into the grand, ornamented rooms.

"Let me take your coat," Wesley said. He closed the door behind them and hung the minister's coat from a brass-hooked stand. Then he followed the minister into the hall. "Like something to drink, sir?" he said.

The minister shook his head.

"Not even a cup of coffee?"

No, the minister said quietly. He did not want to impose.

"Of course not, Reverend. If you change your mind—"

But Cora was already leading him up the stairs, whispering as they advanced step after step, intently and cautiously as if the widow might be lying somewhere in ambush. The minister listened and nodded his head, mumbling in agreement. Later that evening Cora would tell Wesley in a fury: "What kind of a darn minister is that humble-pie, bowin-and-scrapin jackass supposed to be? You know what happened? You know how much good he did? Well, I'll tell you. When we stepped into the widow's room he just stood there for a while like he was in some kind of trance, looking round at the paintings, the dressers, everywhere except where the widow was. She was sitting up in bed with the covers folded over and her hair suddenly brushed and tied back, and just playing the part of the gracious hostess until I thought I'd go and shake her by the collar. That minister was too scared even to look at her, so she went and got them talking about the things he was looking at, about who handed down what from who, and where all them fine things come from. Then she said how it was so thoughtful and kind of him to pay a visit, and *she* started asking *him* questions about his church, his troubles, and what all, which he commenced to babble on and answer, sitting in that chair by the side of the bed like they were old cousins or acquaintances at least, and forgetting what he was supposed to be about, he was having such a high good time playing the gentleman.

"Finally I said to him, 'Reverend, ain't there something you wanted to talk with Mrs. Peers about?' Well, she stares at us both, confused, like she can't figure out what tricks we might be up to but she doesn't like the sound of it. She looks from the minister to me and back to him again, waiting for an explanation, and she draws herself up in her best high-toned look and folds one arm under the other and raises her chin like a presiding judge. And that minister, well, he sits straight in his chair with those clammy hands balled up and he tries to smile and go about it the easy way, so he asks her: 'Mrs. Peers, I understand you've taken ill these past few weeks. Are you improved?' Know what she says? She says, 'Very much, thank you, Reverend.' And she moves directly into gossiping questions concerning leading members of his parish, asking him whatever happened to Colonel Lowell's girl, the one that up and married that boy from Green County that the law was after for some kind of robbery where one man got knifed and another roughed up pretty bad, lost an eye, I believe, and about the divorce between Mr. and Mrs. Crane and how surprised everybody was after thirty years of marriage, and about the little scandal they had at the courthouse, where Mr. Crane was found in the men's room drunk and howling like a dog, and how they had sent him to the sanatorium to recover, it was very hush-hush, and so on . . . Well, you get the picture. She prattled away while he sat there nodding—'Mm-hm,' and 'Yes ma'am'—all the time rubbing those useless hands of his so that I thought they would fall to pieces, until finally she just plain runs out of steam, sits there for a while in a state of satisfaction—oh, she's very pleased with herself—while he drums up his courage to see if he can get a word in edgewise. 'Mrs. Peers,' he finally says, 'you know I don't mean to pry, but I was wondering if you'd like to join us one day, when you're feeling better, of course, and perhaps we could arrange a memorial service for your late husband, rest his soul.'

"She looks at him and says, 'Yes, I believe that's a fine idea.' A fine idea, she says! I could of murdered the two of them right there in cold blood. Of course, I might not of had time, because he just bolted up and scurried at her first tired sigh, which was a poor piece of acting, I can tell you. He thanked her for her hospitality and excused himself about a dozen times and he promised to come back some other day to see how she was feeling. Some other day, he says! Well, I didn't even bother telling him what I thought of him. When he was finished with all his niceties, I walked him down the stairs without a word, opened the door and let him run for his life. I never seen a man so mortally afraid of an old woman before, and so neglectful of his duty."

For a moment she stood tongue-tied with outrage, while Wesley added kindling to the woodstove, making shadows leap along the cottage walls.

"Probably it was a good thing you kept your thoughts to yourself."

She gave him a cool, superior smile.

"Some people," she said, "it's just better to let them go."

"So what are you going to do now?"

She flashed a mischievous grin, at once composed and determined.

"First thing tomorrow," she said, "I'm going to see Reverend Claxwell."

"Claxwell? Are you crazy?" The Reverend A. J. Claxwell was pastor of an evangelical nondenominational Negro church which met daily in a small, rickety schoolhouse out back of a lonely farm road some three or four miles out of town. He had a reputation for cruelty but also for getting results. He had effected more dramatic turnarounds, converted more wayward criminals and backsliders, saved more unrepentant souls, than any man of God in the county. Wesley had been dragged to hear a Claxwell sermon on several occasions over the years and always came away with a more vivid appreciation for the specific torments of hell and the complicated nature of the plan by which he might escape them. But for all that Claxwell's view of human beings was markedly uncomplicated; there were probably between fifty and a hundred people in the whole of Zion

County, Virginia, whom he counted among the saved who would enter into God's kingdom; the rest of the world would perish in fire.

"You can't bring Claxwell here. A black preacher?"

"Why not?" Cora said. "Ain't nobody going to know."

"What about Mrs. Peers? You want to scare her half to death?"

"Maybe scared is what she needs most. I'll tell you the worst thing I can think of, she settles into that bed and nobody to do anything but coddle her, tell her what she wants to hear, and before you know it she's too darn comfortable to change, and we're getting ready for another funeral."

"Cora, I won't allow it," he said.

"Well then, you better go fishing tomorrow."

Wesley sighed. He saw that it was no use trying to argue. An image passed through his mind of a box turtle drawing its head under a quilt-patterned shell and he grinned in spite of himself, expelling the tension in the air.

"All right," he said, shaking his head. "But ten dollars says she hollers bloody murder the minute he steps through her door."

"Fool, I ain't gonna let him in the house," said Cora dismissively.

The next morning she left before Wesley was finished shaving. When he realized she was gone he laid his razor down, padding a towel under his chin, and came onto the porch in time to watch her disappear down the hill, wearing her same hat and gloves but with a wool scarf coiled against the hardening chill, its frayed ends waving back gently in the breeze.

He spent the first hours of the day cleaning up around the cemetery, raking leaves into piles and pulling what weeds remained out of the rust-colored soil while overhead streams of ragged, dark-edged clouds blew by at high speed, riding a stiff northwesterly wind. After a while he went to check on the widow but found her napping and so left her alone. Better if she slept all day. As he returned and looked over the rolling land, he breathed in the sharp, smoky autumn air. A purplish grackle rooting in the yard fixed him with the bead of its eye, morbidly distrustful. It took small, jerking steps forward, dipping its beak into the grass; suddenly the bird flashed up and disappeared over a stand of half-bare hickory trees. Soon Wesley began hearing the sound of a straining motor over the gusts. It's only been a couple of hours, he thought. But sure enough he saw Claxwell's blue pickup come rambling slowly up the road like the head of a traveling circus, braking constantly to ease the violence of the ruts and bumps, and displaying a rough-hewn, hand-painted sign attached to the front grille by means of oversized steel bolts, reading TRUST JESUS.

Wesley went down the hill to meet them, feeling cross and out of place, mashing his hands together in his trouser pockets. Meantime the blue pickup clanged and wheezed as it came up, as if any moment it might shake to pieces. Large, gaping holes flecked with rust had worn through the side panels and an oily, burnt-metal odor leaked out from the exhaust pipe.

They parked a short distance from the gate and sat there a moment, apparently conversing in private while the engine continued running. Wesley could see them inside the truck, two flat shadows behind the bright windshield. The wipers had worn a pair of inverted crescent smears into the glass, obscuring his view. Finally Claxwell shut the engine off. The doors swung open with a shrill creak and they stepped out of the truck, Claxwell grinning broadly as he came forward over the path. "Hello, William," he said, stretching out his hand while still many paces away. He had grown fatter since the last time Wesley saw him, his cheeks belling out to contain his vigorous, confident smile, while his chest filled the drab brown suit he'd always worn and which seemed more hastily thrown together each day.

"Reverend," Wesley said, nodding.

The minster's grip was like a blacksmith's.

"I hear you're keeping well," said Claxwell, glancing at Cora out of the corner of his eye.

Wesley said that he was doing just fine and inquired after Claxwell's young wife, who the minister reported was in the flower of health. Suddenly his face clouded over and he snapped, "I haven't seen you at church in a long, long while." He looked Wesley dead in the eye, awaiting a response.

"Well . . ." Wesley said lamely, "the estate keeps us so busy . . ."

"Too busy for God? He ever too busy for you?"

"No sir," Wesley said.

That settled, they proceeded uphill toward the cottage. Wesley followed sullenly behind, feeling like a child scolded by his father. He noticed a dark, plug-shaped growth on the back of Claxwell's neck. It looked just like a wad of tobacco. "A fine-looking cemetery," Claxwell noted, "it makes you sense the peacefulness of death." As they stepped up the porch stairs Cora paused, unsmiling, and insisted that they wait inside while she checked on Mrs. Peers. "She's asleep," Wesley offered. But Cora said she would only be gone a minute.

"William, fix some coffee," she instructed.

They entered with a clamor of foot-swishing and remarks about the chilly weather, after which Wesley urged the minister to catch his breath. "Sit on down," he said, motioning to a small but comfortable chair at the table. He set about fixing the coffee while Claxwell worked himself into his seat.

"I had a nice talk with Cora on the way over."

"I'll bet she had lots to say."

"A fine woman, very high principles. She would of made someone an excellent wife." Claxwell shook his head sadly, inspecting the tablecloth.

"Well, Cora, she's all right."

"What's that supposed to mean? Ain't there nothing better than 'all right'?"

Wesley put the coffeepot on the stove, irritated. The minister's inability to make small talk was one of the traits Wesley found most exasperating in him. Not every conversation could be life-altering. He didn't want to have a life-altering conversation with Claxwell but he knew that's where they were headed. Then again, maybe the minister was just warming to the task at hand.

"I guess you must be right, but I wouldn't know," Wesley said.

"The shame is, there's only so many people with really high principles, understand, like your sister. And when a woman like her goes unmarried, childless, it fails to pass down through her children."

"I heard of many a case where high principles, like you say, failed to pass down to the children. You take that Colonel Lowell's girl—"

"Ah"—he waved his hand in dismissal—"white folk's troubles. Spoiled kids, looking for a thrill. She'll come to her senses, you wait and see."

Wesley looked at him, leaning back against the stove. He'd heard the rumor many times that Reverend Claxwell was part white himself, on his mother's side no less. Behind him the coffee was heating to a boil.

"Well, you know how it is . . ." Wesley sighed, bringing the subject to an end. He turned and, with his back to Claxwell, checked the pot on the stove. The coffee was good and steaming. He poured two cups and joined Claxwell at the table.

"Thank you," the minister said, wrapping his hands around the cup to warm. They were thick, powerful hands, heavily callused. "Maybe you could tell me what you think's the matter with your Mrs. Peers?"

Wesley didn't like that "your." He sat back and waited a minute before answering. "Can't say I know. It's like I told Cora, I never thought she loved her husband enough to grieve like this, if grieving's what her trouble really is. Maybe she's just got sick of living alone with nobody to pester."

The moment he said it he wished he could take it back, and indeed the minister threw him a critical look. "And her temperament these past few weeks? How would you describe it?" he said, deciding to move on.

"A little strange. She seems . . ."

"Distracted?"

"Yeah."

"Fearful?"

"Well. Not exactly."

"Hard to put up with her?"

"She's a natural bossy type of person."

"She ever talk about God?"

"No," Wesley said.

The minister nodded, a mental note.

"Doctor seen her yet?"

Wesley shook his head. "She won't allow it."

"Good," the minister said. He took a long, slow sip of coffee. "I've seen this kind of thing before. People like to walk through life without paying no attention. Before they know it, friends and family, maybe a husband, passes away, and they realize for the first time, they come smack up against the truth: I'm going to have to stand before God and answer for my life. Well, that is a shock. Of course, they *known* it all along, just haven't bothered to think about it." The minister paused and looked at him. "Know what I mean?"

"Then you agree with Cora," Wesley said, ignoring the intent of the question. "You think she's got this . . . sickness of the soul?"

"I guarantee it," Claxwell said, digging the end of his finger into the table for emphasis. His hard ivory eyes widened and retracted, showing the intense self-certainty that Wesley found so intimidating in him. Then he regarded Wesley coolly, with a mild disdain. "Of course, even the prophets failed to bring in all their sheep out of the wilderness." He took a long, drawn-out sip of his coffee. "I take it you don't see things the same as I do."

"I don't know what to think," Wesley said honestly.

They sat in silence for a couple of minutes, looking around the cottage at the various trinkets hanging from the clapboard walls, lining the mantel where that old photograph of brother and sister stood centered between clay jars and magazine clippings. "This is a nice place you got here," Claxwell said. Wesley explained how it was constructed at the same time as the main house but had been vacant for several years before he and Cora moved in, so that the very first thing they did was clear sheets of cobwebs from all the corners of the rooms. "Not just them nice, silky ones neither," Wesley said. "Some big spiders were running loose in here, I can tell you." He told about the new pantry and cabinets they built and how they cleaned up the woodstove and repaired the porch, which had been falling to pieces. Claxwell nodded along for a while, then asked where Cora had been living all the time before Wesley joined her. "She had a room in the main house," Wesley said. "Mrs. Peers has always treated her kind. They seem to get along real well."

The minister nodded. "You get along with her too?"

But Cora's feet on the porch steps spared him from answering. The minister and Wesley both glanced instinctively at the door, relieved when it opened and showed Cora's bemused, patience-seeking smile, her head tossing back and forth in disbelief. "That woman is a handful," she said, unwinding the scarf she had wrapped round her neck and draping it over the back of a chair. She went straight to the stove and poured a steaming cup of coffee, chuckling under her breath at something apparently ridiculous, then joined them at the table where they all sat (so Wesley thought) with a false, casual air, appearing like old friends who haven't seen each other in many years. "She's lying back in that big old bed, got her legs tucked under a blanket and one arm 'cross her forehead to keep the light out of her eyes, she says, and she's just acting more injured and piteous than you can imagine. I told her go back to sleep." Cora looked at the minister frankly, her hands spreading open like a fan. "Reverend, it's like this every day, only getting worse. She's pale and skinny; she can't weigh more than a hundred pounds. I don't know what to do with her anymore."

The minister nodded authoritatively. "Why don't you tell me," he said, "a little more about her."

"Well, how far back do you want to go?" Cora said, grinning slyly. "I've learned a lot. There's letters, journals, and she's told me plenty on her own." Noticing Wesley's astonished look, she said defensively, "What now, are you gonna accuse me of snooping? I like to think of it as research. From the very start Mrs. Peers took me in her confidence, Reverend, and that's the way it's been ever since. Some of these letters she read to me herself, others I just happened to find while I was straightening up, and maybe a few I actually looked for myself. But understand, it was always with a reason." With a mild expression, Claxwell told her it was only natural to show concern. "That's right," she snapped, looking at Wesley, "so whatever I tell you, I've got some kind of backing for it. I'm not making anything up but only sticking with what I know. Would you like something to eat, Reverend? I could warm up biscuits in half a minute . . ." But Claxwell waved her off, saying he'd had plenty at breakfast that morning. Regarding him suspiciously—he might not admit to his appetite—she continued:

"I don't expect there's a soul living that doesn't keep some secret to herself, and hides it from the world. You take Mrs. Peers. Why, I had her figured all wrong at first. I figured she was just your average rich lady. But it turns out she's one of the unhappiest women I ever knew." Cora paused and looked at them both sincerely, as if appealing for a fair judgment of the facts. "It didn't take me long to see this but I've spent a while trying to understand. See, the way it started was, she began making remarks about how she was gonna leave nothing in her will, how nobody was looking to get a dime. She'd say something like this and snap her fingers, just so. That was long before her husband died, but you remember he was often ill, which is why I came here in the first place, so she must of thought about it plenty. Anyway, when I'd been here a couple of years and when she kept making remarks like that, I asked her one day, I said, 'Mrs. Peers, don't you got any family round here?'

" 'Ha!' she says. 'Them crocodiles?' And for a long time, she wouldn't say nothing more. Then one evening when we were alone together, the cat came out of the bag. Mr. Peers was away that night on some kind of business, and I guess she got to feeling lonely and mistreated. So she put down the book she was reading and told me the story.

"She grew up on her grandfather's farm, in a pretty white farmhouse, and the family was prosperous and grew all kinds of things—but mainly tobacco. Now, the way she talked on and on about her childhood, it was maybe too nice, too happy. She might of got some wrong kind of idea about life, like it was all long walks in the sun and picking cherries from the tree. But as the case may be, she grew up thinking the world of her grandpa—there wasn't nothing he couldn't do—but mainly afraid of her daddy, who she said wore a big brown-rimmed hat all the time, no matter what the weather. Said that was the one thing she really remembered about him, that big brown-rimmed hat and the sharp edge of a moustache sticking out from underneath. He'd ride from here to there around the farm and she'd follow along in secret, hiding behind fenceposts and watching him between the slats, like she wanted to spy something out that couldn't be found out directly, by asking questions. And what she told me, her daddy never regarded her much but always seemed awkward and skittish whenever she was around. Now, she had a couple of younger brothers named Ab and Sherwood and he mainly spent his time with them. They'd go around the farm together and he'd show them things, put them to work. And Mrs. Peers, she took it hard. When she grew a little older, about thirteen or so, and still feeling left out, she took to following them with the purpose to catch them doing something wrong, so she could run and report them to her grandpa. But one of the brothers would always see her and point or wave, it was like a game for them to find her, and she'd have to run away with a high-pitched voice chasing after her: 'I seen you! I seen you!'

"She was kind of a tomboy, it sounds to me. Didn't take to women's things until she had gave up hope of ever being close to her daddy, and by that time she was just plain bitter. I've known other women who were just the same as Mrs. Peers and they always had rotten luck with men, like that first hopeless love just ruined their luck for good. Now, her daddy, he had his own ideas about farming and he got frustrated with the way the old man ran things. He was always running on about 'keepin up with the times,' you know, and that meant more machines. He was just hot after the latest machines and there was forever some contraption he wanted to buy, but the old man wouldn't let him. Also he thought the sharecroppin familes were bleeding them dry. 'Bleedin us to the bone,' he used to complain, when the old man was out of earshot. He said the whole sharecroppin arrangement was outrageous and unfair and he aimed to change a lot when he took over, starting with the way them workers got their loans practically for free, paying low interest and then letting the debts drag out over years." Reverend Claxwell glanced across the table, raising his brow and smiling acridly at the familiar, uncharitable words. Cora let a sly, mocking light dance in her eyes before continuing: "Well, her daddy got his chance soon enough. It was just days before her sixteenth birthday when grandpa collapsed while riding his horse one morning, just clutched up his arms like he was cradling a baby and fell out the saddle in the middle of giving orders. Doctor said it was a heart attack.

"Now, Mrs. Peers was at that funny age when things get

mixed up in your head real easy. You feel so strange and so aware of yourself and you imagine everyone else in the world must be just as aware of you, and that everything they say and do is directed at you in one way or another, is a response to you or an attack on you. So when her grandpa died so close to her birthday she took it real hard, like it was a kind of secret sign from the heavens. Maybe she felt singled out for punishment. At least that was the impression I got from the way she told the story. But whatever craziness she was feeling at the time, however lonely and out of place, one thing's for certain: she took his funeral all wrong. Even now—well, it was a couple of years ago when she was telling me this—I could see she had it all wrong. You should of heard the way she told it. She said the truth is most families are cruel to one another, and when she saw her daddy standing there somberly beside the casket, conducting himself with perfect respectful manners when she knew, they all knew, how relieved and pleased he must be in his heart to finally have his chance at running the farm, well, that was the greatest lesson in cruelty a father could teach. She said they learned right there, all them children, how to love one another with fingers crossed behind their backs."

"Sounds to me like she's got into the habit of pitying herself," said Claxwell sharply, stretching his arms behind his head.

"Oh, that goes without saying," Cora continued, "but then you ain't heard the whole story either. Now, soon after the funeral Mrs. Peers had her sixteenth-birthday party and her family spared no expense. She was shy, and she felt uncomfortable, and here her mother was dragging her away from her friends and introducing her to all these young men, and some not so young, who were loafing around their living room and talking about the baseball games, so that she hardly knew what to say or how to behave at her own party. That was the night she met Mr. Peers. She said he was just one of many dull, older men she curtsied to that night. Said the only thing she recalled about him was his ruffled, distracted look. And funny thing, but somehow that made her prefer him to the others. Now, I know for a fact she had a crush on some other boy. I know this because she wrote about his 'Arabian eyes,' in her journal, which I read through one day like I said, though she never did let on who he was or how serious she was smitten. It might of been one of the sharecropper's sons, who she'd never really meet on equal terms. Or it might of been some boy from her school, who knows?"

"Arabian eyes?" Wesley interrupted.

Reverend Claxwell let a long, low chuckle rumble out of his belly.

"I assume she got that out of some book," Cora said, annoyed. "But the point is, she had something to lose when she married Mr. Peers, even if it was only a young girl's romantic dreams, and even if she held him off till she was eighteen. Now, what made her marry him after all? That's where we start getting to the root of the trouble." She paused and sipped her coffee, looking askance at the two as a card dealer keeps an eye on suspicious characters. "Now she told me all about them losing the farm, even showed me a couple of letters she kept just to prove how awful it was and how poorly her daddy handled his accounts, and if I remember right it went something like this. They'd been in debt for a while, actually, though none of them really knew just how far until after her grandpa's funeral when her daddy got his hands on them account books. Well, he just about went crazy when he saw the figures. According to Mrs. Peers, he came out of her grandpa's study just spitting fire and carrying on about 'ignorance' and 'ruination' and it took all her mother's strength to quiet him down before he took the roof off the house. Even after she settled him down, he kept mumbling under his breath and insisting that he would save the farm, no matter what. The difference was, her father blamed her grandpa's poor management where her grandpa had blamed the market decline. Her grandpa always swore that the railroads charged such sky-high prices for shipping, it was barely worth growing surplus to sell. But whatever the case, her daddy set about changing the farm to suit himself; he let half the sharecroppin families go and said how they would concentrate on raising tobacco for those little cigarette factories that were popping up all over the place like mushrooms at the time. So he took out a bank loan and bought a couple of those machines he'd been wanting so bad, he got things running to his satisfaction and then sat back waiting for the price of tobacco to rise. Only problem was, it never did. And soon enough those big factories came along and gobbled up all the local ones, and he lost the majority of his buyers and was having to ship everything out by train, paying those same sky-high rates her grandpa had always complained about . . .

"Meantime, Mrs. Peers was accepting visits two, three times a week from this sweet, dull man she met at her party, and he was very gentlemanly, he behaved himself and showed consideration for her feelings and for the difficult position her family was in. He came from old money, with good prospects. But more than anything, she told me, he seemed like the kind of man who would love and care for his children and not cherish his own ambitions more than his family ties. So when the day came and he kneeled down in their parlor and asked her to marry him (she said it was awkward, embarrassing, and she was happy when it was over), she surprised herself by accepting him. Well, you can just imagine, her folks were delighted. They naturally thought she'd made out pretty good. And it was one less mouth to feed." Cora aimed a sardonic glance at the minister, who smiled faintly. "Now, where the trouble got started was after she'd been married a couple of years. You can imagine it's no easy trick, suddenly moving into a strange house across town, getting along with your husband's folks (they were still alive back then), and all the time reassuring everyone that you're exactly as happy as they expect you to be. Then imagine on top of all that, one day your daddy shows up fiddling with his brown-rimmed hat, his moustache grown a little wild over his lip, and he says, 'Well, darling, we're throwing it in.' "

"He lost the farm?" the minister said.

"Turned out the way they survived, he had the whole place mortgaged, and when he couldn't keep up with the payments, finally the bank foreclosed."

"Nothing new in that story."

"Maybe not. But the point is, this business here is what led to the whole split between the family and this is how she comes to say those awful things about her will, how she's gonna hold it all back so that nobody sees a dime."

"You mean to say she broke with her daddy on account of he lost the farm? Because he wasn't no kind of natural-gifted businessman?"

"In the first place," Cora said, "she says it wasn't *her* that broke with *him,* but the other way around. Now, I've read letters from her brothers that say it didn't happen that way. But the fact is, her daddy had got a new idea stuck into his head, and he was dead set on moving the family to Florida. He wouldn't hear no other argument. Just said that Florida had opportunities which you couldn't find in Virginia and it was a chance to start over again with 'a clean bill.' According to Mrs. Peers, that's what he worried about the most. So anyway, soon as he got his problems straightened out, he bought a one-way train ticket and got the family packing. By this time Mrs. Peers was close to desperate. She couldn't stand the idea of her family moving so far away, especially her mother. So she went and hatched a plan of her own. Sat down with that rich new husband of hers one evening and came away from the table with a promissory note big enough to pay what sum was owed the bank plus back interest to boot. Believing she'd rescued them from a miserable life of toil down in 'that godforsaken swamp,' as she likes to say, she drove out to see her family early next morning. She went running up the stairs of that empty-looking farmhouse all excited and bubbling with joy. But when she waved that promissory note in her daddy's face, instead of greeting her or thanking her, she said his eyes turned flat and hard and he looked at her with contempt, as if he wanted to strike her. 'Go give it back,' he says, and went right on helping her brothers pack what furniture they were taking."

"Well, that don't surprise me," the minister said.

He glanced at Wesley for concurrence, but he was only watching Cora in open amazement at all she had learned.

"But don't you understand?"

"I've heard plenty of sad stories in my time, Cora," the minister said, straightening his back. "Children killed by lightning, husbands and wives tore apart, men sent to prison that never did nothing wrong, one woman strangled her son because he appeared like a warthog to her. All of them beloved of God. Now your Mrs. Peers, her family might of ran out all right. When was that? I gather some thirty, forty years ago."

"That's the whole trouble. Time ain't the same, not for her. You have to imagine a woman like her shut up in that house, nothing to do, she's got no children, no nieces or nephews growing up around her, how's she supposed to measure time? What she's got is the bitterness of that parting stored up inside her and it never changes. It never wears away. She's got that parlor with all them pretty teacups, she's got the stairwell that nobody's weight is making to creak, a sewing room with yellow drapes and that bedroom where her husband has disappeared from . . . and it's emptiness. No memories. No voices except ours, William and me. Letters stopped coming a long time ago."

Wesley could hardly believe the extent of all that she knew and felt and understood, of what must have started as a secret between them, whispered stories pieced together on quiet nights when nobody was around, when the widow got to feeling lonely and mistreated and needing some stitch of compassion on a wound still raw and bleeding through the age-old scab. So needy of attention that even Cora, her nurse and house servant, would do. Wesley felt the nag of some impropriety. It seemed a violation of sorts. But then Cora herself, a willing conspirator, apparently went right along, was drawn in to where she believed, sympathized, sided with the widow even if her story was not without a self-serving taint, a smacking of half-truth. And Wesley wondered: is it something wrong with my heart, that I don't believe her for a minute and that even if I did it would be with a coldness and unwillingness? He could imagine what Cora would say. But then this was something new and unfamiliar, this concern and sympathy for a white person. It felt out of place, unnecessary. Maybe even dangerous.

"Reverend, what should I do?" said Cora, with a tone of appeal.

For a while the minister sat and considered this, his eyes fixed and intense like a tiger's. "Can't let her go to Judgment with a will rigged against her own family," he said with a sudden pounce. "No matter what she says they done."

"I know it."

"Then you got to minister to her. You got to make her see."

"What if I can't? She's so stubborn, Reverend."

"Then she's aiming for the fire," he said flatly.

Cora nodded, staring at the spiderweb cracks on the tabletop. Unfolding his hands, Reverend Claxwell pushed back his chair: he had spoken. Later, when he'd left them to their separate ruminations, Wesley would recall the severe tone of the minister's voice as he gave detailed instructions to Cora about what she ought to say, and how best to say it, about the tactics the widow would use to evade her and how to turn those tactics against her. It was war. The minister was a General Sherman. He hunted and burned the corrupt without regard or mercy. Finally he told Cora, with a hint of concession, "Of course, she may quit on you rather than face her own sinning." It was an admission that made Wesley think: *He doubts, he feels the same as me. Doubts her need, her sickness, this whole mess* . . . And he told himself that this proud, spoiled, spoon-fed woman could not possibly accept the rigor of Claxwell's repentance, the harsh terms of his faith, and that even if she could it was no business of theirs—was it?—to meddle where her own minister had failed.

And the long, slow weeks afterward, Wesley following with his eyes Cora's light footsteps up the curving stairwell, her slender hand cupping the rail, and the worry weighing on her neck as if she were carrying a sack of stones up and down the stairs, until she arrived at the widow's bedside where she would bend, whispering, and the widow whispering back in her harsh, phlegmatic rasp which was getting worse and worse by the day, to the point where Wesley finally said, "Cora, we got to bring a doctor." So she knew then that he'd been standing outside the door, listening, and she fixed him with a caustic look that told him to mind his own business. In the mornings he watched her cooking and scrubbing and in the afternoons climbing those stairs again, their secret conversations growing longer and more exhausting. She came out around seven o'clock, sometimes later, and flopped down on her bed, looking ragged and weary as if she'd taken a part of the widow's sickness into her own body. Wesley warmed their supper in a frying pan. Weeks turning into months again and the days slowing down, stretching out like gray Sunday afternoons, becoming focused and insistent and intolerably quiet while the business of reconciliation and conversion went on in the now-wintry bedroom, until the day when Cora entered the cottage in tears, saying, "She's going to change the will. She promised me . . ." And Wesley, shocked by his own concern, taking advantage to say once again, "We got to bring a doctor," then riding the distance into town, kicking the old sorrel mare indignant at being urged to a canter, now that the widow had finally relented and would allow the doctor to visit, because she was feeling better, she said, was even up and around a bit looking content and pleased with herself, yet untrustworthy, Wesley thought, and his bad foot beginning to ache, to throb like it often did when the weather turned cold . . .

At the snap of a twig Wesley came awake, slumped over in his chair. His foot was asleep, filled with stinging bees. "Aah," he said. He lifted it gingerly off the porch rail. Again he heard a crack coming from the cemetery woods. He peered out into the darkness. A stirring, a slight swishing movement in the trees. Instinctively he reached for the shotgun, leaning propped against the doorjamb. Empty, he remembered. Then: what a lot of foolishness. Raccoon was all it was. He cradled the gun under his arm and waited in silence. The dreaming, the memory, still echoing. The way that doctor finally looked at them, shaking his head at the childish folly and superstition dogging modern medicine, which he dispelled like an exorcist with the word "pneumonia."

There again, the crack. Where's the crickets gone? Quiet. Raising the empty barrel, he stood. Glaring now. Fingers in the darkness reaching for him, stretching through the wall of hickory and oak. Maybe curling a flat metal trigger, like him. Slowly, like a man looking over the edge of a crag, he backed into the doorway and stood flattened in the shadow of the frame. His breath came dry-tongued and shallow. Quiet. Shamefully he felt his knees begin to twitch, then lose all feeling as if they would crumble. He thought of Cora sleeping alone in the next room. Cora and him all alone out back of this pretty old estate by the river. All at once a humiliating terror seized him. A terror of living too well for what they were worth in the eyes of their neighbors. It made him long momentarily for the safety of degradation, some ramshackle dirt-floor shack on the side of a highway. Someplace no white man would ever want for himself. He thought: *They could of parked a mile down the road and doubled back on foot.* But then—sweet music—the crickets began to sing again in the bushes and trees. A cool sweat came out on his forehead like a fever breaking and he shut the cottage door, bolting it tight behind.

6

Not the thing but the idea of the thing. Since the last time she'd been to Oscar Wedge's office the front stoop had fallen into an even shabbier and more scandalous state of disrepair. She counted sixteen colored bottles in an open cardboard box and four bags of uncollected garbage clouded with gnats. The building itself was bathed in a warm evening light that revealed the general dishevelment of the neighborhood. Against that sordid backdrop, Oscar Wedge's newly painted sign stood out in stark contrast—a stab at respectability. Common, she thought, and just then heard someone coming to the door. Rapidly she climbed the stairs and knocked. A moment later the door slid open. "Elza Childs," said the secretary, impartial and businesslike. It was the same tall, gaudy woman who had surprised Elsa at the ball, only she now wore a tight-fitting navy blue dress with long vertical stripes that only exaggerated her morbid height. She thanked Elsa for making room in her schedule and asked her to please come in.

In the foyer hung a portrait of a judicial old gentleman seated in a red leather chair. He leaned forward and stared intently from the canvas as though fixing to rise and deliver a lecture upon some eminent subject. Beneath him a vase of wilting flowers sagged over the rim with the stems bent like soda straws. "We don't even know him," the secretary said, pointing with her thumb. "It was just there on the wall when we moved in. Why not keep it?"

"Very distinguished," Elsa said.

"Mr. Wedge don't care much for art. But after all, we didn't have to pay nothing." As she dropped her hand Elsa recalled the gleam of silver from the dance.

"You're engaged . . . congratulations."

They both stared in silence at her ring, the secretary as if she were only noticing it for the first time. "Oh," she said, "how sweet of you. Let me show you in."

They proceeded down a narrow, dimly lit hallway over a strip of faded Oriental carpet, passing between paint-crusted walls that showed bare nailheads in the wainscoting. Elsa reflected that it was the sort of place that mice might choose to inhabit and wondered how these people—Yankees, strangers, of questionable social standing—had managed to insinuate themselves into the most glamorous and infamous event of the spring.

When they reached the door to Wedge's office the secretary stopped and announced Elsa absurdly. As she entered Wedge was just rising from his desk. The first thing she noticed was that his pipe tobacco smelled exactly like her father's; next the stifled, musty heat of a room seldom aired. Also, there were hardly any books or papers on his desk. His bookshelves displayed a collection of pawnshop curiosities, school pennants, autographed baseballs. The few books she could see appeared to be old college texts with spines cracked and nearly illegible. Everything about the room seemed utterly careless and self-confident, like the domain of a wealthy uncle who doesn't give a damn what the rest of the family thinks.

"Miss Childs," he said, "such a pleasure," his voice warm and easy. He extended a hand and smiled. It was a curiosity of his features that he had almost no lips at all, just a row of gleaming teeth suspended in the cavity of his mouth.

She said the pleasure was all hers and he motioned to a worn leather chair set at a slight angle before his desk. She sat and leaned her briefcase against the chair legs and glanced out the room's only window onto a view of the street through slatted blinds. Outside a decrepit figure with a cane was walking a noisy terrier puppy, whose barks and whines penetrated the room with alarming clarity. The figure paused beside a sapling, allowed the dog to sniff and urinate, then shook a scolding finger and dragged it complainingly away.

"I apologize for not calling you sooner," he said, extinguishing his pipe in a square glass ashtray, "and for the sweltery afternoon. There's one thing I don't like down here, it's the summers. I was never much for the sun." He wore a white button-up shirt, short-sleeved, with a handkerchief in the pocket and sagging collar at the neck. The shirt was nearly translucent and his breasts showed through like an old woman's. "My secretary, Frieda, is from up near Canada. God knows what she thinks. But I don't ask, I don't want to know. There's enough trouble as it is. Now you're from right here in town, aren't you? Then you must know my friend Mr. Sweeny—a friend of your father's?"

She nearly groaned. She felt the blood draining from her face.

"A banker," he continued, "your father. Well, that's something to be proud of, given the times. Sweeny and me, we go back a ways too. Has he ever told you about our adventures in Manhattan? He likes telling stories."

He paused and gently laughed. Then he took the handkerchief from his pocket and dabbed at his forehead.

"Where is your family, sir, if you don't mind my asking?"

"I was born in Harper's Ferry, a country boy, but I've spent most of my time in New York—a religious conversion of sorts."

"And Baltimore," she said.

His face assumed an expression somewhere between startled and amused. "Made some phone calls, huh? So what did they all have to say about me?"

"Namely, you don't hold a license for this state. But a state's attorney Callaghan had some other interesting anecdotes he didn't trouble to conceal."

"Well, that's all water under the bridge, as they say. Did he happen to tell you about the corruption scandal in which he was implicated and subsequently and fraudulently exonerated? No, but I guess he wouldn't have thought to mention that. So goes the world. I can say truthfully that I don't have any theories on it and if you've got some of your own I'd be more than happy to hear them out."

Elsa crossed her legs and folded her arms. "None that apply to the case of Mr. Wesley, I'm afraid."

Wedge smiled again, a sharp fracture in the placid mold of his face. There was a wrinkled deck of playing cards at the side of his desk and he took them up and began idly to finger their edges.

"I've got a joke," he said. "It goes like this: I'd rather be barefoot in a blizzard than a nigger in a property suit. What do you think?"

"You just admitted you have no case."

"Oh no. I've only indicated the difficulties inherent. But there are certain indisputable facts. The Wesleys hold a quitclaim deed to their cottage. The main house and graveyard, of course, aren't included in that document, but we can indirectly assume intent by the grantor that all properties should remain as a whole, given the condition of caretaking."

"That deed can be attacked from so many angles they're hardly worth listing."

"True, but the burden of proof would fall on the county."

"In a Virginia court."

"True again, but in which court and before what judge. Let me suggest that were it ever to go that far—and I hope it won't,

Miss Childs—I would make sure it was the last wishes of a deceased white woman on trial and not the Wesleys' claim at all. After all, it's perfectly legal to grant proprietorship of land in consideration of a promise to render services, and in order to justify cancellation of such a deed there must be an entire failure or refusal to perform the agreement, which is hardly the case before us. The Wesleys have been model caretakers of the Peers estate. And there are witnesses who will vouch for them."

Elsa watched him shuffle his fingers along the edges of the playing cards, coolly and almost disinterestedly. He even appeared slightly bored. As the sun angled down, the room filled with light suspending like an orange sheet from window to wall. It was yet a while before the opposite rooftops would relieve them into shadow.

"What concerns me here," she said, "is not the county's ability to make a case. I'm not a lawyer, after all. I happen to know your defense won't hold and I believe you know this as well. Because the only thing the Wesleys may actually own is their cottage. Everything else—the cemetery, the very ground the cottage stands on—falls under a restrictive covenant made up by the late Mr. Peers, binding all heirs and assigns—let me read from a copy of the actual document—" She raised her briefcase into her lap and withdrew a sheet of typing paper from the inside. " 'That no part of the said parcels shall ever be used or occupied by or sold, conveyed, leased, rented, or given to Negroes or any person or persons of the Negro race or blood, except that colored servants may be maintained on the premises, for a period of twenty-one years.' "

"Exactly my point. Colored servants performing services agreed to in the quitclaim."

"But they have no real rights," Elsa said, "none, at least, that the county is bound to respect. The Peers relations only permit them to stay on because they haven't thought to do anything with the land. The moment they decide to do something, the covenant can be enforced."

He wiped his forehead and gave an amused look as if he would begin laughing any moment.

"You say you're not a lawyer? Well, there are issues we haven't even touched on yet. The cemetery, for instance. Does the county really think it can get away with exhuming a prominent family's remains? Moving their graves?"

"The county has no such plans."

"Then why not let the Wesleys stay on?"

"It's a problem," Elsa said, fumbling, "a question of who takes care of the grounds once the company moves in. I'm not involved, so I can only suggest that they reapply through the company."

"Reapply for positions willed to them in a deed."

"A questionable deed."

"Competing with white applicants, I assume."

"I imagine so."

"Miss Childs, this is where your case falls apart. What the county fails to understand is the conveyance of a life estate, though this particular language may never have been used. This is a conflict of interpretation and the judge would have to reach his decision in consideration of the grantor's intent—not the county's dredging up of old restrictions that may or may not apply."

Elsa slapped a flat hand on her briefcase. "This is all academic," she said. "We're not getting anywhere."

"So what concerns you, as you put it?"

"Mr. Wedge, perhaps you're unaware of the public mood regarding opposition to the turpentine plant. Have you considered that you may be talking the Wesleys into something very unpopular?"

He shrugged and cut the deck, shuffled with a swish. "The law's never been much of a crowd pleaser, that I've ever seen, because there's always someone on the losing side."

"But it won't be any skin off your neck."

"How about a cold drink? Iced tea with lemon?" He pushed

his arms against the desk and briskly stood. The stack of cards where he set them spilled in a fanning arc against the ashtray. "Frieda," he called, striding across the room, and was answered immediately as if she'd been waiting just outside. As he mumbled his request through the half-open door Elsa wondered absently why he troubled about hospitality if intent upon sabotage. When he returned his body flickered redly, passing before the window. He sat judiciously and relit his pipe. "Miss Childs, here's how I see it," he said. "We could sit here debating technical points of law all night and still be at cross-purposes in the morning. I've always been a practical and reasonable man. You've got your concerns, well, I've got mine. For one, there's this office to run and it's not easy. Especially being new in town. It's every crook and shyster for miles around and not one of them without his last dollar's vanished down a pint of Seagrams. Now the Wesleys come along, they're good people, colored, but they've managed to put a little aside. They can actually pay for services rendered. So you have to understand my position, that you're asking me to drop a paying client and an interesting case. All right, I might be willing to consider that, but there's got to be some room for cooperation."

"There might be something . . ." she began, but just then the secretary entered with a tray of iced teas and Wedge sighed, "Thank God," wiping the handkerchief over his brow. The glasses were quickly distributed and they each drank heavily before continuing. But this time, to Elsa's surprise, the secretary did not withdraw; she simply stood near the door like a pale, watchful lampstand, sweating and crunching softly on ice cubes.

"There might be a word I could put in for you," Elsa said, "with the chairman, that you were understanding and all, but I can't make any promises."

Wedge was leaning back in his chair, alternately sipping his iced tea and puffing at his pipe. His expression had taken on a kind of authoritative smirk, as when an important man is questioned by his inferior.

"Let me tell you about a time when I was your age," he said, "maybe a few years older. There was a club in Baltimore where I liked to play cards, and this one man was always winning. A tall skinny chap that had everyone in a fright because once upon a time he had shot an enemy and spent some time in jail. But in any case, whatever he was or wasn't, the man was a cheat. I saw the way he cut and marked the deck, defying anyone to accuse him. So one night after losing my way into a hole I went up to him during a break. He was standing on the porch drinking and looking out into the night, smoking a cigar. We stood there a minute in silence and then got to talking. He was aloof, keeping his distance. I played the hard-luck kid. Finally, I broke down and confessed myself the meanest cheat in the world, real hangdog as though I were all torn up inside, and said that since it had availed me nothing against his skill I figured to repay my wrongful intentions. He looked surprised and angry and asked how I meant to do that. So I said I'd just show every man inside exactly how and by what methods a cheat like myself could be spotted. Well, while I prattled on he went white in the face. Soon, though, he looks at me and reaches a conclusion. He pats me on the arm and says it's all right, he won't rat on me. Doesn't want to see any trouble for me. In fact, if I'd just lay back and stay real quiet, he'd be happy to help me get back on my feet."

Elsa looked away out the window. The decrepit old man and his terrier were coming back along the street, the dog whining and straining at its leash while the old man cursed and wiggled his cane in the air.

"I'm sorry," she said. "You'll have to excuse me."

"I didn't mean to imply—" he said, as a knock sounded, soft and muffled, beneath the warm drone of his voice. The secretary set her iced tea on a clear level of the bookshelf and moved briskly for the door, the clip-clap of her shoes sharp and quick as hammers. Elsa shot a look at Wedge. He showed no traceable expression. "Just an old-time story, half apocryphal—" he was muttering, but she hadn't been paying attention. In a moment the doubled sound of footsteps returned through the hallway and then the secretary entered in awkward silence. Her face had assumed an abstracted expression that took no part in these affairs. She led Wesley into the room.

At first Elsa could not believe it, this was so beyond the pale of everything professionally acceptable, was at once so audacious and so cheap, that it absolutely had to be a coincidence or a joke. But when she saw how Wesley stood slumped, hat in hands, eyes down, as if brooding over one of his graves, she felt palpably and for the first time his loss of dignity in such a way as left her speechless. He did not even look at her or at anyone in the room. He might have been a statue dragged in for their amusement or pity.

Wedge was standing behind his desk, smiling congenially, everyone's friend. "Wesley," he said, "how you doing today?"

"Fine, thank you, sir."

"How's your sister?"

"A little under the weather."

"Mmm. Sorry to hear that. You'll give her our best."

"Thank you, sir, I will."

"What do you say, huh? All together now in one room, maybe we can sort this out."

"I hope so, sir."

They were all three watching him from their various positions but he seemed wholly indifferent, even unaware of their scrutiny.

"Well," Elsa finally managed, "this is a surprise."

"I felt the same at first," said Wedge, "and I worried about propriety of course. But the more I thought about it the more it made sense. Why not fan out all the smoke and see where we stand?"

Elsa gave a surprised look.

"Oh no, it wasn't my idea," he said. "Wesley insisted."

She looked at Wesley in amazement. A slightly perceptible

movement, a wrinkle at the corners of his lips. She had been resting her glass on the flat side of her briefcase, balanced like a tabletop on her lap. Now she lifted and gently set the glass on the floor. She put down the briefcase as well, leaning it against the legs of her chair. Then she turned back to him.

"What's this all about?" she said.

He hadn't looked at her since he walked in and did not dare look at her now. Rather he tilted his head a little in her direction as if indicating that he knew she was there. Nothing else. His eyes glazed and his hands nearly crushed his hat. It passed through her mind that he was old enough to be her father and that he should not be standing before them like some errand boy. Yet there was a part of him she would not reconcile to herself, which stood separate and alien though their blood might be the same, their capacity for love and suffering the same.

"Just wanted to ask a couple of questions because there's been a bit of gaming going on."

"Gaming?"

There was a curious disjunction of his posture, submissive and shy, and his speech, which came out clear and direct like the firing of a gun. "Every night this past week a car drives up and down the road by our gate. Comes by near to midnight, we can hear the engine gunning from a long way off. Once we heard a shout like a wildcat. You know the sound, like a woman shrieking. It's got Cora afraid to sleep and myself sitting up till sunrise."

Elsa felt a flush of heat in her cheeks.

"Then a county man comes by to tell us our well water might be bad. Says he'd better check it for contamination."

Wedge shifted in his chair and coughed. He made a pretense of fooling with his pipe and Wesley paused in mid-thought. A square of sunlight moving slowly down the opposite wall quivered between them like a sheet in wind.

"We just wonder," he continued softly, measuring his words, "if it has anything to do with the land sale."

Elsa shook her head. A humiliating thought was beginning to occur to her, but it couldn't be true unless they had no trust in her, unless the chairman expected her to fail. "It's the first I've heard of it," she managed. "But that's not important. What we ought to be talking about is what price would be fair . . ."

"Maybe we could have more time," he said.

"No," she said flatly.

He gave a strange smile, a fluttering contortion of the lips. "Seems like you could hold off a while longer."

"Hold off? This has already taken too long," she said, thinking: *Is that what's going through his mind? That April has slipped into May, and somehow May will slip into June, all for the benefit of him, his sister, for Wedge?*

"All my life," Wesley said, still without expression, "every time I thought something was mine, a white man came and took it."

"That's enough of that," said Wedge.

There was a long, numbing quiet in which nobody moved or spoke, except to sigh or wipe a forehead, as though weighed into inertia by the evening heat. Outside the bell of a church clock rang five times. But Elsa kept her eyes on Wesley, whose only sign of life was a vein swollen and worming at his temple. She didn't believe in his allegiance to the lawyer. It was false naïveté. She thought that he must have an ulterior purpose and only wondered what it was. Almost as if he were using Wedge to get at her, as if banking on her influence and efficacy. But if this were so, of what did he imagine her capable? Was he so desperate? It was the right moment to disillusion him.

"Mr. Wesley, you need to understand that nobody wants to take anything from you. There's a difference between 'take' and 'purchase.' Do you remember what I said before, that you may as well argue with the river? Well, you've got an opportunity to do what's right for everyone—white and colored—and I don't need to tell you there's a whole lot of families hurting for work."

"Can they really force us off?" Wesley asked, addressing Wedge but keeping his eyes on the floor.

The lawyer grunted. He blew out a trail of blue smoke through which he cut an equivocal glance in Elsa's direction. He wiped his thick brow and said, "These are complicated matters, out of your hands completely. In my opinion you have a fair chance in court."

"That all?"

"If it's one thing I do know, there's no sure bets in the law."

"I'm sorry," Elsa said, and heard the official in her voice like the voice of another person. "Mr. Wesley, there's nothing I can do for you."

At twilight the next evening she stepped out of the Paramount onto the darkening street. She had gone to clear her head, to sit a while in the back of the theater, lost in the anonymity of the audience. But *The Prisoner of Shark Island* was a bore and she hadn't paid attention to it at all. It was a fleeting seclusion; for what seemed a moment later she was back outside under the glower of tall, hook-shaped street lamps, following the jagged brick sidewalk toward the diner where her father had agreed to meet her. The evening was cool and calm, filled with the ghostlike voices of people idling about, catching a breath of fresh air after the day's heat, couples slouching on porches and strolling along the avenues, joined together by an intricate architecture of shadows. A night breeze was blowing faintly off the river, fanning the shrubs and trees. Very suddenly a man was walking at her elbow.

"Miss Childs, how you doing? Been to the picture show? Did I scare you?" He was an unctuous, undersized man, meticulously dressed in a plaid suit gone threadbare at the sleeves. A faint moustache topped his pouting, elastic mouth. She recognized him from the office, a new hire, but she couldn't remember his name or his job. For some incomprehensible reason he was whispering. "I'm just crazy about the pictures, spend all my money there, every night, they have to practically drag me out of the theater. You know I didn't see you, where you were sitting?"

"In the back row—" she said, and clipped her words mid-sentence. She had the distinct impression that he'd not been in the theater at all but had just come up from the other side of the street.

"Gloria Stewart, she's too much, and that Baxter's not half bad himself—a little stiff, but not bad. I've been to all his pictures. So what'd you think—"

"About the picture?"

"Sure, did you like it?"

Elsa picked up her pace. "It was all right, maybe a little dull."

"Exactly what I thought," he said agreeably. "Dull and flat, as if the actors were tired out, but I liked it anyway. Hey, are you in a hurry?"

"It's just my father's waiting for me."

"Ain't he a banker?"

"Well, yes."

"You know, he'd be furious if he heard what all everyone's saying . . . I'm pretty upset myself, plus I'm new yet and don't know how to take things."

Elsa stopped. They were standing just outside a broad cone of lamplight cast limpidly upon the sidewalk. "What do you mean?" she said.

He appeared alarmed for her sake and dropped his voice even lower. "Oh, just a lot of babble," he said. "I wouldn't let it trouble you one bit. Of course, I don't have to tell you there's always some guys looking for their first chance to jump all over a lady and run her down, say she's fooling where she don't belong, and what all. Naturally, they just chime in with little things they've noticed, and they fan the fire, to use my mother's expression, and it's all a lot of babble and nothing will come of it."

"I don't understand." She felt a strange fluttering in her stomach.

He watched her keenly, expectantly, like a muskrat.

"What are you talking about?" she said sharply.

He held his hands up in self-defense. "I shouldn't have said anything, it was stupid of me—"

"You started, so finish."

"Really, I shouldn't—"

"No." She gripped him by the sleeve. "Don't go—" She was whispering now.

"Well," he said, adopting a confidential tone, "I can't name names—can't afford to—you understand. And I don't believe a word of it all, but they say you're the one holding up that land sale. At first out of . . . well, incompetence—now on purpose."

She was silent a long time. He shifted politely out of her grasp and stood almost indifferently as if to impress upon her his cool turn of mind. Then she asked him if they would try anything against her. He seemed to consider this a while. "No, I don't think so."

"Then let them talk themselves blue."

"Still, you could use a friend," he whispered. "Your father's waiting—I know, just a minute—they say he's protecting you but only so far."

"I'll be fine, Mr.—"

"Just mention my name . . ."

"What?"

"I've been in offices before, dealt with this sort of thing. Throw them on a wrong trail is the best idea. Get them beating the bushes, kicking up smoke, making fools of themselves—only tell the chairman I wasn't with them, I helped you . . ."

"I appreciate your concern, but no, thanks."

"Hold on—" he hissed.

"I don't know you. Good night."

"Miss Childs—" he began again, but she walked away from him under the puddled streetlights. She heard him take a few steps forward, his shoes scraping the brick sidewalk, then stop, muttering under his breath as if consulting with some invisible person. Finally his voice lisped out from the thickening darkness: "Suit yourself!" Startled, she turned and found him gone. Vanished. For a long time she peered into the umbrageous twilight as if unraveling a dim script of shadows, then she fled in a breathless jog up the remainder of the street.

But when she arrived at the diner her father was not there. The one man in the world she absolutely did not want to see was sitting in a booth, waiting for her.

"There you are," he said, and bit into a pinkish hamburger, dribbling bloody juice down his chin. He wiped himself clean with a paper napkin. "Come on and sit down a minute, I'm almost done."

"Mr. Sweeny," she said, walking up to him but not sitting, just standing there awkwardly. "What happened to dad?"

"You look kind of pale."

"Do I?"

"That picture must have been too scary."

"Is everything all right?"

Sweeny chuckled. He was famous for his monotone laugh and for his endless clowning, and with his flushed oval face and gleaming eyes he might have been some adoring uncle, quick with a joke or smile.

"I'm sorry, the way you said it. You've been watching too many horror pictures. He's fine, fine. Just this business at the bank is making him crazy."

"He told me."

"At ease, Lieutenant Childs. You may experience cramps in your legs." He took a huge gulp of soda pop and his throat puffed out in swallowing. "It's all right. I'm done anyway," cramming the last bite of hamburger in his mouth. "Besides, I promised to get you home on time. Heard that line before?"

He put his money on the table and said thanks to the waitress, a pretty young redhead with a capitulating smile. Elsa noticed that he did not leave her a tip.

They left the diner and walked to her father's Chevrolet, parked just outside with one wheel halfway up the curb. The car's interior was immaculately clean: streetlights quivered on the seats and dash, reflected as if in pure water, and a smell of leather polish hung decadent in the air. Sweeny fired up the engine with a look of tenuous self-restraint. "That'll put the fear of God in you," he said, and they jolted toward the highway with the streets stretching away on either side like blurred and elongated tunnels. "Hoo-wee," he called. Elsa saw the face of a passerby swivel to follow their progress, round and ghostly white like the face of a barn owl. Sweeny was in the midst of a joke from "about the time I was your age," something about a farmer's first automobile and his attempts to mate it with a mule. Most often his stories were accompanied by dramatic voices and gesticulations and dazzling shifts of character, but here he only droned on by rote and could scarcely keep his own interest from wandering. He was in an unusually subdued and cynical mood. And now, abruptly, he switched gears and was talking about her father.

"Truth is, he's worried about this man escaped from jail."

"What man?" Elsa said.

"This fugitive. He got over the wall somehow and disappeared in the woods."

"I hadn't heard. Is that why he sent you?"

"Well, you know your father. He's one that's got to worry. If it's not this business with the bank then he's got to find something else."

"I tell him all the time."

"He's got to push that stone up a hill," Sweeny said, shaking his head. "I'd hate to be there the day they tell him to retire."

"Retire? He's not yet fifty," Elsa said. She watched the town dissolve into rushing shapes of trees, glimpses of fields awash in moonlight.

"But he looks it, I'd say. He's got the worries of the world." A patter of buffoonish chuckling: "He thinks you've gone and turned socialist on him. So I confessed how I spied you passing out Red leaflets at the country club and making secret hand signs with the nigger stableboy."

She looked out the window at the stark fringe of clouds along the western horizon. Above the stars appeared to blink and waver like a net of fireflies encircling the earth. "That's funny," she said.

"Don't get cross with me, now. It's not my fault if he can't take a joke. But you know, I tend to agree with him. Certain ideas, they don't sit right with a lady."

"Neither do certain men."

He cracked an equivocal grin. "In any case, I'm only saying this because I'm concerned for your father's health. With all he's got on his mind these days I'd hate to think there was any unnecessary bother."

"No reason to worry, Mr. Sweeny."

"Well, I'm glad to hear that."

They drove on a while in silence. After a short time they turned off the highway and the car bounced and jostled on the rutted country lane leading to her house. The world outside seemed to Elsa strangely distant and isolate as if she had returned to the dark of the Paramount, the passing of a phantom landscape.

"I spoke to a friend of yours yesterday," she said suddenly.

"Really," he yawned.

"Oscar Wedge."

He broke into long, exaggerated laughter.

"Then he isn't a friend?"

"No, no—"

"He claims all kinds of familiarity."

"No, oh God—"

"Something about Manhattan . . ."

"Well, that's a story for another time," he said in mock confession. "We've run around a bit, had some little adventures. Oh, I could tell you some stories."

"Why don't you tell me something else?"

Sweeny shot her a sidelong glance. "Almost home," he said, looking away through the windshield. "Your father will think I forgot all about you."

"He involves himself in a dispute he can't win. He makes allusions to some sort of deal. The only thing I can figure is he means to get himself known and this whole song and dance is some kind of sick advertisement."

"Lucky Strikes Are Less Acid and Oscar Wedge! National Beer Brewed for Flavor and Oscar Wedge!"

"Except," Elsa said, "it isn't funny."

"What do you want me to say? He's a mercenary, a con man. I know for a fact he once took the case of a woman who believed she came from outer space and was unable to make rent because she sent the money home. And you say he isn't funny? What planet are you living on?" He pounded his palm on the steering wheel yet looked secretly annoyed, like a vaudeville minstrel before a crowd of stiff-necked Baptists. "Let me give you some advice," he said. "With men like Oscar Wedge there's only one thing you need to know: how to keep him in his place. His kind can be a lot of fun, at a proper distance. But it's a question of nature and you can't fight it even if you wanted to. The nature divides us from him, him from the lower breeds. There's nothing else to say about it. Just be thankful he's not your relative, for Christ's sake."

"Uncle Wedge," she said.

"Just imagine him in your kitchen."

"Only it's not a joke," she insisted. "His clients are depending on him and the only question is how high can he drive the price?"

"Well, I guess they should have found themselves a better lawyer. I honestly don't see why you're so worried for him and his clients when you've got troubles of your own—that's right, I've heard a thing or two. So if you think like I do"—he flipped his hair back in limp, oily quills and lit a cigarette without pausing—"it's again a question of nature. It's a plain fact some people can't look after themselves. Now I'm just a horse vet, but once I heard a doctor from the university give a talk on the human brain. What he said about people wasn't all that different from animals. There's different sizes and weights to the brain and some are less developed than others. Undeveloped brains weigh less and are shaped differently too: smaller and more angular, not so elaborate, and the front end of the corpus callosum relatively swollen. This means the colored man stands on the evolutionary scale far apart from you and I and closer, in fact, to the higher anthropoids."

"A science lesson," Elsa said, tired of this ride, this endless night where even the fields and houses looked worn-out and pained.

"Just a minute. The point this doctor got around to was you can't expect these people to act like you and me. You can feel sorry for them, try to help them along, but if they're just naturally backward you can't fairly expect them to know what's best for themselves. See what I mean? So maybe in this case you've just got to take up the burden of a steward. Maybe that means making decisions you'd rather not have to make. It's like a mother does when her children don't want to take their medicine, she makes the decision, they might cry and complain, but everyone stays healthy. Everyone wins."

She leaned back and shut her eyes. "Aren't we home yet?"

"Right on time," Sweeny said, and flicked his cigarette out the window, a firefly sucked into the rushing dark.

He turned onto the long dirt drive where her house stood broad and dark, in moonlight a luminous blue. The air was stagnant, weighted with the promise of heat, and it seemed very clear that there would be no relief for some time. In the same moment she felt a flutter as if something delicate and very precious had suffered its death at last within her. She felt it as her own heart beating, as the pulsing of her blood. Then it seemed to finish. A sigh escaped her and she looked out to where the window of her father's study glowed from its curtained frame. She wondered what he would say, who had always believed in fidelity and duty, to the living and the dead. Who had raised her to believe the same. At last the car jerked to a stop and Sweeny pulled the handbrake. He came round and opened her door with ritual manners and she stepped past him and walked up the porch stairs through a cloud of tiny gray moths and mosquitoes circling the muted light. By turns they buzzed and charged the bulb, spinning like an implacable wheel. " 'Night," he called from behind her. "Tell your daddy I got you home in one piece." She heard the car door slam shut and Sweeny whistling as he walked away up the drive.

But halfway through the door she paused as if struck. The slightest breeze listed and shivered in the yard, provoking within her a sudden new idea.

Did they catch the sonofabitch?

No sir, they didn't. Figure he made it to a train and they passed word down the railway.

Won't catch him now.

I don't expect so.

How's your mother?

A little shook up. She's kind of wondering—

You can quit early if you like.

Thanks.

So what happened?

With mama?

With the sheriff, son. Quit looking over there.

He's been standing there a while—

Let him stand, for God's sake. What excuse did he make this time?

Says the dogs were no good, drove them in circles, and the trail was weak . . .

Dogs, eh. Too bad they can't tell their side of things.

That's what everybody's saying. But he claims he ain't worried, they'll just nab the fella somewhere else and send him on back.

Huh. We'll see about that.

Well, I should be going.

You see what's happening downtown?

Nothing. They all gone home to their families. Hell, there's a killer on the loose. For all we know he didn't get on some train but he's hiding out somewhere nearby waiting for the coast to clear.

That's a fat chance.

Well, I should be going.

Go on, I'll see you tomorrow. Eight sharp.

Night, Mr. Sims.

Wesley, you been standing there long enough. What can I do for you?

Twenty minutes, sir.

What?

Just twenty minutes, sir.

What do you need, son? I don't have all day.

Ax blade, skein of rope.

Taking down a tree?

Yessir, a dead oak.

That's mean business for a man your age.

Yessir. I need some shells too.

Shotgun?

Two boxes, number 7 shot.

Hunting quail with that?

I also need cartridges for a .32-20.

Loading up, ain't you? Worried about this fugitive? All right. We've got 'em around somewheres. What kind of rifle?

Stevens, thirteen-shot repeater.

You ain't looking to sell it? I've got a boy's birthday coming up and he's just the right age. Says his friends have all got real rifles and now he's got to have one too, you know how these kids are. I'd pay a fair price—

I like the gun just fine, sir.

Well, then. Here you are. I expect you'll want it on credit.

Nosir, I'll pay cash, thank you.

7

The dead oak rose high over the yard, scarred by hundred-year-old lightning. The trunk had split in infancy and curled half around itself in contrary directions so that it formed two separate trees joined by and dependent upon the selfsame root structure, unwilling partners in an unbrokered truce. Forty feet in the air the span of dead outer branches bobbed and creaked precipitously. Wesley set down the ax. The main house shone behind him in the late morning sun and away down the hillside the roof of his cottage appeared angular and worn. He took the coil of rope in hand and circled the oak. Woodpeckers had been at it. Ants quivering in sinuous files. He wanted to fell it away from the main house without damaging a young chestnut that spread its gentle umbrella over the lawn. Come autumn squirrels would take the spiked round shells in their teeth and crack them effortlessly apart.

He made a slipknot in the rope and cinched it around a palm-sized stone. Then he set his ladder against the base and climbed to the second step and holding the trunk for balance tossed the stone high into the air. He was aiming for a solid branch, something to provide leverage and stability, but the throw went wide and the stone came crashing down and hung itself in the lower reaches. He got off the ladder, yanked the rope free, threw and missed again. Again the rope hung up in the tangle and he had to pull with all his strength to loose it. He launched it immediately in anger and was nearly struck when the stone glanced off the trunk and came whistling back, landing with a hollow thump in the grass. "Damn," he said. He stood blinking and sweating in the sun. Up high a crow traced unhurried figure eights, impassive observer of the farce. Wesley waved it away. But the next time his aim was true. The stone arched over and hooked a solid branch and he cheered as it fell until the rope caught a protruding stub and the stone swung loose in the air, snowing him with barky debris. He climbed the ladder steps and strained upward. It was just out of his grasp. "Cora," he called, his voice carrying over the yard, but she'd already left for town. Gone to meet an old friend who worked for the C&O Railroad. He tried catching the stone with his ax, but his balance was too precarious and the blade too heavy, so he returned down the path and rifled through the toolshed until he found her garden hoe, warped and forlorn-looking in its musty corner.

Returning to the tree he discovered an entire family of crows settled among the sagging limbs. One of the birds was pecking experimentally at the rope end while the others watched with apparent interest, as if hit upon a novel form of mischief. Wesley hollered and clapped his hands; the crows croaked and fluttered away, malignly resettling on the main house roof. From atop the ladder Wesley reached with the forked edge of the hoe and caught the stone in its notch and stepped carefully down. The rope dragged free and the stone fell to earth.

He loosed the stone and set it with the hoe against the side of the house. Next, with a hammer and garden stakes, he pulled each end of rope away from the house as far as they would stretch and drove them into the ground. The tree groaned and light branches snapped but the twin crowns remained erect, unimpressed. What I could do with a son, he thought. It was nearly midday and the sun's heavy web was draggling about the yard. He went down to the cottage and drank a glass of iced tea, then he looked through the toolshed again and returned with his bow saw and a can of oil. He laid them beside the trunk and looked up, shading his eyes from the glare. The tree seemed to bob and sway serenely as though all were well with the world. He took up the saw and dripped a pale thread of oil down the steel-toothed edge of the blade, first one side and then the other, and climbed the ladder and began taking off the lower branches, everything within easy reach. The bow saw sliced straight through the rotten wood, which crumbled with a suspect odor as he worked, until at the foot of the tree a ring of strewn unhealthy limbs lay spread out like excavated bones. When he'd finished cutting he stepped down and piled them out of his way. He rested and fingered the axblade. It looked good and sharp. The bare metal surface was hot. Already his shoulders ached and he was breathing quickly and shallowly, thinking of the years he'd stripped pines in Appalachian lumber camps and hauled scrap trees to the mill for a dollar and twenty-five cents a day. For a young man in those days it was a good opportunity to rise in the world and make enough to marry and care for a family, even if you were never at home to see them, even if the one girl you loved wouldn't have you on that account.

When he had rested a while he folded the ladder and laid it on the grass and sawed a level notch in the trunk to use as an eye mark. Then he raised and swung the ax. He laid into the tree and hacked at the tough outer bark, balancing the effort and angle of his blows. Periodically, he stopped to rest his arms on the upturned ax handle and gazed down over the steaming green yard. No sign of Cora. As he worked he felt at once acutely aware of and separate from his own body, as though a part of him in concentration had stepped outside the bounds of blood, muscle, and skin. He scarcely noticed the passing hour, the depthless meridial sun. All time was measured by his progress through the tree. When at last he broke into the rotten core he had to sweep the loose chipping as he worked or else shower himself in a cloud of pungent dust. The tree began to lean with the ropes and he quickened the tempo of his strokes. Once when he looked up he thought he saw a figure slipping from the cemetery into the woods. He snapped straight and waited for a while but neither saw nor heard a thing. Finally, the oak shuddered and groaned. It split along the line of the cut and the ropes bowed and fell slack in the middle and he stepped away, expecting the weight to drag it down. But it held stubbornly. He went out and pulled the stakes and ran them sharp as clockhands and came back and looked up at the tree, still expecting it to give way.

It was leaning at a bizarre angle, the twin crowns wavering slightly as if dazed, sagging against one another, and he felt the mixed sadness and exhilaration that comes with the wrecking of once-beautiful things. Yet it was part of the natural scheme, the duty of a caretaker. He swung back the blade and drove it hard to the mark. Three sharp hits and the crippled tree gave, snapped, and fell over with a hollow thud and violent flailing of limbs.

When he took the first armful of kindling down to the cottage it was midafternoon and Cora was not yet back from town. He stood listening for the blend of casual, satirical laughter in her voice, and all at once a wearisome thought occurred to him. He let the kindling fall. And he was right: he'd sensed it all morning. As he rounded the cottage she was just coming into view along the cracked dirt road, walking side by side with TJ in the wavering heat.

"Goddamn," Wesley muttered. He returned to chopping wood. As if she hadn't never said she was finished with him. Hadn't never sent him packing and told him not to show his face when he came through town, no matter if he stopped over on a late train and needed a place to spend the night. All of which had been a long time coming, for Wesley. After all, it was Wesley who time and again intervened in the middle of the night to keep them from strangling one another over some inarticulate dispute comprehensible only to the local gossips, who clicked their tongues at Wesley and said, "They're just in unnatural love with one another, and there ain't a damn thing you can do about it." And as if he hadn't asked her just yesterday to remember what always happened whenever she weakened and agreed to see TJ, to hear him out—the apologies, excuses, his sweet promises and youthful smile. Youthful though he, too, had aged—they'd all grown too old for this nonsense, which better suited lovers at the start of the line, with the whole of life's misfortunes before them yet like some unexplored territory. Wesley was tired of it. Even the gossips let it alone.

Now here they were, their voices already ringing inside the cottage. For a while Wesley waited with a grim sense of helplessness. He swung the ax hard and steady in repetitive strokes, splitting branches from the trunk.

"Hey there," a voice called.

He paused and looked up. TJ strolled up the lawn slow and easy, with Cora beside him. "Well, look here," he said, smiling, "if it ain't old Wes."

Wesley let go of the ax handle. "How's the railroad?"

"Ah, forget that business. Looks like you're keeping busy though." TJ eyed the long, decrepit trunk of the oak with amusement. "Big sister's got you chopping down trees and everything."

"Well, you know she runs a tight ship." They both turned to Cora; she grinned with obvious delight, the three of them together, it had been a while, and Wesley wondered if she was maybe lonelier than she let on. "You laid over tonight?"

"Couple of days," TJ said, squinting in the bright sun. "Then again . . . who knows?" And to Wesley's questioning, discomforted look, Cora added: "Says he's thinking about settling down, but you know how he likes to talk."

"Yeah, right," Wesley said.

"Only I might be serious this time," TJ said.

"You know there's not a lot of work these days."

"What I hear," TJ said, "there may be some jobs right here in Zion."

Wesley looked quickly to his sister but she was studying the tree, which had already settled into the grass like an old log that has been there a long time.

"So they say," he said.

"Don't sound like you believe it."

"Well, you know. Before turpentine it was furniture, and before that it was textiles. And all it ever amounted to was talk."

"At least you can have a good meal, and a few days' rest," Cora broke in. "Now, dinner's ready in an hour. You going to be long?" she said to Wesley.

"Nah," he said, lifting the ax. She turned back toward the garden.

"I'd give you a hand," TJ said, grinning, "but my bad back . . ." And he chased after Cora, a mock cripple limping over the summer lawn. Playing a kid's game of teasing, pursuing, seducing. "Goddamn," Wesley said to himself.

At dinner TJ was in a high good humor, telling jokes and stories, talking in outlandishly squeaky and deep booming voices, adjusting his face to match the part he was playing. He had Cora in stitches and even Wesley was laughing, he couldn't help himself, and all the while TJ gorged himself on an incredible quantity of rice and butter beans, ham and mashed potatoes and corn bread—a regular feast. And Wesley caught himself thinking: the two of them together, Cora and TJ, it's not so bad . . . But then it always started out this way and went downhill fast. He recalled in particular the brief time when they had lived together in a little two-room house along the riverbank, not far from where he was living at the time. He'd taken one look at that place—the cramped, ramshackle rooms, nowhere to get away from each other even for a minute, "comfortable," she'd said—and sensed they were in trouble. But he knew better than to tell Cora what she should or shouldn't do. They'd had to fight their way through it, Cora and TJ, until finally she'd had enough. Wesley had helped her move her things, TJ standing long-faced and worrisome in the doorway, now and then rousing himself from a stupor to plead his case. But it was over. Soon after she'd found her position with the estate and he'd gone back to his job at the C&O. Now, sitting together at the table, Wesley wondered . . . the sly looks passing between them, the crescent-moon smiles and laughter like dueling clarinets. But then Cora had told him on many occasions how she was done fooling with men and only lived with Wesley because he was family. How in the end it's family that matters.

They'd met years earlier on a train bound from Zion for West Virginia. A steaming passenger car, huddled with men. Long faces grayed and blacked in grime. Smoke sludging from the engine and from the parted lips of passengers, teeth tobacco-stained, hands clasping the greased iron walls and wilted cigarettes. "What's your name?" he said. The train shuddered over a bridge and Wesley clutched his belongings, looked out over the passing ravine. The thin man looked at him imploringly and lit a Lucky Strike with dark, trembling fingers. "Hey there, you heading for the pine camps? Know if they hiring anymore? I got a mind to let off a here. I can't stand it anymore."

His cheeks were neatly shaved and his dress a blue porter's uniform and company cap.

"Ever worked a Pullman?" he said, sucking the smoke. "Christ, but it don't get any worse. They say it's a decent living but it's all the time serving and scraping, holding out your hand for a nickel. And the sonofabitch manager breathing down your neck. Make one little mistake—don't matter what—and it's 'Ride in the smoking car, with the rest of the no-'counts, and don't come back till you learn how to act.' Thinks he's teaching me a lesson."

He glared at the sullen, silent men.

"Come on," he said, "do me a favor."

"What can you do?" Wesley said.

The thin man clenched his hands and his eyes flared wide, giving the impression of a hunted man. "That's right," he said loudly, ostentatiously. "Ain't nothing you can do about it. It ain't worth the effort if the job is rigged against you. You might as well stay at home."

"I mean can you strip pine, swing an ax? That kind of thing."

The thin man paused. "Sure," he said, "why not? I used to chop firewood every morning for my aunt Luz—after she had her stroke the whole right side of her body got stiff as a board. But hold on—what do they pay?"

"Dollar and a quarter a day."

"They pay on time?"

"Yeah."

"They don't jerk you around?"

"No. It's a standard wage."

"And they don't keep expense accounts?"

"I just pay cash for what I need."

"What's your name?"

"Will Wesley."

"All right, man. I'm TJ."

They shook hands.

At Mill Creek they got off together, Wesley pursued by this strange yammering shadow, stepping down the corrugated iron stairs through plumes of gray steam that billowed and hissed from the side of the boxcar, then leading him with the other men toward the end of the platform, flour sacks thrown over their shoulders or clutched by hands worn into arthropodal shapes, wearing broken shoes and blue jeans, with wads of soiled dollar bills stuffed in their front pockets or rolled into a sock, and eyes hollowed and longing for a home they had left behind and which they would only return to in dreams for the next several months until work or luck ran out, whichever first. It was Wesley's seventh trip. The first time he was sixteen and his father took him and then he'd not gone again until he was twenty and on his own for good. From then on, steadily, each fall and winter, the money was there, in Appalachia. He considered himself a veteran logger and was accorded something approaching that regard by the white manager and his underlings, a dangerous crew of blood relations and ex-cons whose numerous pistols and shotguns were like inseparable parts of their bodies, protruding from waistbands and shoulder holsters. He was there now, the manager, a short squarish man in a slanted cowboy hat, mulling and squinting at the end of the platform and chewing on the burnt stub of a cigar. His name was Robbins. Come on, Wesley said to his shadow; it slunk along as such. They crossed the platform and a cool wind blew hard though it was yet September and Indian summer in the mountains. When the manager turned from his silent appraisal, counting heads on his fingers while a second man scribbled in a ledger, a hint of recognition crossed his eyes exactly as a computation and he squared his shoulders and gave a curt familiar nod.

"Hey tha, Wes."

" 'Morning, sir."

"What you say? Ready for another crop?"

"This man here wants to work."

"Put him to it, then. What's his name?"

Wesley looked at TJ, he looked scared. He muttered something that neither of them understood.

"Well. What's he say?"

"I don't know."

"Jefferson," said TJ. He choked on the word, looking at his feet, and seemed about to explode.

The manager spat out the slobbered end of his cigar.

"What's that now?" he said.

"Jefferson, sir."

"Ever stripped a pine, Jefferson? Tied a catch-cup?"

He shook his head.

"That's all right, son. We're gonna learn you how. Wes, show him where the new fellas sign up. And see he gets fitted at the company store."

Mid-afternoon they loaded onto a flatbed truck squeezed man against man, kept from their deaths by a few narrow planks penned to each side and a chain draped across the doorless back. Some of the men squatted, grasping their knees. Others merely stood, serene and unfazed. Wesley and TJ had got on early and they leaned against the cab, smoking cigarettes and talking with the other men. Wesley spoke easily of his home, of places he'd been, of other autumns with other men where someone was killed or ran into trouble with a woman, some complicated affair ending in a comic footrace to the train station. Occasionally, they were interrupted by the violent pitch and sway of the truck slipping off the rutted dirt road, and everyone laughed and peered over the edge in desperate abandon of their lives to a circumstance no longer under control. Meantime the white driver kept on grinding and downshifting gears, and leaning from the window every so often he cursed and sent a long copper-colored strand of tobacco juice floating on the wind.

They were climbing through ragged hill country past stands of dark, shaggy trees. TJ kept stiff and uncommunicative. He watched the ground whip by in a trance. They rounded a steep mountain crest and turned onto a road that went flat and easy for a while, then changed and became rocky, and on the opposite end of the valley could be seen broad patches of stripped mountainside in dark, irregular shapes, and long wires of soot funneling from lumber mills and alkali works, hazing the sky a snowy gray. Eventually, the road gave off to what was little more than a poor dirt path and they were thrown against one another with increasing violence and hard feelings and the air became silent and gloomy. The storytelling stopped. Somehow they managed to smoke. As the truck strained and quivered up a yet steeper grade, wheels alternating from the brink of one plummeting gulley to another equally terrifying and absurd, flanked by the sheer stone wall of the mountain from which the road had been gutted out, Wesley leaned and watched the exposed layers of sandstone, worn by the ages into delicate creases and folds, pass them by.

At the crossroads of a company town some hours later, they passed a group of miners returning from their labor underground, lugging pales and short iron picks; worn-out, cadaverous whites who stared malignly and suspiciously over their shoulders and frowned at the loggers through heavy beards. One of them no older than a schoolboy raised his fist, shouting some insult, and several of the loggers leaned out from the truckbed to spit at him. A cry went up but nothing came of it. The driver sped away, obscuring the miners in a dense fog of exhaust, through which their limbs appeared here and there waving picks and shovels like a troop of escaped lunatics. A gap-toothed man standing beside TJ shouted, "You know how they call them people round here?" TJ shook his head, grinning. "Call 'em white niggers."

"No kidding?"

"Yeah, I heard 'em in town."

"Hey," TJ said. "What else do they call them?"

"Crackers, rednecks, white trash . . ."

"What else?" TJ was delighted.

Gaptooth shrugged. "I ain't ever heard nothing else."

By evening they entered a bowl-shaped valley that bottomed out in a network of logging roads, forking and twisting through longleaf pines. A stream drained from the hillside into a slow, muddy creek, and the truck slowed and came to a stop beside a row of lean-to shacks thrown up along its bank. Soon as they were able, the men jumped or swung beneath the chain before the driver could get around to unclasp it. Grinning, he asked if they'd enjoyed the ride and they all told him to go to hell. He claimed he was only concerned for their comfort and, appearing shocked and hurt, promised to install sleeping bunks for the trip back. Then the manager got out of the cab and told them all to shut the hell up. There was work to do. Someone go and pitch tents in the clearing yonder and someone gather wood. Fun's over. Get a fire going, I'm hungry. Wesley started with the men pitching tents, staking and raising them in the blueing twilight, the canvas husks sprouting with the speed of an army encampment—and it was not an hour before someone pointed out TJ slouching on a log with his hat in hand and said: This one better watch himself. Already he was moping about with a perplexed, resentful look on his face. Wesley went over to him. The sun was nearly down and new firelight quivered in the hollows. He explained that there were many unwritten rules to camp and that he would help him in every way he could but that he'd broken the first by slacking off before supper. Was Wesley kidding? TJ wanted to know. No, he was not—and the manager was eyeing them.

At dawn they rose from their makeshift beds and stretched and stepped out into the clearing. Early fires were starting and shadowed forms stood obscured in the chill, rising mist, hunched over basins of cold water or pissing against black stumps of trees. When they had cooked and breakfasted the boss divided them into groups of six to eight with a foreman at the head of each who, it was made clear, would report any troublemakers directly to him. They were to work at different tasks in different parts of the woods and there was to be little truck between the groups except at mealtimes. They were to listen to the foreman and do exactly as he said. Robbins glared, squat and bullish, from man to man. After supper, he said, they were free to do as they pleased. It happened that the foreman of their group was a man Wesley knew by reputation. His name was Albert LeClaire and he was a mixed-blood cousin of Robbins's who wore eyeglasses and an immaculate pair of leather boots that he brushed and waxed each evening on a chair outside his room. He had the pinched, comfortable expression of a clerk at his counting desk but he was rumored to settle his troubles with a razor blade. Before they started out he made note of each of their names in a ledger, scribbling with a black fountain pen. He also took down their age and hometown and asked whether they had any prior experience with the company. For some incomprehensible reason TJ answered, "Yeah. Long time ago." When LeClaire looked him over dubiously and asked for dates and references, TJ stammered, put on a blank look, and said he couldn't remember anymore. LeClaire tucked away his ledger and led them into the woods.

They trudged and stamped over a succession of timber paths, dragging axes and buckets and coils of rope up the side of the hill, following stiffly LeClaire's regulated pace and speaking in low tones as they passed from tree to tree through the piney straw. It was full light before the sun finally broke the opposite crest. They lowered into a dark hollow littered with bracken and scrub, where huge spiderwebs gleamed and wavered like banners, and little spiked burrs clung to the legs of their jeans. LeClaire showed how to shave the bark from the tree and make the diagonal crosscut and set the catch-up underneath, where the sap would collect and drain into barrels to be hauled now and then to the still. Then he divided the workload, assigning the tenderfoots to Wesley, and said: "Get to it, boys."

There were two besides TJ, brothers from North Carolina. One was but fifteen years old and the other was older and walked with a decided limp. "Look here," Wesley said. He showed them the cut LeClaire had made and had them put their fingers inside to feel the depth. "It's shallow, see. That's good. It's like blood. You don't have to hack your hand off just to make it bleed. Cut it quick and clean. But there's one thing wrong. Look close. Walk around the tree." The younger brother saw it, his eyes opened wide and he smiled. "It should be over here," Wesley said, pointing to the mossy side. "Because here the pine isn't so tough. LeClaire knows it, he just wasn't paying attention."

On his first attempt TJ made an awkward, hacking cut and set the catch-cup too far down and Wesley corrected him gently and showed where he was wrong and how the sap would grow polluted the farther it ran. Next the older brother went and then the younger brother and of the three it was he who had the knack. Soon he was working on his own while Wesley labored with the others, showing them again and again. By noon they were sweating and sticky with sap and there was sap in their hair and on their clothes and their hands were glued with sap and it was in the air they breathed. They had covered roughly half of the area assigned them when LeClaire appeared out of the woods and rested one foot on a broken log, watching them with untroubled eyes. He wrote in his ledger and kept on watching for a long while and left without speaking. As soon as he was gone TJ turned on Wesley.

"Who's he think he is, anyway?"

"Ignore him," Wesley said.

"Wearing them shiny cowboy boots."

"It's gonna be a long autumn so get used to it. Don't go looking for trouble with LeClaire."

"It's him you should be worried for," TJ muttered.

Wesley let it go. By night, in the tent, with a full stomach and maybe some guitar playing outside, these things generally resolved themselves. And if that was not enough there were other ways, other diversions and amusements that took place just beyond the ring of firelight in the stands of dead trees surrounding the camp, or at the company sawmill two miles down the road. The important thing was to form a habit: whether dope, dice, or romantic poetry, it didn't make a difference. If you cut your daily load it was laissez-faire democracy. And the habit would be what pulled you through in the end, what made the terrible loneliness of living among strangers bearable, and the paradox was that often the very habit you formed to escape the drudgery of toil would be that which kept you coming back, year after year, like a convict doing his time.

What sense of time as exists in such a setting quickly breaks down, since there is no common standard to measure against but a fractured, disjointed count of the passing hours, days, weeks, in which different people would come and go according to the chiming of their own highly particular and individual clocks, and to the whims of their fancy, which led to more than one tragic and mysterious conclusion, becoming thereby the stuff of legend out of which the living kept themselves amused, instructed, warned. If Wesley lost all sense of time, if it became a plain stretching out before him in flat and uncharted distances, barren of signs or coordinates, through which he kept on steadily nonetheless like a traveler through a fog, then for others it retracted, condensed, became a minutely measured cycle of episodes that repeated one upon the next—a multiplied, monotonous time, playing through its series of tedious and unvarying events with all the originality of a stuck phonograph needle or a dripping spigot. Which did not mean the weeks passed more slowly for one man than another. But for some the experience of time was more severely dwelt upon, its prone body continually examined and dissected on the slab, so that every least detail became glaring, horrific, luridly felt, and the stink of corruption was forever in the air.

For the practical-minded the hours were measured by a succession of backbreaking tasks needing to be accomplished, at which they labored every day from dawn to dusk, clearing land, cutting wood, draining the sappy residue that would in other hands become a salable chemical, hauling scrap species of trees to the mill, cooking, cleaning, walking the same muddy footpaths, burning brush, repairing shoes, tools, and tents. Then eating, tending sores, arguing, drinking coffee, getting high, falling into bed, and beginning all over again the next day at first light. A crude instrument but more or less precise. You carried it in your body. As individual, as personal. Out of such a variance of flesh-and-blood witness is the one true narrative formed.

In the mornings Wesley would wake early, as the first risers were beginning to stir. Always he lay there looking up; a dull and gradual gray dawn light crept between the seams and illuminated the flat canvas walls, so that men passing the tent stood in dark relief, inkblotted shadows, and the sounds they made might have been mistaken for opossums or raccoons. Half listening, a weight seemed to fall over him, denser than his grandmother's quilt under which he slept coccooned each night. After a while he would hear sharp commands and the clanging of metal buckets and know that the cook was taking his station in a whirlwind of hasty preparation as though they were going to war. Wesley would rise then, quietly, and pull a gray wool sweater over his head. In the tent some were beginning to stir, others still slept undisturbed, breathing in the rundown manner of the dreaming. Outside he felt the snap of cool mountain air and looked up immediately to gauge the sky, whether clear or clouding, whether likely to rain.

Sometimes the night watchman was coming down the road, yawning, with a lantern swinging from one hand, and he would nod to Wesley and perhaps say good morning. Other times he was asleep in his chair, snoring gently, and the cook, returning from the well pump with two heavy buckets in tow, would splash a fistful of icy water over the watchman's face and rush away cackling in the direction of his pots and pans. Being the only cook among them, he was granted a sort of unspoken immunity which he daily repaid in proportionate crimes. Brisk and carefree, he blackened his skillets with bacon fat and grits, slopped his biscuits with an unidentifiable gravy, a gray glaze over cornmeal the consistency of sand, whirling and shooting his arms rapidly through the haze of firesmoke that was his element—he lived, breathed, preferred it to all else. When the meal was done he started right up smoking and devoured an entire pack of cigarettes, sucking at the butt ends as though they were candy canes or licorice sticks and spitting them out in a trail that fell all around him, until the squashed ash specks became a part of the earth itself, like the caterpillars you might find under a rotting oak leaf.

Wesley washed down his breakfast with a cup of strong black coffee and then wiped off his tin dish and cup and placed them with the clothes and tools alongside his cot. He wrapped several biscuits in old sackcloth which he would carry throughout the day, his only food until evening, when there would be meat of some sort, however, dubious in appearance. Then he put on his work jacket and headed to the woods.

He passed his mornings in a virtual trance, unselfconscious and unaware of the hour as he worked through stands of longleaf pines marked for catch-cups and scraps damned to the mill, moving steadily and scarcely speaking a word to anyone until noontime when they would rest a while on slowly crumbling logs in the shade of what hardwoods they had left unassailed. And as much as Wesley disliked the circumstances of life in the company camp, he found that the work itself came naturally to him. And often as he sat sprawled out against the dusty husk of some vanished hickory or sweet gum tree he would think that if only he could find a way to go into business for himself, to find some small lumber or turpentine interest that would contract out to him at such and such a rate, with the understanding that payment was determined by the size and quality of the harvest and not through such random and malleable calculations as the hours or days employed, which to Wesley signified nothing at all, other than a lupine cleverness on the part of the managers to keep wages at a fixed and general low. And while he went on lost in his thoughts, men would start rising and brushing themselves off, stretching and laughing at one another, and Wesley would return from his daydream to the perpetual cycle of afternoons running before him like a mill wheel, grinding and sawing and sweating for a fraction of what his labor might be worth . . .

But there was no use going on about it. And so evening found him winding back through the trampled footpaths with an ax and a coil of rope slung over his shoulders, with sawdust caking his jacket and hands and the shapeless cap he always wore to keep the splinters out of his hair. The mountain peaks would redden and begin to go dark, while from the east a sheen of silver-blue twilight washed imperceptibly over the sky, and the thickets resounded with thousands of humming crickets and cicadas. By the time he arrived at camp and was washed and seated with a plate of food balanced on one knee, the night had settled down, the moon come out overhead, and faces of friends and strangers alike were blurred in dark anonymity until the firelight worried them again into view. About this time Wesley would take out his pipe, cheerlessly stuffing and lighting it and then drawing in slow and easy while all around him the evening chatter began. Sometimes he would join in and talk about his home, his sister, and about the pretty girl he'd left promises and assurances to and his hopes of returning soon to make good on them. More often he would say nothing at all.

At full dark there was a certain man who made his rounds, when the foremen had retired to their shotgun houses and Robbins's light could be seen blandly squared and fluttering in the window frame. He would join in the banter for a while with his big horselike best-friend's laugh but soon everyone would grow quiet and uncomfortable waiting for him to begin. And he was the last man the bosses would have suspected. They had their eyes peeled for what they thought a communist should be: some wiry, gaunt, unhealthy-looking sort, with an intense firebrand's stare, who was always slinking off whenever something went wrong, when men were fighting, or when someone was injured in a freak accident. The bosses took their cues from newspaper cartoons and what the organizer called "capitalist propaganda," those editorial diatribes that railed against the Populists and former Alliancemen as stooges of foreign powers and a threat to the very Union itself. Referring to these depictions as he so often did, in a mixture of ridicule and condescension, the man with his jovial grin and heavy black cheeks puffing out like a trumpet player's would start in quietly with what seemed to be sensible questions. He asked if anyone had ever seen a fellow human being with a tail and horns. Of course not. He asked if anyone would therefore contest him when he said that the newspapers and the industry bosses were feeding them lies. And they would shrug, for naturally it was so. He would seem to grow confused then and suggest in a slightly chiding fashion that he wondered why there were so few converts to be found when they themselves admitted who it was telling lies and who was telling the truth.

"Nobody said nothing about your truth," a man might say in the general silence that ensued. "You're putting words in our mouths."

He would smile then, patient, even grandfatherly, for he was going on forty years old among younger men, the majority of whom had yet to see twenty-one. Wesley might open his eyes and watch the conversation then, noting who was waiting patiently for the apostle to wear out and who was listening with interest. Recovering from the rebuff, the man would glance round the fire seeking some ally in the eyes glistening white and troubled thereabout. "You there." He pointed to TJ. Startled, TJ looked toward the others and then back to the man whose raised finger trembled slightly like a fat copper cord. "You understand what I'm talking about."

"Sure," TJ whispered.

"Where are you from?"

"Tidewater."

"And what are you doing here?"
"Same as everyone else."
"Working," the man said.
"Yeah."
"Come all the way from Tidewater to work pines?"
TJ let out a dry, rasping laugh.
"I wasn't aware of any shortage of pines back in the Tidewater. In fact, I thought that was the one thing they had in plenty. But here you are. Because you couldn't get a job back home?" And before TJ could answer the man was lecturing them about the practice of hoarding jobs and capital into the hands of a few. "So your boss, he's got to watch you real close. Because if he lets you alone even for half a minute, you might decide to pick yourself up off that dirt floor where he's holding you down—and *organize,* see—and you can bet that would spell trouble for him. Then you might take that precious capital right out of his hand. See what I mean?"
The organizer paused, let his eyes roam around the fire. "Sound like someone you all know?"
TJ smiled, long and lean. "That goddamn Albert LeClaire."
The organizer looked back to TJ.
"Yeah?"
"He's always got his eyes on me. I never did anything to him. Who does he think he is?"
"Look out for that one, anyway."
"I'd like to slug them goddamn eyes."
"But I was thinking more of the manager, Robbins . . ."
Later, when he could no longer keep himself sitting up, Wesley would lie awake in his cot for some time before falling asleep. He had always envied and admired those who could close their eyes and begin snoring right away, as if shutting off a switch, but he'd never had the talent for it. There would be night sounds outside the tent drifting on the air like contrary breezes, someone strumming a guitar, late talkers muttering and breaking into laughter, and occasionally, distantly, the cry of a

great horned owl from somewhere deep in the hills. So hollow and mournful. He would have to flip onto his side and crush the blanket roll he used for a pillow over his ears.

Near dawn Wesley undreamed himself. Opened his eyes. All around him the sprawled men breathed deeply and muttered a garbled language of sleepers. The sound of the crickets droned like tin violins. Then the tent flap blew open and someone came in and rustled out of his pants, shivering and wheezing in the dark, someone gone to be sick or to warm himself over the ashes of the fire. Turning, Wesley caught sight of TJ slipping back under his blanket. His gaunt limbs and shadow of a praying mantis. The black knot of hair on top of his head.

"Hey," Wesley whispered.

TJ lay there motionless.

"You awake?"

He pretended to quiver and stir in his sleep.

"Hey."

"What," TJ said.

"You see the moon?"

"The what?"

"It still waning?"

"I wasn't paying attention."

"Didn't you look up at the sky?"

"I didn't see no goddamn moon."

"Then it's a new."

TJ said nothing. He flipped onto his side with his back facing Wesley.

"Know what my grandma used to say?"

"No. What."

"New moon, frost soon."

The line for the first month's wages began outside of Robbins's office and stretched down the hill, past the foremen's shacks and the loggers' canvas tents, ending in an unseemly gathering by the outhouse door. Every now and again the door blew open and shut with a wind-tossed clap. Each time it did so the crowd of tensely expectant and hopeful-looking men smiled and spat tobacco juice and made bad jokes to cover their nerves. It was chill and bright and the leaves were turning a burnt-orange color. Wesley and TJ stood near the back, along with the Carolina brothers, watching fleets of clouds drift across a glacial-blue sky, flat and serene, like icebergs in a polar sea.

The older brother complained about his game leg. He claimed it always ached when the weather shifted.

"You tried rubbing vinegar?" Wesley asked.

"Yeah, that didn't make a difference. I know a lady back home who swears by the stuff. Uses vinegar for head colds, fevers, stomach pains, broken limbs, it doesn't matter what the hell's wrong with you."

"I've known some to mix it with ginger."

"Yeah, I heard of that too."

"And kinnikinnick."

"Kinni-what?"

"It's bark from a dogwood," Wesley said, "crushed up in a stew."

TJ wagged his head in amazement. "You backwoods niggers are just too much," he said.

"Who you calling backwoods?" the older brother said.

"You." TJ pointed at Wesley. "Him. Let me ask you all a question—ever hear of this thing called a doctor?"

"Yeah, they're the fellas that charge so much."

"We got Negro doctors in town."

"Those are just the ones I mean."

"There's more than one kind of doctor," Wesley said.

"All right, drink the voodoo stew," TJ said with satisfaction.

"Look, what are you always preaching at me for?" The older

brother tramped away, crunching dry, curled leaves under his shoes. "Hold my place in line," he called back darkly over his shoulder.

Wesley watched him disappear into the outhouse.

"Lord," TJ said, "what's got up his ass?"

A high cloud blew them into shadow. It glided southeast along the ridge and slowly the sun resumed and with it a man came strutting down the hill waving his money and whistling like a schoolboy. How much? TJ wanted to know. But the man only laughed and continued on down the road in the direction of the sawmill. Wesley smiled and said: "Don't believe we'll see him again, at least not for a couple of days." They looked at all the backs of heads craning and bobbing in front of them. The line seemed to stretch on endlessly without motion. Wesley remembered feeling that way as a child, when he'd waited hours for a ticket to a traveling circus. And they were feeling more and more like overgrown children as the line edged closer and closer, in a position of application or even supplication. Wesley felt it instinctively, despite his good standing and years of hard work: the gnawing, rotting knowledge that his money was never guaranteed. It was a blow to the pride, even to think it.

"Looks like we're moving up," TJ said. He began chattering volubly about the various deceptions and stratagems employed against the railroad managers during stopovers in order to slip off duty and spend some money on a good time. Naturally, the managers had counterstratagems of their own, as well as snitches and spies in the ranks, so you never could be sure the fellow you'd gone to town with wouldn't rat on you when you returned, or conversely, that you wouldn't find yourself in a position where due to some unforeseen circumstance you'd be forced to rat on your friend. While he was busy explaining this state of things in an attitude of lighthearted self-confidence, the older brother rejoined them in line, rubbing his hands together. "It's right cold," he said.

"Try keeping your pants on," TJ said, and continued with his story.

As he did so, the line suddenly and without apparent reason lurched ahead, so brisk and efficient that they could not help wondering what had held it up in the first place. At its front several armed foremen stood guard, arranged with bored expressions around the squat wooden table at which Albert LeClaire sat scribbling in his ledger and counting out money from a padlocked strongbox, touched at all times by the fingers of his left hand. Wesley noticed that the closer they came to the cash box, the more TJ's manner of storytelling changed. The narrative slowed, slumped, split into fragments, grew secretive and glum, took on a bitter tone, and finally drowned out altogether in cursing some obscure member of the railroad crew whose name he'd neglected to mention. By the time the Carolina brothers were called by turns he was stone silent, staring fixedly down at the tops of his shoes.

"You want to go ahead of me?" Wesley said.

"Nah," TJ said.

"You sure?"

He nodded.

"All right then."

"Listen," TJ said.

"Yeah?"

"Forget it."

"What's the matter?"

"Nothing."

"Come on, what's eating you?"

He glanced away at the foremen, who observed the proceedings with a scornful gape, their jaws slightly unhinged.

"Nothing," he said again. All his avid energy seemed to have retreated behind the glazed surface of his eyes.

They watched in silence as the Carolina brothers received their money and moved a few steps off, conferring in private. LeClaire was busy making a lengthy and concentrated notation in his ledger while his henchmen gaped and spat long brown wormlike threads of tobacco juice in the dirt, squinting and muttering complaints about the cold. Alternately, they fixed sour looks on Wesley and the remainder of huddled men, as if seeking to erase them from existence. Out of patience, Wesley stepped forward. LeClaire looked up in surprise.

He was wearing a white collared shirt and short-brimmed hat, looking every inch the boss's accountant. The joints of his long fingers bent around the niggling pen. "Wes," he said, and his lips vanished into the slit of his mouth. "I haven't finished recording . . . just hold on a moment and I'll take care of you." Crouched over his ledger and staring intently, he scrawled onto the smooth white pages such a script as was almost impossible to decipher. When he had finished with his notations he looked up again, as if seeing Wesley for the very first time. "All right, Wes," he said. "A dollar and a quarter per day, times twenty-four days employed, comes to thirty dollars total wages. You got to sign the paper here to receive it . . ." He reached into the strongbox and counted out thirty dollars in cash while Wesley scrawled "W. W." on the line beside his name. Then LeClaire recounted the money as he handed it over one wrinkled bill at a time. "Next," he said, when he was through. That was all there was to it. Wesley looked over his shoulder as TJ stepped to the table.

"What do you say?" The younger brother smiled.

"Not bad," Wesley allowed.

"Pays the bills. Hell, more than pays them."

"It ought to."

"Another month or so and between the two of us I figure we'll make it home for winter."

"Good," Wesley said. "I'm glad to hear that."

At the same time they each became aware of a closing sphere of silence at their backs through which TJ's voice echoed alone, empty, outraged: "That can't be right," he said. They turned and looked. He was leaning menacingly over the desk and staring at LeClaire's ledger as though he meant to smash it over his head. LeClaire, detached, gave a meager shrug. He picked up his pen and began scribbling. By the time Wesley could return and ask in a subdued tone of voice what was going on, TJ simply pointed, unable to bring himself to speak. LeClaire's pen was intently whipping across the page, leaving bizarre marks the likes of which none save himself could possibly translate or comprehend, as if he conducted his business affairs in another language. When he'd finished he leaned back in his chair and said: "Twenty-one dollars and forty cents—" And he gestured for them to measure their complaints against the evidence of written figures. "Now hold on," Wesley said. But LeClaire preempted him: "Jefferson," he read aloud, "twenty-four days employed, at a dollar and a dime per day—" Wesley interrupted him: "You mean a dollar and a quarter." Summoning the guileless, open face of a schoolmaster, who signals by his patient lack of criticism the crucial detail his students have overlooked, LeClaire explained that for Wesley that was indeed the going wage, but he—Wesley—had a documented work record and had been with the company for several years. For novices there was a starting wage. And that was just the way they kept accounts, so that loyalty and longevity would be rewarded. Now if Jefferson were to stay on another year . . . All the while he spoke his henchmen were narrowing about them in a half-circle, simian, slow and deliberate like wrestlers, breathing heavily to impose the full weight of their presence over the dispute. It occurred to Wesley: it has been seven years. He felt himself beginning to flush through his cheeks and the lobes of his ears. "Even so," he said, "don't you still come up short?" At this LeClaire fixed his small colorless eyes directly on TJ, who stood transfixed in a state of outraged mortification like a stone representation of a soul suffering in flames. "It's all right here on paper," he said. "If you just follow the figures I'm sure you'll see it plain as day—" and he ran the tip of his pen slowly down the page. TJ followed blankly with his eyes as though he were staring down the murky shaft of a well. "There's this matter of a broken ax blade. I see that you know what I'm talking about. It's true, yes, we generally let the handles go. Part of the price of doing business. But the blades. Mr. Robbins is very strict on blades."

All at once TJ seemed to come out of his trance. "How much did you charge me for that ax blade?" he said. Wesley had been lost in the officious tone of the words and their utter lack of significance: now he remembered the incident. TJ crouched against the trunk of a knotted pine, cursing and holding his thumb between his teeth, the blade cracked a hairsbreadth at the tip, running up the back end and widening to a jagged gap that unhitched where it met the handle. They had turned it over in their hands and remarked upon the unlucky break and TJ, who was yet cursing and sucking on his bruised thumb, let it fall in disgust. They had finally moved on and left the blade lying in a pool of speckled, glaucous sunlight on the forest floor. LeClaire pointed smugly at his figures and said, "Five dollars, son."

8

Five dollars?" Cora said. Where her outline leaned through the thickening dusk a crescent paper fan passed languidly back and forth, chasing the bugs from her face. "What were those axes made out of . . . gold?"

Wesley eased back and adjusted himself in the rocking chair from which comfortable position he'd been telling the story. The firewood was all chopped and set out back of the cottage and the evening air smelled fragrantly of buttercups and wild onion. After dinner, a couple of whiskeys, and endless complaints about the railroad life, TJ had collapsed in a heap onto Wesley's bed, murmuring something about love. "It's time for my evening smoke," Wesley said. He fiddled about his pockets. When he'd succeeded in locating his pipe and packing the tobacco to his satisfaction, he lit a match and breathed in, watching the faint red glow begin to expand and retract, throwing a ring of lazy light out from the center of the bowl. Through this light he could see spotted moths beating the screen door and mosquitoes darting by on mysterious trajectories. Meanwhile the extremes of his sister's features—her watchful eyes, the curved bones of her nose and cheek, a flash of grimacing teeth—stood out from among the shadows like the exaggerated and expressionless parts of an Indian mask.

"Gold?" he said suddenly, picking up after a silence. "I suppose you might say so, if there was such a standard for common jealousy. Truth is, LeClaire and TJ hammered away on that ax blade surely as if they'd agreed beforehand to work in perfect union and harmony till its completion."

"But it's plain who started it by the story."

"The question of whose idea it was, which one of them came up with it first and by what means suggested it to the other, I've never been able to figure out nor really cared to try," Wesley said. "Most probably they dreamed it up together the very moment they laid eyes on each other, maybe even passing a bright little smile between them the way you might say Aha! to something clever you never thought of before. Of course, I was asking myself a different question at the time—why didn't he tell me he couldn't read?"

"What difference would that have made?"

Wesley shrugged. "Probably none. I might have been there from the beginning, though, instead of interrupting when it was already too late. Maybe at least I'd have found a way to explain—"

"Cover up, you mean."

"If you say so. I'll admit it crossed my mind that way as well. But then you have to understand what can happen in a place like that, out from under the eye of the law, with nobody around to gainsay whatever LeClaire might pass off as the truth. Those stories the organizer told about the manager watching us and holding us down—well, that was used to advantage as you might say. But part of it was true: they did keep their own code of law out there, a vigilante code, and it could go bad for you to run the wrong side. I remember when they found a man crawling in a ditch one morning and couldn't get him to stand, he was so badly whipped. And some disappeared, though I imagine mostly they just ran away for loneliness.

"There were plenty other signs," he continued in a mute, comfortable tone. "Phrases, codes, you get to know them. You get a feeling for it. And deep down in your gut you know when something is told in warning and even if you have no intention whatever of heeling, obeying them, if you fool around—well, it's best to have no illusions about what kind of people you are dealing with and how your own friends will hang you out to dry. And that was the thing. He had no idea, no notion of it. He was carrying on with the most amazing confidence in his safety, the most stubborn belief that no matter what he did another man could not just stamp him out of existence, make him disappear."

Cora snickered. "And so you felt obliged to look after him."

"It was that or start digging him a grave," Wesley said. "But I haven't finished telling, you still don't know the whole story."

"I can see where it's headed, though. I expect you took him aside, advised him to accept what they gave, don't want no fuss with the managers."

"Well," Wesley said, and took a slow drag on the end of his pipe, illuminating for a moment the fixed red scowl on her face. "That's a serious thing, to tamper with a man's wages. I've already explained—or tried to—the anticipation, how we waited for our pay nearly holding breath, because so much was depending on it and so much already given up on its account. TJ had given up his railroad job. That's not so much as some others, who left wives and children behind, but it ain't trifling either. The trouble was the twist. And the twist was that LeClaire told the truth about that base wage—those brothers from Carolina had received the same dollar and ten cents per day. I suppose I'd just forgot the difference, it had been so many years.

"But that business with the ax blade, that was a slap in the face. It was also a very intentional, unmistakable message. You could complain and make threats if you liked or you could stop and look at the problem in a more practical way. If you did, you'd probably see that the only solution was for someone, most likely myself, to go and have a quiet talk with Robbins and see if we couldn't work something out. Because I don't believe the message came from him. I don't believe he ever knew a thing about it. It had to do with the understanding between TJ and LeClaire which, as I said, they seemed to have worked out beforehand"—he waved and pointed idly with the blackened stem of his pipe—"the way a pair of these moths, according to their instinct, bang themselves against the screen door until one or the other gives out."

"All very well and good, very fine-sounding," Cora said, "comparing a man to a kind of bug. But then you're only telling it that way to make yourself come out the better."

"I'm just calling things the way I saw them."

"Or maybe you were just a little bit afraid for your own skin. And since it shames you to remember and since there's no one handy to say otherwise, you're trying to lay that shame on TJ."

"Wait a minute," Wesley interrupted, sitting up in his chair. "Let me explain: it wasn't his politics that bothered me, I'd heard all that before from guys more serious about it than him—or his posturing, we were all guilty of that in one way or another. But the fact was since I'd brought him to camp and more or less stuck up for him ever since, anything foolish that he might do ended up a reflection on me. I still needed that job. At the time I didn't have anything else—you remember those days. I couldn't afford for him to go messing things up. But as it happened TJ neither threatened LeClaire nor sent a soul to make amends. Neither did he let the matter die. He saw after it in his own way, I suppose, according to his instincts. Let me finish . . ."

He kept real quiet. All the rest of the day he wouldn't speak a word. It was the one long day since we'd arrived earlier that month that you didn't hear him yacking and carrying on about whatever troubles passed through his head. Like when a neighbor's dog suddenly stops barking in the middle of the night. I remember staying with him throughout the afternoon and into the evening while he sat there humiliated on a pine chair outside the tent, staring at the tops of his shoes. Meantime the temperature was falling and a sharp wind had come up from the northwest, with a moon so bright and slivered it might have been pared from the setting sun. The cook greased his skillets, got dinner going, and doled out some kind of charred gristle cakes—I could barely force them down. At first I figured that TJ wouldn't have an appetite, but instead he came out eating like a prisoner kept under rations. His spirits even seemed to lift a little—he mumbled a few words about the meal through his teeth, but scowled at me when I tried out a joke.

"Twilight came on with a mess of rain clouds bedding low on the horizon. I sat and smoked a while and waited for it to begin. It took about an hour if I remember correctly, and the hickory started swaying and, between the hickory, the pines. It looked like it was going to be one hell of a night. Pretty soon the wind was gusting so hard and cold it blew out the fire. Then pine needles started zinging through the air and the dirt was blowing up in your eyes and everyone was running headlong for cover or else checking stakes and ropes to make sure they would hold through the night. It hadn't started raining yet when I decided to go inside. Them brothers from Carolina were lying there so completely wrapped in their blankets that I could hardly tell one from the other. I stepped over them and got into my bed and sat up a while watching the shadows play on the walls of the tent. Then I heard the first patter of drops, big and thick, coming in clusters, like the sky was just spitting them out, and I guess I wouldn't have gone out there for the world.

"The next morning I would realize it was just that which allowed TJ to move unsuspected around the camp and take his revenge without ever attracting the attention of a single eyewitness—but there was no way of knowing at the time. It rained all night, a nasty, violent storm, so he would have been soaked through and half frozen, in danger every moment of losing his way in the woods or turning his ankle on a stone. As it happened he made it back in good time, slipping in just before sunrise. I remember being aware of movement and a strange smell, but I was exhausted and just turned over in my quilt. Some time later the brothers from Carolina started shaking me and whispering, 'Wake up, Wes. Hurry up.' And then I just knew. And I'll admit that I tried to push them away but they kept tugging at my shirt and saying, 'You got to see this, Wes,' and then falling over laughing.

" 'What's going on?' I said, but they wouldn't answer. Instead they half dragged me through the door and over the grass to where I could get a good look at Albert LeClaire. He was standing next to that chair he usually sat on each morning while scrubbing his boots, only now he was limping, hopping around on one perfectly sound tall black boot while he picked over the surrounding earth with a long whipping cane. 'Where is it?' I said.

" 'Gone,' the brothers told me.

" 'Let's get him out of here,' I said.

" 'Just look at LeClaire digging around in the mud.'

"I said, 'Get back inside. I don't want him to see us.' So we all turned around and walked back over the sopping grass to the tent and what do you think we saw when we got inside? He was lying there, TJ was, fully clothed, sleeping peacefully on a bed of soaked and twisted blankets. We looked at each other a minute, those brothers and I. Then I went over and gave TJ a kick.

" 'What's the big idea?' he says, sitting up immediately like he's been waiting for us all along. I told him: 'You better change your clothes and come with us.' He looked up at me with bloodshot eyes and asked what was the matter. 'LeClaire,' I told him. He said he didn't know what I was talking about.

" 'Look at your shoes,' I said to him. They were coated with a layer of slick orange mud and pine needles broken into stickles. I asked him what he was going to say if LeClaire walked in and found him looking like that.

" 'I didn't do nothing. Besides,' he says, 'what are they going to do? Hang a guy for having a little mud on his shoes?'

"Well, you can imagine the scene we had in there: me yanking him to his feet while the brothers stripped off his clothes and found a pair of dry overalls and a clean undershirt, which if I recall the younger one supplied from his own store, and all the while TJ complaining and making it hard as possible for us to help him. It was about then we started to realize he wasn't looking so well, and by the time we got his shoes and socks peeled off—that was no kind of pleasure, I can assure you—he said, 'What's wrong with my feet? I can't even feel them.' They had turned the color of a corpse. I said, 'What the hell did you do?' But he just started yacking on about how he had to jump in the creek to throw the hounds off his trail, and when I put my hand against his forehead I realized how cold he was, and we began to try and rub him down. Meantime he kept on about the hounds and how he'd heard them barking and closing in, how they would have treed him like a common animal if he hadn't gave them the slip. By the time we got him dry and reasonably dressed the other guys were mostly finished with breakfast and we had to hurry out to get ourselves something to eat and bring back coffee for TJ, who by now was too sick even to think about food.

"Of course, we wondered what to do next, because there would likely be a degree of suspicion whether we took him to work half draggled and dead, or told the foreman—who was naturally LeClaire—that he'd taken sick overnight and was too feverish to leave his bed. As it happened, TJ made the decision himself: he was going to work just like everyone else, and even though the brothers both said he was crazy he didn't give a damn what anyone thought. Myself, I didn't know what to do. But the coffee seemed to do him some good—he was speaking somewhat like he was in his right mind, and a little of the color had come back to his face, though I worried about him trudging around in those same wet shoes. But there was no helping that and we would all of us be in similar straits inside half an hour, so in the end we put our jackets on and got our tools and left together, hoping to keep ahead of the group and, more then anything, out of sight of LeClaire. But we had only gone a little ways across the camp when LeClaire came out of his shack in a pair of old Indian moccasins he sometimes used for slippers and looked right at us without any trace of what he might be thinking, without any expression at all.

"It was the worst situation you could think of: he nodded good-morning and followed us into the woods. Why did he have to come out just then? The very moment we were passing by his door? Or maybe he was waiting for us, I don't know. Anyway, we went on acting natural while he walked with us, trying to make the regular remarks about this and that without drawing any attention or even looking down at the flimsy moccasins he was wearing, which after fifty feet of trail had completely disappeared under a blob of mud, and trying at the same time to keep him as far separated from TJ as possible, though between TJ's sickness and LeClaire's bad shoes they were naturally disposed to walk at about the same slow pace, which made the rest of us slow down so much that soon we were all going along about a leisurely stroll and I was starting to think there was no hope of putting off disaster. Of course, at this time I still didn't know exactly what it was TJ had done with that boot, whether simply buried it somewhere or dropped it in one of the campfires or sent it floating down the creek. And then there was the question of how, by what possible method, he could have got hold of it to begin with and I didn't even want to consider that, it was so beyond what I could imagine at the time. And all the while we walked on, I was aware of them both aware of each other.

"Their hatred was a friendship, a brotherhood. I never saw anything like it. In any case, pretty soon we came upon a man jogging back the other way—a foreman, one of LeClaire's bunch. He stops and stands there a minute kind of dumbstruck and then he asks LeClaire has he seen the clearing yet? The clearing—that was the area we were working on, and we were almost done with it as a matter of fact, about another day to go. So LeClaire, his face pinches up and he says obviously he hasn't seen the clearing since we haven't goddamn got there yet, and the man looks at him again like he was stepping careful around a rattlesnake and he says, pointing: 'Yonder.'

"Well, that just pissed LeClaire off. He yells out in a screechy, trembly voice: 'What the hell is that supposed to mean?' And he shoved the man aside and went on his way, only moving a little quicker now. About then I noticed the older brother whispering in the younger's ear and something about their expressions—the one demanding, ordering the other, who was attempting to resist—gave me a good idea what was going on. Every man for himself. It was a terrible thing to watch and I let them fall behind. Besides, I had to hurry to keep up with TJ, who was pushing along now like he was afraid LeClaire might get ahead of him, like they were in some kind of race to get to the clearing and find out what it was the foreman had been too afraid or stupid to say. Soon the path forked downhill, very rocky and steep, and pretty much washed out of sight. By now our shoes and pants were splattered front and back with mud and every other second we were slipping on our hands and knees, sliding a couple feet before coming under control, though we continued right down, and picked our way around the stumps, logs, and piles of woodscrap, till we bottomed out in the hollow where it was easy ground, flat and full of puddles.

"By now we could see the ring of men gathered in front of some sap barrels at the base of a tall, dead cedar tree. It was a tree that served for a landmark of sorts, since the hollow all around us had been pretty much cleared to the last hardwood. On either hillside, though, the pine woods were left more or less intact since they were longleafs and gave quality sap. Anyway, these men for whatever reason didn't seem to notice us coming down the path, and they were having pretty good fun joking around with one another in the loose and loudmouthed way that was usually reserved for the off-hours, and so it was that by the time one of them happened to look up and notice LeClaire and pass a sign to the others, we had come into earshot and clear as a gun heard someone laugh: 'Done hung him out to dry.' To which LeClaire, shoving his way briskly into the circle, says: 'Who said that?'

"Nobody answered.

" 'Hung?' he says. 'Did I hear hung?' Then he begins to pace back and forth like a tiger in a cage, and without seeming to look up he had somehow already taken in what I, only now, following the rest of the men's eyes up the base of the dead cedar, past scraped-away strips of bark and a few rotten branches, saw: LeClaire's boot, nailed upside down to the top of the tree, dripping rainwater from the ruined leather ends. And in the hush that had snapped into place, LeClaire squints around and he says calmly, quietly: 'The one and only thing you need to know is I'm gonna hang the guilty sonofabitch by the same godforsook tree.' That dead hush went on for a while, with everyone scraping their heels in the mud and looking innocent as they could be, until one man couldn't stand it anymore and made a move like he would take out his ax. But LeClaire just holds up his hand and whispers: 'Leave it. Don't anybody so much as lay a finger on it. Until I have the name of the sonofabitch, the tree stays up, and every mother's son of you is paying with your backs.' "

Git," Wesley said, and whizzed the broken end of a garden trowel through the air. It sailed high and came angling down dead to rights, but the dog made a simple unhurried adjustment in its path and the missile landed with a harmless thump in the grass. Unimpressed, the dog came trotting into close range of the Wesleys' porch, looking curiously and expectantly at the man and woman talking there with its ears and tail turned up like antennae.

"Go on back to Atwell's," Wesley said.

The black dog stood for a while, flicking its tail, its eyes dull and eager; then it turned sniffing the air and trotted away toward the bushes, sucked back into the darkness of the yard.

Cora was quiet a moment, he could feel her stiffness.

"I'll clean those guns in the morning." Wesley took the pipe out from between his teeth. "You want something to drink?"

"Glass of lemon water would be nice."

He banged the screen door open and went into the kitchen and poured two glasses of water, sliced a lemon in half and squeezed it dry as a stone, adding an impromptu nip of whiskey to both glasses and returning through the door with a kick of his shoe, scattering moths like flakes of snow.

He handed a glass to Cora and sat in his rocker again.

"Mm," she said, still leaning against the porch rail.

While he was away his pipe had snuffed out and he tried halfheartedly to light it again, then gave up and knocked it out against the side of the chair.

"That story," Cora said, pausing to take a long, easy drink. "I guess you must of told me before."

"Sure I told you."

"It must of been years and years ago."

Wesley nodded. "About the time of the war."

"That long. Seems just yesterday, for you."

"I still haven't finished," Wesley said. Her laughter came sniggering at him from across the porch. "Well, I guess it's pretty funny, in some ways," he continued, "though more than a couple of guys didn't think so at the time, LeClaire set to working them so hard, clearing brush and dragging barrels from here to there for no good reason other than to satisfy his revenge. I remember looking up now and then and seeing that boot hanging there and thinking, trying to imagine, the effort he must have gone through to get it there: in the rain, the wind, with the lightning flashing and what he thought was the barking of hounds, and on top of all that him climbing the tree, of all people, who was noteworthy above all things for his dislike of physical work. It was the kind of tree he wouldn't have looked at twice during the day and that if someone had ordered him to climb he would have stood there and laughed, but that night he must have chosen it for the very difficulty and prominence of it, the way an army captain plants his flag on the highest ground. He would have gripped the boot—how? in his teeth?—pulling himself by main strength up the high tree trunk which as I said was nearly stripped of limbs, until he got to the point where he could nail it—how again? With what tools?"

"Maybe he took along a hammer," Cora said.

"And a couple of nails? Did he really think it through like that, or did he get to the tree with the stolen boot in hand and then stop, thinking: what next? And did he maybe stand there soaking and shivering—it was pretty cold, I can tell you—until he got the idea in his head and went scrounging around the woodpiles, searching for a discarded wedge or maybe even a stone that fit in his pocket without getting too much in his way, and then prying the nail from one of the catch-cups, which would have meant looking a good distance to find one in the dark and then hurrying back? Did he do all this before he could begin to consider what might happen if he slipped halfway up the tree, or got himself stuck at the top, unable to climb back down?

"I don't know, I never asked him. But when LeClaire said that business about hanging the sonofabitch from the same tree, I knew that he knew and that TJ knew, that it was unspoken between them, a kind of understanding as I've said, and that it was only a matter of time before someone decided to tell LeClaire what he already knew and then he would be able to set his own wheel in motion. And that would go badly for TJ.

"So straight off I began thinking, wondering about those

other times where men had disappeared, just run away, and since it was the company trucks that took us out there in the first place and since it was a healthy distance back to Mill Creek and no road you might feel particularly comfortable on within ten or twenty miles, I figured those guys must take a hitch on one of the late trains passing along every night, since they carry heavy freights and generally run slow enough through the mountains. But LeClaire had the watchman move down close by our tent, and all night long you could hear him playing low on a harmonica he used to keep himself awake. In any case, TJ wasn't ready to pack his bag just yet, though I tried talking him into it. He was having too good a time enjoying his joke. And naturally the word or at least the suspicion of it had gone around a bit, so everyone was grinning at him and paying him compliments every other minute of the day, which was another bad sign as far as I was concerned.

"And what worried me more, those brothers from Carolina, ever since that morning when the boot was found, when I'd noticed them arguing under their breath, they'd kept their distance like we were lepers out of the Bible. Well, that was as much as standing in the middle of the camp and pointing fingers. But there was nothing I could say to them—they made their choice.

"It was a day or two later when I came across Robbins, the manager, relaxing on his porch and scribbling in a little half-sized book that he held balanced on one knee. I remember he was wearing a pair of reading glasses, which made him look funny, kind of grandfatherly, and overalls and shiny black leather shoes the kind you buy in one of the better stores in town. It was evening and I was just coming in from the woods, so I had my tools slung over my shoulder and was more or less covered in mud from the waist down—it was still wet out there, still a mess from that storm, because the streams had overflowed and the runoff had nowhere to drain. Anyway, he looks at me and sort of raises up his eyebrows and flags me over with his pen. 'Hey tha, Wes,' he says. I asked how he was doing and he says, 'Fine, fine,' and starts telling me how he's keeping a diary about life in the turpentine camp because it's occurred to him that one day he might want to publish his memoirs. And if he ever decided to do it, then it would sure be helpful to have a diary, now wouldn't it? I guess I must have looked surprised because he breaks out in a big laugh and says: 'Didn't take me for the scholarly type, did you?'

"So next thing I know he's asking me if maybe I can help him with a problem he's having, which is that he wants to put in a little something from a logger's perspective—he called us loggers even though we mostly cut down only what was in our way and sent almost nothing to the lumber mill. I told him I could probably help him as good as anybody, since I'd been working there for seven years straight, and he said was it really that long and I said yeah, it was. 'All right,' he says, 'then tell me this—and tell me the truth, mind, even if you've got to be impolite, because it won't help me if you lie to keep from saying something ungentlemanly, besides which I won't hold anything you say against you. I want to know what you loggers think about the company men we've got working in the field and, more particularly, I want to know who is the single most yellow-dog hard-ass slavedriver of them all.'

" 'Sure,' I said, 'that's easy.'

"He opened his book again and pretended he was going to write down what I said for his diary, memoir, whatever he called it. 'Go ahead,' he says.

"I said: 'Albert LeClaire.'

"He slapped a hand against his thigh and began wheezing so hard and dry I thought he would choke. 'That's good,' he says, between wheezes, 'just what I would of thought. Of course, I won't tell him you said that—but since you mention him, I wonder if you know any good stories, something I might want to put in here that if I ever published the book would serve as a kind of amusement.'

"I was starting to feel stupid for blurting that out, for telling him what he wanted to hear. So I told him: 'I never heard nothing funny about LeClaire.'

"It was just around dinnertime then and I was tired and now it was all settled. The shadows grew long and sharp, falling over the porch and over Robbins's face, which could have used a shave or at least a bar of soap. He went on for a while longer, asking me about things of small concern, things I couldn't have remembered half an hour later because my mind had stopped, frozen, right where he meant it to, just like when a watch runs down. Finally he says, 'Well, I could talk all night but you've got things to do.'

"And I did. By that time it was nearly twilight and while I walked down the road into camp the evening star came out and you could smell the smoke from the cooking fires. First thing I dropped off my tools in the tent—but nobody was there, it was just empty. I got a bad feeling right away. Then I looked outside but I didn't see anyone I could talk to. So I went to wash up, figuring that wherever they'd all disappeared to, they'd be back for dinner soon. I drew a bucket from the well pump and found a bit of rough soap to wash with and I remember watching a couple of mockingbirds yelling at something in the field—probably one of the cats a guy would take along for company and then let loose to fend for itself. It wasn't till I turned around that I noticed one of the foremen had followed me out there. He was standing about fifty feet away with his foot up on a rock, sucking on a cigarette while he watched me scrub my face and neck over the bucket. We stood there for a long minute looking at each other. He was a tall, foreign-looking guy with a pockmarked face and a smashed-up nose. When finally I threw down the bucket and started back, he kept on following me like he was some kind of a prison guard. So I got fed up and hollered: 'Ain't you got nothing better to do?' And he came over then and I waited for him, feeling sick. We were by the outhouses, away from the others.

" 'Get inside,' he says, and I looked at him like he was crazy, and then I was through the outhouse door and he was panting in my face and I realized he'd shoved me in there. It was dark and close with only a little light showing between the slats. His hands were working up my collar and he was saying something I didn't understand. Then the stench hit me and on top of that the smell of his breath while he muttered. I tried to push out of there but he grabbed me by the neck and squeezed. I understood, then. I was standing there thinking, *He's choking you, Wes,* while he was squeezing me and it seemed to take a long time for the message to get through. I was thinking, *Robbins wouldn't do this . . . ,* while the man pulled his right hand away and came back with a shaving razor pressed against my cheek. He was moving me back against the seat, pushing me almost gently like he was a friend or father showing me where to sit. And the awful thing was, there was a moment when I might have let him. I don't know if you ever felt anything like this—it's strange to say, but it would have been so easy. And during that long moment I felt a strange kind of attraction . . . that I've never felt before or since. There's something very satisfying in resignation. And it's a shame to say, but I'm not going to deny it—it was the very devil of a temptation. It even seemed logical, practical. After all, they like to say it about us—frightful, weak-natured. But I grabbed his wrist and bent it backward. He gave a little squeal and I heard the plop in the bottom of the pit.

"Then he was out the door and I remember seeing him flying over the field, his arms pumping like a track star, like Jesse Owens. I started to chase after him, thinking all the evil things I'd do in revenge for that nightmare, but I gave up after a couple of shaky steps—I was never much for running."

In the flat night sky a gibbous moon was rising. It was getting late and the early active sounds of night had lapsed, receding to a faint, constant drone of insects repeating in the azalea bushes and the grass.

"Short legs," Cora said.

"Yeah, and too wide in the middle."

"And what happened after, it was lucky you didn't get the lockjaw."

Wesley laughed, he felt her look of disapproval. "You can be sure that it hurt plenty," he said. "And then having to walk the tracks all night, hobbling from tie to tie on the ball of my foot—I can tell you it's never been the same."

"Well, you sure begged for it. Your whole story, all it goes to prove is what a couple of children you were."

"I don't know what it proves."

"So what next?"

"That's all there is to tell."

"No," Cora protested, "go on and finish."

Wesley leaned back in the rocking chair. "What's the use? That all happened a long time ago like you said. And you know the rest besides: how I found TJ back at the tent looking about as white and cold as a bottle of milk, sweating just the way a bottle sweats in summertime, and how they'd been following him all afternoon, two at a time, just keeping him in sight for fear he'd try and shake them, which of course we went ahead and did. And you know how we cut out the back of the tent late that night, how those brothers from Carolina just lay there watching without saying a word or doing nothing to help us, which made me so hot I had to lean down and whisper something I won't repeat in the older brother's ear, and then us running through the clearing as fast as we could, a lot like that man I chased off, only crouched down so the watchman wouldn't catch us in the moonlight—it was shining then like it is tonight. It was real quiet, too, and still. And we slipped into the woods, hugging the edge of the road as it ran down to the sawmill, because the tracks as I understood it were just a mile or so beyond, a little to the southwest of us. I'm telling you it wasn't easy on the mind either, dragging our bags and tools and giving up a week's pay and wondering the whole time if those Carolina brothers would give us away, or if someone had spotted us and sent word to LeClaire's goons, or if maybe LeClaire had thought to place a lookout by the sawmill or even by the tracks, and by the time that occurred to me I knew I was more than a little spooked.

"And the *noise* we were making: me stepping on every branch and kicking every stone and TJ hissing and whispering every other second, 'What was that? Did you hear anything?' If the two of us had played the drum and bugle I'm sure we couldn't have made any more of a racket. And then hearing the sawmill with its wheel creaking away—you could hear the rush of the stream that powered it still overflowing from the storm. Pretty soon we got to fighting about which way to go, but I wasn't listening to him. We picked around the mill and found a lumber path which we took for a while till it bent in the wrong direction and from then on it was straight through the woods, cluttered and easy to get turned around. And you can imagine, those woods were dark and strange, they got to your head, and you would look at a tree and think you saw someone hiding there, and every now and then we would stop and point and listen, both of us, crazy as a pair of graverobbers. And sometimes I actually thought I heard those hounds TJ had talked about, only far off and never really gaining, never clear enough to know . . .

"And then scrambling down the kind of rockwash you find on those mountainsides, where they've stripped out everything with roots, and where you damn near better lower yourself with a rope even by daylight because otherwise you'll end up like us—slipping, tumbling, bumping down on your backside till you manage to catch hold of something solid, and so sore afterward you can barely pick yourself up. About a mile farther and we realized we'd got turned too far westward. And if you ever tried choosing your direction by the stars you know it ain't all as simple as people like to say. Especially when you consider that by now we were in thick woods, with no way to get a good view of the sky. But we kept hurrying along through the underbrush, every minute rounding a gully or a patch of thorns, or else catching a spiderweb in the face and pausing to curse the devil, and it took the sound of a train whistle in the distance to finally get us straightened out. And you know the rest: scrambling fast as we could, running to make the tracks in time because there wouldn't be another train passing until early morning and the one thing we didn't want to do was wait, and coming at last into a clearing where the Chesapeake–Ohio was just about on top of us. Then crouching in the scrub to wait for a coal car, out of breath and shouting to each other above the noise—'this one,' 'no, this one'—and then picking up our bags and sliding in the gravel along the side of the tracks to reach for the stirrups, and I never saw the two-by-four until it was too late, lying right there for no particular reason, just a piece of scrap someone tossed away without a second thought, but landing with that three-inch nail sticking up in the air, just waiting God only knows how long for me to come stumbling along in the dark, and all I knew was a flat, dull ache—not sharp, not what you might expect—but enough for me to give a yell that made TJ freeze while the railcar rolled on by, slow and easy as you please, and pretty soon the whole damn train, gone, goodbye, and no way to ever bring it back."

9

The deputy appeared at the appointed hour scowling inexplicably, hat in hand in the screened frame of the doorway. Behind him, as if resting on the indolent unswaying treeline, the sun weighed down the prone stretch of fields, dried the green stalks to husks. It was exactly quarter after seven o'clock. The deputy was a little early. His squad car—Sheriff Montgomery's battered black Oldsmobile sedan, loaned them for the occasion—stood blazing in its own slick puddle of reflected light.

"Please come in," Elsa said. They reached for and grasped the door handle together from opposite sides; immediately the deputy let go, laughed at his clumsiness, and Elsa let him in with an apologetic smile. "Coffee?" she asked.

"If you can spare a cup."

"Sugar or milk?"

"Better together than alone."

The deputy's name was Reynold Dodd. A trim, rawboned man with a boyish face, cropped wheat-colored hair, and restless hands. He was but two or three years Elsa's senior, yet already he conveyed an attitude of professional ease, contradicted by the erratic and somehow desperate play of his eyes.

"How's your father?" he asked, looking expectantly around the room.

"Fine, thanks. He's sleeping off a headache."

"That's too bad."

"We'd better get going."

"All right if I bring the coffee with me?"

"You're the law," Elsa said.

Inside the stifling hot sedan, shaking and pitching as the car bounced along a road half paved with asphalt that the state had enlisted convicts to build when there were so many people desperate without work, who would now have to go and commit a crime to earn the privilege of employment, Elsa glared out the open window and plumbed the muck of a foul mood. The sedan seemed to run on a steam engine; already she was sticking through her dress to the back of the seat. Her hair, pulled into a tight double knot, tickled the top of her neck. Yes, everything was wrong today, as she'd expected, and now the deputy, juggling his cup of coffee as he drove, began chattering inanely about the run of dry weather. "Ain't nothing gonna grow, that's for sure." They hit a deep rut in the road and Elsa clenched her teeth. She couldn't help recalling what the chairman, hearing her out in patient grandfatherly repose at his convenience in the awkward intimacy of his office, redolent of bourbon and cigar smoke, had remarked at her idea: "I believe it's for the best—the Lord knows they had their chance." But she'd come away with the uncomfortable suspicion that he wasn't the least bit pleased or impressed, as if he himself had tactfully suggested the idea and only waited for the predictable echo from her tongue.

Now she turned the sheet of paper in her hands. She had gone to the courthouse for it and waited an entire morning and afternoon on the bench outside the judge's office, chatting with his secretary and reading parts of a romance set in Ireland, a story about a girl whose heart is broken by a lover who woos her as negligently as one might whistle for a cab or swat at a passing fly, until at last the law clerk appeared in vexed distraction, carrying an odor of misspent and putrefacted youth, and without so much as a greeting fished the document from somewhere in his sheaves, practically threw it at her, and vanished again behind his door after a few garbled and hostile commands aimed in the secretary's direction. Armed with that official sanction and seal of the court, on letterhead racked with carefully imprinted rows of impartial and technical citations of legal statute and precedent whereby a simple serving of notice would translate into authority over domain, she returned to her office as the sun dipped toward the listless Blue Ridge and turned off the lights and went home. From the end of the driveway she watched a warm evening glow settle over the house like a benediction. With its air of inherited gentility, its sleepy verandah and maze of symmetrical whitewashed fences where the ghosts of auctioned horses hung their sickled heads, the house appeared isolated and beautiful, her own private and imperturbable world. And when she stepped through the door there was only her father's hat on the tilted nightstand, a medley of neglected, empty rooms, the faint irresolute echo of his coughing.

"Dad?" she'd said. She found him in his study, looking up from a mess of papers, his glasses resting partway down the bridge of his nose.

"Oh, Elsa," he said. "I didn't hear you come in."

"Have you had anything to eat?" she said.

"Not a bite since morning."

"Well, I can warm something up."

"Better put it on low," he said, "I'll be a while yet."

They looked at each other a long moment in the quiet.

He smiled. "I almost forgot. Did the judge give you what you need?"

"Yes, he did."

"That's good."

She wanted to say that she didn't know whether it was good, if by good he meant some measure of fairness and honor. But his words of a week past still rang fresh in her ears: "The simplest way to stop all this gossip is to do what the chairman wants." Surprised by his sharp tone, she'd asked how he managed to reconcile the divergent interests of his clients and the bank. "You find a way," he'd said flatly.

And now harassed by the deputy's borrowed car, she went over the bizarrely clinical language of the document that had transformed her idea without ceremony into a signed and binding petition: . . . *pursuant to section 2.1 et seq.* . . . *Motion for Immediate Vesting* . . . What did that mean? Suddenly it occurred to her that she'd left her Irish romance on the bench of the court office. A shudder of outrage passed through her; she was certain the secretary had filched it. And so everyone was stealing from her, everyone hounding her, yapping at her heels. And even the deputy wouldn't let up, whistling low as they went: "Ooo, looks like another scorcher. See that ring around the sun?" It was glaring her in the eye, red, roiling, and inimical. She made a placating remark. But he was undaunted and continued: "The worst I've ever seen. Of course, you hear the old-timers say, 'Remember that summer of ninety-nine?' "

"It's a left here at the state road."

"Yeah, yeah," he said. "So you went away for school?"

She muttered and nodded.

"Did you like it much?"

She said that she had liked it very much.

"You studied some law?"

"What?"

"You're delivering that summons."

"It's only a notice. I could have mailed it, I suppose . . . No, I didn't study law. I thought I'd like to be a teacher."

"That's nice." He squinted away down the road, picking up speed as the pavement smoothed. "I stopped at the eighth grade myself."

There was a long, uncomfortable silence.

"You still want to be a teacher?"

"No."

"Guess you got your job with the county."

She thought a moment. "Yes," she said, "I guess I have that."

"Hey, there's a buddy of mine!"

Elsa glanced up from the document, then quickly shut it in her briefcase. They were bearing down on a road crew crouched along the ditch at either side, toiling like miners, like gravediggers, raising and swinging their picks with a repetitive rhythmic flash of sun on metal blades. A single long iron chain ran from ankle to ankle and traced a jagged scar over the pocked orange dirt. As the car slowed they didn't even look up; instead they kept on swinging, apparently insentient, gears and pistons of the machine of State. Meantime a tubby white man with a shotgun balanced on his shoulder came swaggering out from under his shade tree, calling, "Hiya, Reynold—" in a familiar and easygoing voice, until noticing Elsa in the other seat his face twisted and he shouted, "What the hell are you thinking?" And the deputy already picking up speed again, calling through the window, "Gotta go," while the white man shot back, "You ought to know better, sonofa—" before the dust and wind swept him from sight.

Elsa sat rigid in her seat. Reflected in the little rearview mirror the hunchbacked shapes of the convicts were arrested in mid-stroke, their blades poised and flared like figures in a deformed romantic tapestry. "Careful," the deputy said, and accelerated into a hard curve, pinning her against the door at her side. When Elsa suggested that they were not in all that much of a hurry, he only tossed his head back dashingly. "An officer's habit," he said, "I only know one way to drive."

"It's my stomach . . ." she persisted.

"Oh, all right." He assumed a bored expression. "Some people like a fast ride. Ever been on a roller coaster?"

"No."

"As long as you ain't scared. I mean that's what I'm here for—to make sure of that."

Elsa looked away through the window. The sky was steadily losing its color, paling to a vast transparent sheen. Whipping alongside, an etched black treeline momentarily enfenced them, forming a complex canopy overhead, and Elsa was reminded of Wesley's gate: the delicate wrought-iron tracery, the spirals and quatrefoils multiplied in miniature upon miniature, as a spider compresses its pattern ever tighter toward the center of its web. Only not Wesley's gate, the gate of a cemetery. Not belonging to him, nor associated with him, except as a caretaker has reason and right to open it and shut it and perhaps scrape the rust off its face. And she had to impress upon herself that soon he would be utterly dispossessed. By her hand serving this notice declaring the well groundwater contaminated and their property duly condemned—a judgment enforceable through the person of Sheriff Montgomery—she would make the closing move in the unspoken match they'd been playing since that dreadful day in April when she'd first clanged the cemetery gate behind her.

The notice read:

> William & Cora Wesley
> Zion, Virginia
> Notice is hereby given that in the above entitled clause the petitioner, the Zion County Board of Supervisors, pursuant to section 2.1 et seq., of the Eminent Domain Statute of Virginia (VA Rev Stats c 47) did on the nineteenth day of June, 1936, file its Motion for Immediate Vesting of Title in petitioner as to Parcels legally described in petition to condemn filed herein . . .

Et cetera. The idea had come to her through a complicated junction of circumstance and jurisprudence. While at first she pondered a straightforward attack on the quitclaim left by the late Mrs. Peers, a phone call came unexpectedly in answer to the dozens of inquiries she'd sent out over the previous weeks—it was Sherwood Jr., the nephew and sole heir, his voice crackling faint and raspy through what he bragged was the only working telephone in all of south Florida. And so the matter of the estate was cleared up in an instant: he had no interest whatever in the property, the house (which he had never even seen), or what he termed "Ziontown." The only thing he wanted, he said, was "a fair cash offer and no troubles." As to the matter of the quitclaim, he knew next to nothing about it. He'd never even heard of the Wesleys. In response to her pressing him further, he said he didn't and couldn't know what she was driving at, but could she hurry up and wire the money? He was in a tight spot with some investments. Their official relations ended with the phone line cutting off and, a few weeks later, an exchange of signed and sealed papers delivered by the U.S. mail. Now the county's position was significantly improved. At the same time she learned the result of the groundwater test, which had been conducted even as Cora had said, on some pretext or other, with a view to thorough planning ahead. It was as necessary as predetermined, for though the county might claim the Wesleys' property as part of the Peers estate, the judge would require them to pay a fair market price, which every day they stalled was inflating.

"Unless, of course," she proposed to the chairman, "it wasn't worth anything to begin with."

A ladybug inched its way up the inner rim of the window, minuscule, plodding, a spotted teardrop waddling on black eyelashes. In the passing bean fields, roused from the wire fencelines where they posted watch, a cloud of crows flapped upward through the air, caw-cawing. "It's your next turn," Elsa said to the deputy. The dust blew ahead of them and wheeled, backpedaled to either side.

The faint echoes, reverberations, of the town and of its restless sleepwalkers exhorting and chiding themselves through another morning came to her, but as voices speaking in a darkened theater: the butcher trading gossip over his shanks and loins, ugly language spilling from the barbershop window, intimations, circumlocutions, the regular buzz. On the newsreels Hitler marching Europe to the wall. And the incessant local preoccupation with turpentine, as though it were a vein of gold newly discovered in some furrow of the Blue Ridge, which sunburned men slumped in doorways discussed over cigarettes in tones most often reserved for tales hatched of divining rods and conjure bags, so that even the deputy couldn't keep himself from asking: "You think there might be something in that plant for a cousin of mine?" Distracted, Elsa explained that the company hadn't even signed a lease, much less begun to hire workers. The deputy appeared shocked. "But I heard—"

"Oh, they'll sign all right."

"Then I could maybe ring you up sometime?"

Elsa paused.

"For your cousin?"

"Right."

"Well, I expect the company will post those jobs on their own."

"Uh-huh," he said glumly. "I figured you might give me a little friendly advice, what I ought to tell him, if he gets the itch?"

"Here, turn here." But the blurred earth already swung on its hinge: the county roadsign announcing 2 MI. ZION in faded black letters rose out of a tangle of witch hazel and weed-choked crabgrass, where, as if crouching in its secret den, an iron rooster perched rusting on the tip of a junkyard weathervane. Poised as if in the act of scratching, scrounging for seed, its single hacked eyehole stretched in profile along the feathered back of the skull, the rooster appeared ready at the slightest change in wind for flight or attack. Poised like a fierce fighting cock. She craned her neck but another moment and the road of sallow dirt flagging unevenly ahead, sucked curve by curve under the black front grate of the sheriff's car, swept the rooster cleanly from view. Clumps of trees and scrub brush gave way to open fields. They passed the sunken husk of a barn torched some middle of the night.

Farther on the cemetery gate appeared under a sunlit crest, familiar, forbidding, yet unlike the gate she'd recalled. Simpler. Plain, really. The details exaggerated in her memory as the faces of beautiful or unpleasant people remarked out of a crowd. Beyond and around the rising hill the mountains loomed flattened with distance, hazed by tissue-thin clouds that curled and dissolved in the sunlight. Beside her the deputy had gone silent and she could sense him straining and gnawing at his lip. She turned and pleasantly said: "I don't imagine there's going to be any problem."

"You're damn right," the deputy said.

Elsa replied, smiling wanly: "I mean to say we've talked about this before, and I think they understand, they aren't going to resist—"

"Don't worry," the deputy snapped, "I know how to handle a nigger." The car in its heedless onrush made a final whirl in the road, raising a wide arc of yellow dust in the air as he righted the wheels and braked alongside the gate, the engine thrumming underneath and dying with a sudden muffled click-clack.

From the height of the hill TJ watched the dust clouds ballooning over the sunken tips of roadside trees as if blown from a train's engine, as if the railroad pursued him. It was a thought that had often occurred to him. Once it seemed actually to have happened, crossing the outskirts of hills frozen in Appalachian darkness, hopelessly lost until that first shrill whistle echoed over the distance, beautiful, serene, unexpected. And shortly after, the slow, chugging, plaintive groan of the freight cars proceeding at a crawl, the whistle repeating like a night-bird's cry.

He bit the stub of his cigarette, then removed it and smashed it out on the windowsill. He emerged from the cottage, stretching, in time to watch the squad car do its doughnut at the bottom of the hill. Squinting, he spat out a knot of phlegm. He had slept like the dead on Wesley's cot. "Cora," he called, his voice a little high. Two white strangers got out of the car—a man and woman—their bodies warped and faceless in the gauze of heat through which they moved, at first in the direction of the car trunk, which the man opened and as quickly the woman shut, throwing up her arms, and then on toward the gate, which they unbolted and left swinging ajar. Then Cora's quick footsteps, her eyes urgent and harried: "What? what?" But he cut her off and turned back casually into the cottage. "Somebody's comin."

. . . and don't need to be told how to do my job." The deputy, sulking as they trudged up the path, with a sullen, vindictive look, pulled the brim of his hat aslant as he'd learned from the protagonists of gunfight movies.

"Sorry if I offended you," Elsa said coldly.

"I would of kept it lowered at my side."

"Just please," she said, "please try not to exacerbate—"

The deputy guffawed.

"You sound like my mother."

"Reynold, you've got to understand. This is a delicate situation . . . you can't just come riding in here like some kind of Texas Ranger."

"I'm standing on county property, ain't I?"

"That's not the point . . ." she said.

"Well, I don't see how come it matters one way or the other."

She turned on him savagely. "Because I asked you. Isn't that enough?"

He resumed his sulking, his eyes straying over the rounded headstones, at once rigid and desultory. "Anyone might think—"

"The devil cares," Elsa snapped.

They were halfway up the hill now and the main house from its point of seclusion was scarcely visible, passing in and out of view through the jointed latticework of oak branches. The Wesleys' cottage loomed directly ahead. It looked pleasant and well tended in the morning sun. The clapboard walls, rising to the roof, gave off a glow of fresh paint, and a faint ring of bluish smoke still hung about the woodstove pipe. In the yard lay a bundle of what appeared to be garden stakes and on the porch stoop a pair of worn ankle boots put to dry, the leather tops twisted over like flower petals. Elsa felt vaguely annoyed. It was as if he—or else his sister—had arranged things purposely and defiantly in a show of permanence, when they must have known as a matter of practicality what the court and county would decide. Had arranged this display even with the intent of snubbing her, the malicious and wholly unnecessary spitting at the feet of an official representative solely because she was the nearest and easiest to offend.

She was burning, sweating through her dress. It was perversely, sadistically hot. So much the opposite of that distant April morning when rain poured down on the cemetery, and in the close confines of the stranger's cottage, her carefully studied words fell dry and unremarked as splinters from the wood rack, awaiting the stove.

There was the possibility, however, that this show was merely superficial, designed to deceive and mislead, and she hoped that she would get a chance to peek inside. What she recalled—if she could trust herself, if she hadn't altered or exaggerated the details again—were the spare objects indicative of a small space shared by a man and woman of practical tastes and little time for pleasure: a coal oil lamp, prominently set, a pine table still smelling faintly of resin, a black comb (hers) resting on a square tin tray, a handheld mirror (hers again), an open closet revealing its drab timeworn clothing, a patchwork quilt, and finally, insidiously, an advertisement cut from some appalling fashion magazine and tacked to the mantelboard, waxy and wrinkled with age. What the magazine picture in its garish counterfeit innocence could possibly symbolize to the more than middle-aged woman—of course it was also hers, most likely hung over Wesley's protest—Elsa couldn't begin to imagine. Was it hung because the model, young, brown eyes and shapely legs, looked pretty in the sundress? Then maybe Wesley hadn't objected after all. Embittered, she was now prepared to think the worst. After all, they had failed her miserably. Her well-intentioned patience and good faith had been met at every turn with stonewalling and duplicity, evasion and equivocation. Her mistake, she decided, was expecting them by nature to be different from, better than, their white counterparts who came to terms mostly without argument but with seething resentment, with blazing and blinding hatred under the surface. Less protected by law and therefore humbler, compliant, grateful for and not resentful of her intercession, she'd imagined the Wesleys thanking her with a simple gesture of friendship or a carefully chosen double-meaning word. She would know, of course, and insist that she'd only been doing her job. But they all would know. And there would be the check from her father's bank to prove it to whosoever cared to wonder.

But instead their stubborn refusal, apparently intractable, by the day grew more and more to seem like a personal insult.

Arriving at the foot of the careworn porch, she briskly climbed the stairs and knocked on the door. They waited awhile but nobody answered. After some time she cupped her hand to the screen and looked inside.

"Nobody's home," she said.

The deputy grunted and fooled with his hat. His eyes shifted about the yard with a look of impatient, scarcely concealed contempt.

Elsa cupped her hand and had a second look. Inside, among the sparse bits of furniture and makeshift decorations, which remained unchanged, a fold-out cot had been set to air against the right-hand wall. A dusty bar of sunlight shone through the window and bent down the edge of the cot onto the floor. "There must be somebody around," she said. She turned and looked at the deputy. A listless breeze set the leaves behind him in motion. "Shall we go have a look at the main house?" she said. He shrugged and guessed so.

The yard was drying up and turning a rusted, brownish color. They crested the hill together and the grand old estate came into proper view, set among the numerous calm and wavelike folds of earth, the glades of live oak and mossy tree of heaven. "Jesus H. Christ," said the deputy, "I lived in this town all my life. How come I never even seen this place before?" Elsa explained as they continued that the husband, a local financier, was long since dead, his widow had become a recluse, and the family, if ever you could really call it one, seemed to have died away with them. Or else moved so far away that they were good as dead. She decided against mentioning the nephew in Florida and being drawn into a discussion of the details of the case.

From a ways off she noticed the remains of a large oak tree recently felled, cut and piled for kindling. The job had been left unfinished and the long bleached trunk still spread over the yard like a prehistoric bone. An ax leaned handle-up against the woodpile.

And the main house, in its well-preserved and fussed-over state, arrested in time at the very hour of the old woman's death, yet changing subtly and imperceptibly as all monuments do, stood grandly secluded in the dappled shade. Built—so it appeared to her—a good eighty or hundred years ago. Before the Civil War. Rusty, patterned brick. Wood moldings, bowtelled and painted a light cream color. Dentiled eaves. Two stories with an attic, a cellar, and a broad stone chimney that probably opened on every level. A fairy-tale manor. The kind of house in which planters and profiteers played out their final act, for which they fought so fiercely and stridently and so heedlessly of the cost. "Just imagine," Elsa said, stepping onto the portico, running her hand over the fluted columns on top of which a balcony extended from a second-story parlor. The deputy looked it over but said nothing. She went up the stairs and put her hand on the doorknob and her face to a sun-blazed window. Inside she could make out pieces of furniture, chairs and coffee tables and an imposing bookcase set against the far wall, all covered with what appeared to be bedsheets.

"I wish we could go inside," she said.

The deputy glanced at her and sort of shrugged.

"I'm going to look around back," she said.

"Take your sweet old time."

Shoots of half-wilted clover and crabgrass fluttered lifelessly about her ankles. She trailed her hand over the rough brick surface of the walls, stepping carefully among azaleas and Russian olives and rhododendrons, until rounding the back she came to the foot of a tremendous magnolia tree which held in its cupped palm-sized leaves clusters of bloodred berries and flowers in the shape of porcelain bowls. A second, smaller porch protruded from the rear of the house, with a clay birdbath resting on the topmost step. A pair of sparrows fluttering in the remains of a dirty puddle of water deserted the bath at her approach.

She could scarcely help imagining herself mistress of the estate on a morning turn through her yard; and strangely she conceived of herself, like the late Mrs. Peers, as a kind of widow.

While she reflected on this, a conspicuous scraping noise began grating at her ears, but she resolved to ignore it. She leaned forward and peered into the birdbath and caught a warped, dimpled image of her face in a swath of fiery sky. She smiled and smoothed back her hair. A few drowned mosquitoes floated on the surface of the water with their legs fanning out and along the bottom were little piles of birdshit. Then the scraping noise was split by a piercing screech, followed soon after by a thud and crash. Straightaway she cringed and went running around front again. When she saw the deputy poised halfway through the window, with a knob-kneed leg straddling either side of the sill, she nearly became incoherent. "Reynold," she stammered, "in Christ's name . . . that's private property." He only grinned in a sullen, inveterate way: "You said you wanted to."

He hauled his foot over the sill and disappeared. At first Elsa thought he had broken the window, but on second glance she found that he'd merely raised it and pried out the screen. But in getting the screen unstuck and hoisting himself through, he had succeeded in tipping over a flower vase which lay shattered on the hardwood floor. The little blue and white shards were strewn all about like the fragments of an eggshell.

"Just look what you've done," Elsa said.

But the deputy was already gone. She could hear his footsteps clattering and echoing through the house; another moment and she realized he was fooling with the dead bolt, unlocking and pulling back the front door. She stepped briskly and trembling onto the porch. When he appeared in the doorway, grinning conspiratorially, she lost control of herself and swung her briefcase into his knee. "Ow," he yowled, limping backward to make way. She pursued him into the foyer.

"Just because we're delivering a court notice," she said in a jumble, "that doesn't give us the right . . ." They stood for a moment breathing hard and staring malignly at one another in the semidarkness.

"I thought you wanted to," he said lamely.

"Are you going to pick up that vase?"

"Hell, what's done is done."

She dismissed him with the faintest edge of a glance. Yet she knew all the while that she was secretly pleased, that her anger toward him was as much an attempt to quell her own rising sense of curiosity.

"Come on," he sulked, "let's see what it's like in here."

Astonished and yawning, the rooms of the old house opened before her like the rooms of a museum, with that same sterile untouchable quality to the portraits and pieces of furniture draped in white sheets, to the voluminous bookshelves and Oriental rugs peeking out from under tables like pools of wine, the various and bizarre accouterments of wealth displayed on mantelpieces and end tables under a dead buck's glowering eye. As she went from room to room she recalled the appraised value of the estate as they had represented it to Sherwood Jr., and found herself thinking: *It seems a bit low*. The deputy in his own way must have been absorbed in monetary calculations, for he suddenly burst out in an appalled tone of voice: "They left all this in the hands of caretakers? Lucky there's anything left. I'd expect it stripped to the nailheads."

Elsa ignored him and moved into the living room. Someone had been doing work here recently and a toolbox still lay open beside the fireplace. Above the mantel a framed illustration copied from a travel journal or book of maps hung slightly askew. The illustration depicted an Indian village set within a misshapen topography, under which the inscription read: *How the Savages Live*.

"This place stinks," the deputy said.

"The rugs are beautiful antiques."

"I don't care how old they are."

"Well, one of these sheets may have gone musty. Probably if someone opened a window now and then . . ."

"It's like some kind of haunted house in here," said the deputy gloomily. He lifted the corner of a bedsheet and ran his hand over the surface of a plush velvet couch. "Well, if I suspected these so-called caretakers were living it up, I guess I was wrong. It looks plain-ass dead, all right. Probably they ain't so much as touched a feather duster since the old lady went to glory."

"Where are you going?" Elsa said.

"Upstairs." He went back down the hall to the foyer, where a broad carpeted staircase rose to the second floor. Elsa followed, running her hand along the cream-colored banister. The staircase made two sharp right-hand turns before opening gently onto a dark hallway lined by a long, narrow carpet. "Look here—a library," the deputy said, peering into the first room. His voice rang loudly against the wood-paneled walls and Elsa felt a momentary cringe of fear: what would she say if Wesley discovered them prowling about inside?

She stood in the dark book-lined room and looked at the desk with its lamp and inkstand still ready for work. The shades were drawn and a few benign paintings of ships at harbor hung on the walls. She ran her fingers over the spines of the books and dust peeled off like ashes. "You're better educated than me. Ever hear of these books before?" the deputy said. Elsa grazed her eyes indifferently over the titles. They were mostly books about finance and law, with the occasional biography or company history. One fat, outlandish volume was titled *The Rape of the Taxpayer.* "No," she said in a hushed tone, "I never—" But he was already moving back into the hall and heading toward the next room with an air of manic inattention.

"Look, Reynold," she said.

"The bedroom," he announced gravely. He went and stood straddle-legged in the center of the room with his hands hitched to his narrow waist. "Well, well. What did I tell you?" Elsa looked in from the doorway. First to catch her eye were the numerous photographs of family members lining the walls: ghostly, enigmatic faces staring out of gray and white backgrounds, some smiling, others with that stern, inflexible look of authority natural to grandfathers and matriarchal old aunts. Against the center wall stood a huge double-door cabinet, the kind that takes two or three men to budge an inch. A nightstand draped with lace doilies still held a water pitcher and pair of glasses turned top-down. Next to it, surrounded on three sides by faded rugs worn flat by years of treading feet, was a broad mahogany bedstand and an empty space where the bed used to be. A pair of thick, embroidered curtains were closed over the windows at either side. "What did I tell you?" the deputy said. "They're just starting small and working their way on up." In a fit of malign inspiration he crossed the room and yanked open a closet door. "Nothing," he said with a grunt. "Well, it looks like these so-called caretakers got the 'taker' part of it anyhow."

Elsa tried to smile but it died out halfway. It passed through her mind that this was a dangerous sort of man to go wearing a badge. "You know, Reynold, we can't just assume what the reason is—"

"Assume, hell. What's there to assume?"

"Well, it could be anything at all. Maybe bugs got in the mattress and they had to burn it. Maybe they packed things away in the attic."

"That's a little too much 'maybe' for me," he said. He glared about the room awhile, then walked over to the cabinet and pulled at the doors. "Uh-huh," he said knowingly. As Elsa came slowly forward, he began to rifle through the topmost drawers, taking out sheet after sheet of dusty paper, scanning and thrusting them away as fast. After a while he picked up a worn-looking journal which to Elsa's horror he opened and began to read aloud in a mocking tone of voice: " 'January 1. We all danced and kissed and said Happy New Year, but really it was with the most terrible sadness that I—' "

"Reynold," Elsa said sharply.

He looked up at her. "What?"

"That's private," she said.

"Oh, yeah." He grinned in his sullen, give-a-damn way. He flipped randomly to the middle of the journal: " ' . . . because I'm afraid Ab's children have turned out a bit wild and untrustworthy. The eldest may actually have stolen a fishing boat, according to Sherwood at least, and then there is the problem of locating the others because they have developed that crocodile habit of hiding back in their mudhole with only their eye-slits and nostrils above water—' "

"That's enough," Elsa said, flushing.

"What?" he said again.

Elsa glared at him.

"I think we should go back now."

"Whatever you say. I thought you wanted to look around some."

"I've seen enough."

"Okay with me." He snapped the journal shut and put it back in the drawer and closed the cabinet doors with a loud whump. He appeared perfectly content and satisfied with himself. "I guess it don't really matter one way or the other," he said. Then he paused and looked at her askance. "This place gives you a creepy feeling, don't it?"

On their slow way back over the yard (not speaking, not even glancing at one another, passing by the old oak that lay dismembered and bleaching), the deputy suddenly broke into a caustic laugh. He stiffened and pointed toward the cottage. "Well, I'll be damned," he said. Elsa cupped her eyes and saw a silhouette clearly outlined in the window frame. It flickered, vanished for a moment, and returned. "We've been played for a couple of suckers," the deputy sneered. High above the dry lawn, above the opulent treeline fencing them ahead and behind, the sun weighed down like a blazing stone. As they went on, trudging in the direction of the cottage, Elsa's briefcase seemed to grow heavier as though it were packed with stolen goods.

"Let me do the talking," she insisted as they drew near.

The deputy mumbled something grudging and mostly inaudible.

"Hello," Elsa called. "Mr. Wesley, is that you in there?"

But to her extreme displeasure his sister, Cora, dressed in a shapeless pair of man's pants, emerged and without word or acknowledgment simply leaned across the rear doorway, drinking from a tall, sweating glass of what appeared to be iced tea. She was composed in an attitude as though she had nothing whatever to do with her surroundings, neither the cottage, the parched earth on which it stood, nor especially these pale apparitions fast approaching under a burning sky. In her impassive expression of self-removal, Elsa caught shades of other faces glimpsed at other times—a bored history teacher reviewing the Spanish-American War, her mother's druggist fiddling with the radio antenna, Oscar Wedge's towering fiancée—experiences joined in memory by a shadowy network of underground roots. And Wesley, her brother, their shared features running deeper than the reach of human memory, out of the darkness of an unknown past.

And even as she considered this, a stranger in a blue porter's suit appeared at Cora's side as if twinned from her.

"Miss Cora," Elsa said, glancing nervously at the thin man. His eyes and lips had a muddy, pasty look as if he had just awakened from a long sleep.

"Miss Childs," Cora returned.

"I've come to serve you this notice," she began in a rush, and then paused abruptly and asked: "Is your brother home?"

"He's in town," she said machinelike.

"Oh. Perhaps I'd better—you see this is an official notice of the court and I wouldn't want anyone to say it was presented improperly."

"My name's on the deed."

"What?"

"You can just as well give it to me."

"She's gonna do what she sees fit," the deputy interjected.

" 'Course she will," Cora said, flatly and apparently without interest.

But Elsa was already making to open her briefcase. As there was no porch or table to lean against, and since she couldn't look at the woodpile stacked against the clapboard wall without thinking of spiders and worms, she had to lay the briefcase flat on the ground and kneel while she unlatched the locks and withdrew the sealed official document. "I should explain," she began, straightening. "This is neither a warrant nor a summons, which would require your presence in court, but simply a notice that the county has initiated proceedings—"

"I know what it is," Cora said. She held out a long wiry hand.

Elsa passed her the document and said, "Miss Cora."

"Thank you, miss."

"Can I speak with you a moment in private?"

They walked to the corner of the house facing a dry little garden of tomatoes and peppers, mostly withered, their stalks crinkled and brown as twigs. It looked as though animals had found a way through the wire fencing.

Elsa said, "I need to speak with your brother."

"He'll be back."

"When?"

"Later this afternoon."

"What I need to tell him," Elsa said, "I need to say in person. I can tell you plainly it doesn't look good for your case."

Cora sighed. "Come back whenever you like."

"Tomorrow," Elsa said.

"Our house is yours."

Elsa flushed. She had to suppress a stinging urge to explain that bit of childish breaking-and-entering. But she couldn't. Not just because it made no sense, or because she felt guilty about the broken flower vase. The fact was that she could no longer afford to compromise her position through apology.

Behind them Reynold and the thin man had produced cigarettes and begun to smoke uneasily. They were looking at each other with a kind of subtle recognition, and the thin man chuckled softly at something that had passed between them. "A relation of yours?" asked Elsa, as they returned from the garden. Cora didn't answer at first, and then she only said: "No. It's nobody."

"All finished?" said Reynold.

"Yes," Elsa said, retrieving her briefcase from off the ground. "Let me just state for posterity that this notice has been served on the twenty-third of June, nineteen thirty-six in the presence of an officer of the town of Zion."

Drawing from the wrinkled white cigarette, swaggering beside her with his hat low, the deputy appeared satisfied, but they'd only gone a few short steps when the thin man under his breath said, "Yessir," and burst into laughter.

Away in the distance a smoke trail hung frozen over the mountain ridge. Three hawks were circling the area, floating back and forth between one another, and Elsa thought it odd that someone would be burning brush in this godawful heat. Then she heard the deputy as if confused by the thin man's laugh saying, "What? what?" At the same instant she felt something inside him crumble. "What?" he continued to babble, turning back and staring, so that she had to take him by the elbow and lead him around the cottage and down the shaded path, while he turned and stared uncomprehending over his shoulder. When they were halfway down the hill, under a cover of wide-flung and gruesome elms, he stopped and said to her, "They can't talk that way to you, goddammit." She tried pretending ignorance but he wasn't buying it. Finally she said, "Reynold, don't bother. He's just some tramp." But the deputy's eyes were set firm and hard like little flints. "Maybe it doesn't matter to you," he said. And shaken, trembling, he looked and sounded the way Elsa felt deep down. "Maybe not, but just wait till Sheriff Montgomery hears about this."

10

The truth was, Sweeny was the happiest man he knew. And that was saying no small thing, because he was friends with just about everyone in town. He had contacts in the big cities too—in Charlottesville, Richmond, and even Washington, D.C.—and he was proud to look them up whenever the occasion presented itself. One thing he liked was talking. He didn't understand quiet types, the kind you see sulking in drab corners of bars or pulling at their moustaches in mixed company as if lost in some obscure inner profundity, then blinking and trembling like startled cattle at the simplest question addressed them. To him there was nothing mysterious or masculine about silence; the quiet were stupid, that was all, and the intricacies of conversation gave them fits. Like illiterates confronted by a library. Of course, there were no quiet women, which was why he preferred and vigorously pursued their company; he also liked the way women saw things, the jokes they made, and believed in his heart that if he were stranded on a desert island without hope of seeing the world again he could be happy with a few decent ladies and a stock of Tennessee whiskey.

Peering from under the shaded barber's awning at the prone,

sun-blasted streets, he knew they were in tough times. Anyone could see it—the deserted houses on the edge of town, the shut-down buildings where businesses had vanished overnight, the dried and wasted crops in the hills beyond. But Sweeny was genuinely and implacably optimistic. There were still things a body could do, after all. There would always be things to do. The world didn't come to an end. All it needed was a little kick-start, spit and shine, a new coat of paint, a fresh start.

Not as if he hadn't took a drubbing himself. He'd lost over half his customers, the horses auctioned or swapped for credit or in some cases—and this particular vice aroused in him the closest thing to true venom—left unattended for want of money. Over the past year out of mere boredom he'd doctored several pregnant mares and a roan stallion plagued by ringworm, entirely free of charge. Of course, their owners had made vague promises, the kind that nobody expects to keep, but which Sweeny nonetheless recorded to the cent and carried about stored in his mind like notes of credit. It pained him something terrible to see the shaggy, neglected coats, the ribs protruding from sunken stomachs. A pasty film of mucous glazing the eyes in sickness would cause him inevitably to have a sharp word with the stableboy. He wondered what kind of a shiftless son of a bitch could stand for it. But then that was the trouble with people: you never could let your eye off them, not even for a minute. An animal—say, your typical horse—so long as you've put it to feed and remembered to shut the gate behind you, you could not bother with it for hours at a time. But a regular person, you better keep your eye sharp and your wits about you.

"What's news?" He hailed a geezer in a wide and scraggly straw hat, walking with a pronounced limp in the middle of the street. The geezer coughed something incoherent back at him. "That so?" he returned.

He made out the words "broke" and "cheapskate" in the

geezer's second volley, to which he replied in high good humor: "They say cheap's twice."

The old fellow wandered off, dragging his boxlike shoes.

Next to show himself was that skinny-ass beggar Leon. He was dressed in certifiable rags and had a slew of pale pockmarks all over his face.

"What's news?" Sweeny said.

"Everybody get to high ground."

"High ground?"

"There's fifty foot of water headed this way from the mountains."

"Oh yeah? Where'd you get that from?"

"It was on the radio emergency."

"Well, which way's clear?"

"Said away yonder."

"That direction you're pointing to is the river."

"You do what you like," Leon said, turning as if to flee.

"Hold on. Speaking of water, I got a joke for you. How do you save a Chinaman from drowning?" Leon looked at him blankly, expectantly, like a ragged hunting dog. Sweeny said: "Take your foot off his goddamn neck."

If there was one thing he liked in the world, it was a joke.

Sidling from his spot in the shade, he left the awning and moved along the uneven brick sidewalk, his head protected by a wide straw hat banded with white ribbon. A large peacock feather protruded from the side, the blue-green eye gazing out from a crimson field. As he strolled he whistled a song he'd heard the Negro stablehands singing earlier; he was a sucker for a good tune.

He tried not to think about the dreariness and downtroddenness of the town, as he tried always to avoid unnecessary confrontations with unpleasant subjects, but it was staring him in the face—the empty street, the sullen storefronts with their few vacant faces in the windows, the quiet . . . And he thought,

That's it, and stopped in his tracks. All around him and in every direction an eerie unnatural quiet prevailed like the thickening of a fog. Where were the birds? The children? Were the trains even running today? He began to walk hurriedly, overcome by a nagging desire for friendly conversation. Arriving at the A&P drugstore he found a mangy cur with bruise-colored splotches sleeping warily in a heap outside the entrance. "Hey there, little fella," Sweeny said, leaning down with his hand outstretched. The cur opened one half-eye and faintly growled. When he tried scratching its head the dog bared its teeth, showing the infected red of its gums. Sweeny pulled back. "You old shitbag," he said, and ducked through the door. A smile yawned easily across his face. Three people were sitting at the soda fountain, an elderly man and a teenage boy and girl on high pink stools. " 'Morning," Sweeny said, gliding in, "is it morning still?"

The soda jerk, glancing at the clock behind him, motioned with his thumb. "Almost noon," he said tersely. He was a sour middle-aged man who suffered from chronic indigestion. "Good afternoon, then, in advance," Sweeny said. "I'll have a double chocolate milk shake. No straw."

"How's the horses?" The old man addressed him in the relaxed tone of a familiar.

"Morgan, I've seen better and I've seen worse. We lost a foal the other day but otherwise it's regular business—"

"Who the hell's Morgan?"

"What did I say? Sorry, Malcolm," Sweeny said. "It's this crazy sun has gone to my head. Next thing you know, she'll be the once and former Mrs. R. P. Sweeny"—he thumbed at the startled teenage girl—"cursing in that bullhorn voice about leaving the kitchen door unlatched and putting out the trash—and don't mind about the R. P. It's none of your damn business!"

He gave a big friendly pink-faced laugh, just to put the kids at ease, while the soda jerk with a glum expression brought the tall cold glass of chocolate shake and set it before him.

"Don't mind Mr. Sweeny," the soda jerk said. But the kids were already getting up from their stools and leaving their bright dimes and nickels on the countertop. It was just as well. Sweeny watched the girl's supple legs snip apart and together beneath her flowered skirt and found himself snickering covetously for those bygone days . . . well, they were done. Once they had even been a memory but lately, when that other nagging prompted him, what invariably came to mind was a motel's lightless room and the habitual, horsey breathing he heard through the wall when he had finished.

"Ned here was just informing me of this fella running for congressman—" the old man said to Sweeny.

The soda jerk swept the change into his cupped palm; he spoke with a pronounced and sibilant lisp. "Figured you might know him."

"Sim Johnson?" Sweeny said. "Sure I know him."

So it was going to be politics. There were only so many subjects men shared in common after all and he'd thought the spinner might fall on the baseball scores or moribund endless speculation about the weather, peppered with stories of natural disaster and death. He breathed deep in relief.

"Is there a dog you don't know upstate?" Malcolm said.

Sweeny fixed him with a secretive grin. "We were in the fraternity way back in college."

"Then maybe you can answer a question for us."

"The recollection's a bit hazy," Sweeny cautioned.

"Just wondering what the hell kind of a name is Sim?"

"Oh, that." He raised the chocolate milk shake and dipped his tongue in the bubbling froth. "It's just like Slim but take away the *l*." A runnel of black syrup dribbled down his chin and he wiped it with the hairless back of his hand. On the wall a thermometer suspended by metal clips read about ninety-two. There was a fan running in the open window but it only blew more hot air into the room and even the shiny chrome countertop felt tepid and uncomfortable to the touch. The soda jerk avoided leaning on his elbows.

"You likely to vote for him?"

"I never vote in elections," Sweeny said.

"Not even for an old friend?"

"Especially then. I don't believe in it, boys. Too much can go wrong. A certain independence of mind is lost in the bargain. You take this flap over the turpentine plant—" He waved a long chocolate-ribboned spoon, the philosopher-king. "If I'd committed myself to voting for this skunk of a chairman then I wouldn't have the right to criticize him, ethically speaking, for making a muddle of things. But if I'd voted for the other guy, the Republican, then I'd feel obliged to explain how he would have done things different and not got himself bullied by a couple of robber barons from Pennsylvania. And it goes without saying that nobody likes a whiner or a sore loser."

Malcolm, his gray eyes half-mooned, glanced nervously at the man behind the counter. "Now the children have gone," he said.

A throttled smile quivered on the soda jerk's lips and he put down his dishrag and sat across from Sweeny on a high wooden stool. "You heard the latest news?"

"Like I was saying, I don't pay much attention."

"Maybe this time you should."

"Listen," Malcolm urged, tugging at Sweeny's elbow.

The soda jerk leaned forward with a conspiratorial look. He had the bloodless expression of a character from a picture show Sweeny had seen the day before, an Arabian magician who casts a fatal spell over the heroine, forcing her into marriage before her lover can arrive. "This fellow Sim, I went to hear him give a little speech at the First Baptist," the soda jerk lisped, his eyes focusing as if to the very pinpoint of memory. "Naturally, there was a policeman there, standing a ways to the back to hear what this fella had to say for himself, which wasn't too much I can report, and to look out for him I suppose in case any of the Democrats got out of hand."

"One of our young deputies," Malcolm said.

"The one called Dodd," the soda jerk said with annoyance. "Skinny kid wearing a cocky smirk. You'd pay cash money just to see it smacked right off his face. Anyway. I got there late, and he was sitting alone in the back pew with one foot up on the benchback, bored to distraction. So I sat next to him. It was a real stinker of a speech and we got to whispering. And listen. This is what he told me. Know why that turpentine plant has been taking so long to get going?" Sweeny shook his head and daubed with a napkin at the blackened corners of his lips. A narrow crease that might have been a grin wrinkled across the soda jerk's face. "There's a couple old nigras holding property on the site, and that banker's daughter—"

Sweeny put down his spoon with a metallic clatter. There was a long uncomfortable silence between them.

"Well?" Sweeny finally said.

"Nothing personal, you understand."

"Of course not. You all know I am a close friend of Mr. Childs. I'm confident you wouldn't dream of sullying his daughter's reputation."

"That goes without saying," the soda jerk lisped, putting on his best placating look. "But it seems the girl has got some queer ideas in her head. Mind you, I'm only repeating what that deputy told me."

The dull cold spoon shone again in Sweeny's hand; he resumed eating and filled his mouth with a blob of muddy goo.

But slipping off his seat with his gray face aflush, Malcolm half whispered, half hollered: "He says the young lady has been helping them stall the plant and that nigra—that Wesley—insulted her right to her face, in plain and open daylight."

"I don't believe it," Sweeny said.

"Well, whether she was fooled or not—" the soda jerk lisped. "That's just what the deputy told—"

"I don't believe it because if it was true, there wouldn't be a white man in six counties just sitting here and taking it."

The two men glanced at each other in mutual discomfort, then lowered their eyes to the scoured and shiny tile floor and made limp gestures with their arms. The old man muttered something about minding his own business. Meantime the soda jerk fell into a gloomy silence and mopped at the countertop with his dishrag. Sweeny watched them with irony and critical good cheer, sucking loudly at the last spoonful of milk shake. He made them wait a good long while before rising from his stool.

"Gentlemen," he said, and let his change drop with a clatter.

"You overpaid," said the soda jerk.

"A nickel for the devil."

"This ain't no damn charity."

"Let him go," said Malcolm grimly.

Outside the sprawled cur raised one pasty eyelid and growled at him again and for just a moment he thought about giving it a good stiff kick in the ribs. It was hard even to imagine such a violation of his scruples but he blamed the heat, the godawful stifling unnatural heat and those no-good jackasses he'd left begging their excuses like a couple of yellow-bellied deserters. Common, his mother would have said. That was the word she always used.

Hat lowered, he clung close to the storefronts. The sweat spread across his chest like a mold. The white front of his shirt had slipped a button at the stomach but he left it open, unheeding. The street was mostly deserted. Two men in overalls were unloading crates in front of a drugstore with typical infernal sluggishness. Here and there a businessman paused to exchange pleasantries with a neighbor on his way downtown. Downtown, Sweeny sneered even at the thought. A couple of stone-and-brick buildings and a grassy square with a single statue of a war hero. His mood had decidedly turned. The implacable optimism that had formerly distinguished him he felt ebbing, draining from his blood, into a discontented haze.

A short ways down the street he met his barber returning from the grocery with a sandwich wrapped in fly-specked wax-paper. " 'Afternoon," the barber smiled, and Sweeny was forced to ask after his children and chatter emptily with a vague smile grafted on his face. Were the boys the right age for baseball? And how were the basset hounds doing? Afterward he proceeded without incident, passing under the railroad overpass and up the gradual hillslope in sight of the square.

He was just coming to the marble steps of the courthouse when he realized he had this scoundrel Wesley dead in his sight. Sweeny knew him well enough to recognize him from the opposite end of the square. The backflung shoulders and preoccupied expression, that particular Negro gait which in his case was a bit too self-confident. Yet for all that a man past his prime. Moving stiff-legged toward a lean sorrel mare hitched to a rail—not a bad-looking animal—he wore ill-fitting brown trousers, a shirt and suspenders, and a rumpled felt hat that seemed to float all on its own as he walked. In one hand he carried what appeared to be a paper sack from the hardware store; the other was occupied in refilling a pipe that protruded from his teeth. And crossing at an angle, heading him off with the pinched look of a schoolteacher, was the young lady in question. An incorrigibly silly girl.

Sweeny positioned himself behind one of the limestone pillars lining the courthouse portico.

He saw Wesley give a start and look both ways. If it had been at all possible he might have fled across the square, but she cornered him as though he were a naughty student. Tense and uncomfortable, he faced her down.

She crossed her arms as she spoke to him, wearing that severely earnest look that always made Sweeny want to tell a dirty joke.

Wesley replied offhandedly, looking at the cloudless sky. She attempted to rein him in but he made another casual reply, slipping out of reach. Now she switched to questioning him with what Sweeny recognized as practiced duplicity, but his stubborn patience outweighed her sense of urgency.

Say what you might, the girl was no kind of quitter. She pursued him with a merciless lecture, talking him up and down even as a prize fighter harasses his opponent, while he untied the bridle and stored the paper sack away in a saddlebag. Sweeny clenched his jaw, listening, but couldn't catch a word of it.

Then without losing composure Wesley seemed to stiffen. The reflex of a blow. Something in him changed altogether and he fixed her a damn near murderous look. Had anyone seen it it would have been enough. But there was nobody at hand—only Sweeny, and he was no kind of fool. Wesley clambered onto his saddle without another word and though she practically tugged at his trouser legs—she was attempting to explain something, it seemed, looking like the spitting image of exasperation—he swung out from the rail and rode the mare at a canter with the street dust mushrooming behind him like a phantom undergrowth.

The mare blustered, its brown eye flared in profile. A horsefly circled away and Wesley waved at it. He held the mare steady and stroked the side of her neck.

"Later, Miss Childs," he said, glancing round.

"Later?" She looked at him disbelieving, appalled. "Are you listening? What I did this morning was I served your sister a court notice."

He paused. "All right."

In a rush she told him how the Peers estate was sold, how the nephew in Florida didn't even want to see it before signing the papers. How some tramp friend of his sister's had to go and run his mouth as if this were all some kind of joke. Wesley's face twisted somewhere between a frown and a scowl, unable to find the expression best suited for a madwoman. Meantime she continued to rant; she couldn't stop herself, it welled up and overflowed, all these months of whispers and Old Mohawk and the cork comes flying out in public, in the town square of all places . . .

"And what's worse, I can't stop that deputy from blabbing—"

"Miss Childs, let's calm down," he said quietly.

And she was thinking, *Calm down?* And what does he know anyway? He couldn't know about that nightmare in the chairman's office: the window thrown open to let a breath of air in, moist and warm like the breath of an animal. The chairman behind his big polished desk, absorbed in scribbling a note of some kind, taking his time in the stilted silence. How the curdled flesh of his cheek wriggled when he smiled to himself, staring down at the page, before he raised his eyes, and focused on her without emotion, bland and official like rubber stamps. Exactly like the stamps they used to sign his name. So that, shaken, she had already made her decision in the infinite moment before he spoke: the Wesleys were obstinate, a hopeless case. And the idea she'd been turning over in her mind was there for her to grasp. Before the chairman could reproach or upbraid her (why else would he have summoned her to his office?), she blurted out that it wasn't worth arguing against the quitclaim deed even if the law was clearly on their side. The case had been poisoned by bad faith. Then she'd told the chairman what she now said to Wesley:

"I had your well water checked."

Wesley looked at her coldly. He clamped his teeth down on his pipe end and swung up on the mare, which skittered sideways a step.

"Yeah? I wonder what you'd find," he said.

"It's no good."

He nodded. Then he nudged the mare with his shoe heels and went trotting away even as she attempted to explain—another act of malice.

At the far end of the square two men stood in front of the grocery with their arms limp at their sides, staring. One wore ill-fitting trousers and a wide straw hat and the other kept a soiled apron tied over his belly. Elsa saw them through the midday heat like warped statues of men. She turned and began walking back in the direction of her office, as if nothing out of the ordinary had happened. But she felt as if her skin were made of paper and might just burn away. Glancing over her shoulder, she saw a third man emerge from the store; he also stood and watched, snapped a tobacco tin, and leaning, dribbled a black thread of spit in the dirt.

The entire morning of the twenty-sixth of June while Elsa busied herself with official correspondence, clicking the teeth of her typewriter like dead piano keys, the gossip fanned door to door through the town, circling the epicenter of her window. Pinched lips almost touched as the word passed along, a sad embrace of affronted righteousness. Overhead the sky trembled with viscous heat; a cloud appeared briefly only to burn away like a whisper . . . At her desk, in a fog of concentration, Elsa typed, "In response to your inquiry," and paused, abstractedly recollecting the extraordinary dream she'd had the night before.

She was walking a rutted dirt lane with her mother. The air, the light, seemed autumnal, weighted with the smell of sodden grass and the sharp onionlike odor that dominates as the woods harden, preparing for frost. As they walked conversation passed easily between them about no particular subject at all and around them an early morning's buzzing of insects and diffuse fogging of the hollows made it seem so real, so undreamlike and plausible that her hopes seemed magically restored. There were the stones crunching under her feet, after all, the individual rounded fragments of quartz and shale standing out like pearls in the rusty clay. There were the shapes of trees inscribed upon the edges of the road which she could have counted one by one and named: shagbark, sycamore, cottonwood. Ahead of them the lane fell away down a hillslope, and they continued on about a quarter mile in the cold dim light of the autumn sunrise. Her mother was speaking again in her low, unhurried way, and even as Elsa listened and replied in the manner of people to whom all time is reserved, she felt an awareness all the same of the hopeless mystery panging like a church bell which she would never lose or resolve and which time could only deepen.

She awoke to the feeling that her mother had only slipped momentarily into an adjoining room.

Unnerved, she silently berated herself for having taken on her father's intractable habit of keeping away from the church. He claimed he'd been "churched out" as a boy and couldn't sit still through mass. But his friends were all Protestants of one ilk or another and she believed he felt conspicuous—and he could never really stand to be conspicuous. In her high-backed chair she groped through the pell-mell corridor of sentences, now obscure and tangled and now wandering in the dark, continuing a while with predictable straightforwardness before stopping with a thud against the forgetful plastered wall, a fresh sheet of paper already catching in the gears, turning to her its blank and thoughtless face while the victims' heads gathered in the dustbin at her feet. The letters might have been written by Latin scribes. She couldn't begin to understand the very logic of phrases that sprung from her own hands. And festering in the back of her mind, there was the court hearing next Monday at which this Wesley business would be finished for better or for worse.

And really that was the end of her involvement. Now it would be up to the county attorney to decide what to do.

Her expectations and sense of her own possibilities had been greatly reduced since failure had dawned, risen, shone on her unsparingly. It was something she had never really considered, intent as she'd been upon the opportunity and as secure about her position as a banker's daughter could afford to be.

But they had undone her all right. A couple of mule-headed old Negroes and her own mawkish sense of wanting to do right by everyone. Stupidity. No longer troubled about concealment—they had been waiting for the chance like a pack of half-starved bulldogs—the junior men and their secretaries now stopped whispering whenever she came around, pretending openly and coldly to fiddle with their work. They did not even say hello anymore but only nodded curtly and looked away till she was gone.

The phone had been ringing all morning. Each time it buzzed she would look into the hallway, startled, and wait for it to go quiet. Now and then one of the others would get up to answer, she could hear the footsteps and vague monologue of Yes, who is it, what do you want, then the face would appear in her doorway and she would say distractedly, "Do you mind taking a message? Tell them I'm out." She was cramped and miserably hot and kept thinking about the bottle of Old Mohawk she'd left at home in her chest of drawers.

Around eleven o'clock she got up and looked through her window. Nothing to see—an empty lot below, a sky as flat and pale as a sheet hung to dry. She walked wearily to the end of the hall and down the set of creaking stairs. In the shade out back they kept a corrugated bin filled with rapidly dissolving ice where she filled her cup, drinking and glancing about from time to time. The only person around was an elderly gentleman with a walking cane who greeted her with a deeply wrinkled, ingenuous smile, chattering on about chrysanthemums. He was apparently an expert on the topic yet was clearly at his wit's end, for the dry spell was causing his garden to shrivel and even his careful watering didn't slow the advancing decay. What galled him the most, however, was how a neighbor's field was specked with wildflowers, brilliant golds and blues wrestling up from the dry dirt without so much as a bit of shade to help them along the way. It just went to show that nothing you do matters against the natural law of nonsense. As he was beginning to flush a bit excitedly, Elsa excused herself and filled her cup with ice a second time.

Her stomach gave a quelch when she entered her office again. In a small and angular hardwood chair the formidable bulk of Oscar Wedge was installed, opposite her desk, with an air of authoritative permanence. His backside drooped over the flat edge of the chair at either side and his shirt luffed outward like a sail. He shifted, turned to her his florid cheeks, the diminutive coon eyes that seemed swallowed up, overwhelmed by the largeness of his face, while his lips thinned to the ironic row of teeth. "Miss Childs," he said grandiloquently. He made a kind of gesture with one hand.

Standing fixedly, she made no move toward her desk.

"I called," he said in his smooth droll tone, "but evidently my messages never reached you. I know how it is. Hard to get help—real help—these days. Slouchers and do-nothings. What's that old-time word? Vagabonds."

"Who let you in?" she said.

"Miss Childs," he said, chuckling a bit, or maybe it was just a cough. He appeared morose and unhealthy, his skin had a slightly pickled tinge. "Please don't stand there looking all wet. I'll only take a minute of your time." She crossed the room briskly and set her cup among the clutter, the scattered sheets of paper on her desk, but remained standing behind her chair. She remembered distinctly their prior meeting in his shabby little tenement office and felt at once markedly superior to him yet uncomfortable with his easy manner, his wry self-confidence in her presence. As though he might have another practical joke up his sleeve. She watched him closely for some sign of maliciousness, waiting and half expecting him to collapse under the strain of his own gloating. But when he spoke he only said with evident complacency: "Looks like I'll be trying my luck somewhere else."

"Really?" Elsa said.

"Giving up the whole, excuse my French, whole goddamn farm."

"And your fiancée . . . Frieda?"

"She'll be coming along."

"Likely it's for the best."

"I'm starting to think so."

"If you don't mind my asking, what made you decide?"

He gave an easy, cynical smile.

"Somebody must have told you."

"Why on earth would anyone—" She stopped herself midsentence. He looked at her, perplexed and even a bit amused.

"You know I don't take offense, I know the score. Some people like to fool themselves into better graces, hangers-on at the cocktail table, so to speak. I've never had any illusions about who I am. What do you think about my necktie?" It was a stringy brown and red spotted affair, dangling like a bloodworm from his loosened collar. Elsa didn't know what to say.

"It's new," she managed. "You shouldn't wear it with short sleeves."

"Well. It was given me by a client."

"Not Wesley?"

Wedge nodded slowly, his eyes squinting. "Really not a bad guy when you get down to it. We had an understanding more or less, of the kind you might have with a hitchhiker. I offered to take him as far as was mutually beneficial, he understood we might not get all the way where he was going."

"A handy metaphor."

"Always said I'd write a book someday. Of course, writing a book is nothing like the law. In the law a little imagination goes a long way."

Elsa said: "I'm really very busy."

"Of all people you ought to understand, Miss Childs. Consider the number of wrecked lives we come across, the poverty and problems, the appalling ignorance of the general population. Consider that more often than not we're working on behalf of the state, and if not the state then the landlord, and if not him, then who? Better to have that gift of obliviousness some of the very best of us have cultivated to an art."

"I'm not a lawyer," Elsa said. "But if your conscience is suddenly a trouble to you, quitting town three days before a hearing isn't going to help."

"Quitting? More like the other way around," said Wedge, in his elliptical, insinuating manner. He shifted his bulk in the narrow chair and, crossing one thick leg over the other, held his chin in a philosophizing pose. "Drumming up business isn't easy to begin with, especially in a new town and with everyone dead set against you, but when you get a phone call in the middle of the night telling you more or less what to expect if you stick around . . ." He looked at her closely for a while, scrutinizing her as if expecting to discover something hidden, and then his coon eyes seemed to root briefly among private thoughts. He finally blurted out: "You've really got no idea, do you?"

"Quite honestly, Mr. Wedge, about half the time you're talking I haven't the slightest idea what it's all about."

"It's funny, you know, but I really thought you were playing along. I kept telling Frieda: This one's a player. You can tell. This one's keeping score. It's so unusual in a county official . . . in a backward town like this."

Elsa sat heavily with a bored expression and glared at him over her desk. The stringy brown and red tie was hanging limply under his neck while long damp stains in the shape of bird wings stretched across the front of his shirt. He continued: "But it seems I had you figured all wrong. There's right and wrong, I suppose. Never deal with the devil."

She continued to glare at him without answering.

"Miss Childs, forgive me for being blunt, but don't you know—have you even looked out your window today?"

"If you wanted to say something I wish you'd just come right out and say it."

"The sheriff's gone to pick him up." Wedge leaned back in his chair and sighed as if relieved of the burden he'd been carrying.

"Wesley?"

"Who else?"

Elsa sat perfectly quiet a moment. "On what charge?"

"It seems a certain mutual friend of ours has been blabbing it all over town that he—Wesley—insulted you in broad daylight, in front of a county deputy, who naturally would have run him in except that he—Wesley—threatened to blow his head off with a double-barrel shotgun."

She looked at him, stunned. The edge of his small mouth was quivering, lipless and tense, somewhere between a smile and a sneer.

"I had it from the soda jerk," he said with measured glee.

"Why, that son—" she said, and even as she spoke she had the sense of something coming into shape out of the darkness, of the faintest echoes of gossip beating, threshing, the air about her ears. "They can't jail him on rumors," she said.

"Better let the sheriff have him," said Wedge. "It's for his own good. Guess you wouldn't have noticed that bunch of loiterers in front of the police station just waiting for their chance to be deputized? Christ, you've got your head in those papers. Even the Negroes are talking about hanging him."

She began to say something in protest or disbelief but at each new attempt cut herself short, bit the edge of her lip, and looked helplessly to Wedge as if seeking his assistance in an unfamiliar language.

He only showed his gray rim of teeth and fixed her with an insolent leer; the wing-shaped stains across his chest seemed to move as he breathed and shifted in his chair. "Naturally you didn't see it coming," he said, "any more than the bull calf that wandered into the hunter's camp."

"Are you just going to sit there making wisecracks?"

"I ought to clear out," he said, glancing down at his wristwatch.

"Come with me to the sheriff's office first."

Wedge guffawed. "And end up sharing a cell with him? I'm not gonna fall for that." He planted both shoes flat on the tile floor and leaned forward with his hands splayed on his knees. Then, as if he couldn't help himself, he said: "You could have done business with me to begin with. I'm a reasonable man. I all but spelled it out to you word by word, even sent my fiancée to make things clear. But you were, how do you put it, not that kind of woman?"

"Get out of here," Elsa said.

"Of course," he said, rising with a phlegmatic wheeze. "No hard feelings, I hope. Have to get the car packed and see about some new front tires—you wouldn't happen to know a good garage? Well, don't bother. If they let you speak to Wesley, remember there's got to be honor for the deputy—don't try and take that away from him. Tell Wesley I said that. He'll listen, he's smart. You can tell the sheriff it's all some kind of misunderstanding, make up any old lie, it doesn't matter what. Montgomery's an easygoing man. But whatever you say, don't accuse that deputy of anything worse than spitting in the grass. Because I'm standing here to tell you, if it comes down to a wager between your story and their honor you will lose the bet every single time. Above all, you know, people want to believe they're better than they are. They even want to believe in their sinning, to believe it's something else altogether. Something noble and beautiful, defending the race from barbarians."

He was already halfway across the room in his appalling necktie, a progress deceptive and effortless as a barrel floating away on the tide.

"To hear you go on," Elsa said, "as if you weren't his damned—"

"Damned?" he said with a smirk.

"His lawyer," she said.

"You mean the second death?" he said.

Elsa stared at him with surprise and horror.

"Don't look so innocent." He laughed in her face.

Then he was gone into the corridor and Elsa was left to herself. She heard his heavy footsteps on the stairs and she heard his breathing, heavy and slow. Downstairs the front door clattered shut and she sat very still and heard nothing at all. The spot where he'd been standing seemed yet to bear the weight of his presence. Mocking her. Above the now-empty chair three flies clung to the ceiling, black ashspecks that stirred, whipped about in a circle, and resettled in a kind of shifting formation. The minute hand moved forward on her clock. Again she had the feeling of something coming into shape out of darkness that she couldn't afford to recognize because to recognize, to perceive and know the thing perceived, is in some way to have known it beforehand. And so she found herself standing and walking briskly through her office and into the corridor and briskly back into her office to retrieve her purse and then standing there, perfectly still, until the minute hand clicked to twenty after twelve. By that time she saw clearly why she'd been offered the job, why the failures and inconstancies which she'd felt so acutely hadn't been failures at all, because she had an unbeatable guarantee, why her father had said—she remembered the very words he used—"they are specifically looking for a woman like you."

At the end of the hallway was an office with a solitary desk and no chairs where the last representative—Zellers, the man she'd replaced—once had worked. Now the room stood empty; nobody had moved in. A hint of cobweb shaded the ceiling corners and the walls were scored with nailheads that once hung noteboards, property maps, pictures of loved ones. And there: a narrow rectangular window which unlike her own opened on the front side of the building—the square. Without even thinking what she was doing she crossed the hall and entered the deserted office. She grabbed the window by its ledge and thrust it open. The outer screen had long been removed and she could put her head partway through and look out from the second story down the street. In the space between the government building and the police station an unreal vision grew before her eyes: a mob of sullen shapes, straw hats aslant, milling and slouching as they waited in the dust and heat of the afternoon, passing among one another in the somnambulent manner of dreamers at a picture show in the moment before the doors swing open. Already a subtle interconnection knit their movements. They joined and parted in loosely associated groups, wearing dust-smudged slacks and sleeveless shirts, and they had the look of men used to waiting with a kind of festering perpetual rage and inattention for something out of the ordinary to happen. Men whose deepest fear was that nothing might ever happen, that whole lives might drain out listlessly in poverty and expectation, in unsatisfying struggle with the land and with themselves.

While she looked on a sudden flash of color moved under her eye. A small rust-backed lizard scampered over the red brickface and stopped rigid near the windowsill with its pronged feet spread wide and its tail jerking.

She stared at the rough alien creature. A relic of the jungle. It seemed to direct the huge black globes of its eyes cautiously upward while its ragged tongue flickered out, probing for danger. Without reason she grew suddenly furious, as though the lizard had tried to bite her. A strong impulse to cruelty moved her and she held out her hand experimentally. But the lizard threw itself sideways in a sudden spasm of movement and snapped to immobility half concealed under the narrow sill.

She saw its tail extending outward like a little fuse and the hind feet splayed and squashed-looking as if its spine had been crushed.

A red pickup truck came swinging round from a side street, raising a wake of pale dust in the air. The bed of the truck was packed with young men sporting military haircuts and a few excited dogs, their black mouths hanging open and yammering. The mob turned to watch as the truck pulled into the police station lot and the men jumped out waving at their friends. Someone hollered an unintelligible word and the rest of the men chimed along, picking it up like a rallying cry. Others, drawn by the noise and wondering if it was a parade or a political campaign, began appearing in doorways, leaning against signposts, mailboxes, observing the show with benign approval. And she could make out the bloated shape of Oscar Wedge skirting the crowd, clinging to the shaded awnings of the storefronts, his shirt luffing out behind him and his crumpled hat pulled low over his forehead, pausing now and again to glance evasively at the gathering as he ambled toward his shabby office, his broken-down motorcar, and the short quick road out of town.

11

Drop it, Wes," the sheriff said. But it was too late and they knew it; the look, the acknowledgment passed between them in a silent flicker and in fact began passing the moment he saw the black Oldsmobile sedan rolling slowly up the drive in the noontime sun. The car parked right in front of the main house, where Wesley had to move away from the window to avoid being seen. He was just finished picking up from the last visit paid them by white men and already here they were again, come to smash something else? Broken shards of the flower vase lay swept in a bucket. His broom leaned against the wall. After a while Sheriff Montgomery and his deputy got out of the car, slowly, unhurried, with a laboring heaviness as if they carried weights strapped to their limbs, and the deputy, lean and sunburned, with his sleeves rolled up, pointed toward the cottage, saying something that Wesley couldn't hear. They began walking side by side, occasionally turning and spitting in the grass. "Comin up from behind," Wesley said. He moved across the hall into the parlor where he could follow their progress through a wide bay window. Or maybe it started earlier, he thought, started passing when that young Miss Childs showed up with her eagerness and nosy questions, or maybe it was Zellers with his whiskey craving, or earlier even, maybe it started way back with the first white man that cheated on his wages or gave him that shining little grin that dares you to contradict his word. Maybe it started with the blood he took from his mother's veins. He continued watching until the white men disappeared over the yard, crossing toward the slanted roof of the cottage jutting up from the hill. "Ours." He repeated it softly to himself: "Ours." And in all the long years of his memory, from yesterday all the way back to when his grandma buried that dog in the garden, whispering words he didn't understand, it was the first time he really believed it. He went out into the hallway and proceeded through the silent foyer, hearing his footsteps creak over the floorboards. A magnificent, a beautiful slowness was overtaking him. He glided through the door and down the steps into the yard. The sheriff's Oldsmobile came closer and closer as if drifting along a swollen river, like the car the old fisherman had stripped. Suddenly his hand was on the hot chrome door-handle. He opened it and peered inside. Crushed gum wrappers and a scribbled pad of paper. A cage separating back from front. Cigarette stink. He wondered what he was doing but his hands, his feet, seemed to know, and he didn't question their purpose; his mind was lost in the sweet slowness that made him smile as if realizing something he'd known a long time. Bending, he pulled the handbrake and watched the car begin to drift, rolling backward, the black hood flashing angrily in the sun while gravel crunched and spat under the tires. Through the windshield he saw the steering wheel spin free as if an unseen hand was yanking it back and forth, while the car backed farther and farther away from him and finally gained speed and disappeared down the drive. For a time Wesley stood, listening every moment for the sound of the crash. But it never came. Perplexed, he wandered a ways down the drive and found the black sedan sitting undisturbed on a patch of crabgrass. Where it had veered off the drive its wheels left a wide swath cut into the grass, neatly avoiding the trees. Wesley smiled; it made a kind of sense. He moved away toward the cottage, keeping to the edge of the treeline. So it was started and there was no unstarting it. All right, then. In the slowness he felt good, right, like there wasn't anything he couldn't do. And there was so much time. Even when he heard the holler, Cora's voice, high-pitched and desperate (warning him?), there was still plenty of time to get to the cottage. Then her voice again, hollering out for him to hear. He looked up at the flat blue sky, clear and shining. He knew why the sheriff had come: the warnings were everywhere, whispering in the leaves, gurgling in the river. But what they knew . . . he would break and run, just like all his kind do, and it would take deputies and dogs to drag him out of the bushes . . . nothing. He walked up into plain view, so calm and free. When finally he arrived out back of the cottage he could hear the mess going on round front, the hollering, the confused, brutal yapping, and TJ's voice now, insisting: "I don't know, I don't know what you're talkin about, I don't know . . ." Like a shadow Wesley entered the cottage through the back door—*Ours,* he was thinking—and walking calmly through the kitchen over to the closet and feeling the iron weight of the shotgun while he loaded it, clicking a pair of number 7 shells into the chamber with the flat of his thumb, he peered through the sunlit window facing front. None of it seemed real, yet it was happening, he saw it happen: they had TJ handcuffed and lying on his stomach next to the water basin, while a few paces off the deputy was twisting Cora's arm behind her back. How did I know? he said to himself. When I saw them through the window and when I freed the handbrake, letting that black sedan roll free, how was it that nobody had to tell me, that I just *knew*? Suddenly the deputy cringed and yelled "Ouch!" and balling up his fist he whacked Cora on the side of the eye. "That's enough, there," the sheriff said, in his low commanding drawl, holding down TJ with the sole of his shoe. Then Wesley stepped out onto the porch. When they saw him everything froze. The only moving thing was a bright red cardinal darting over the trees. They looked at one another, stunned. The sheriff slouching, overweight, his eyes sour with the years of kicking, cuffing, caging, as if ticking off the days till his retirement, while his deputy, hot and frightened and furious, looked on with recoiling terror like a snake cornered in its hole. And Wesley feeling that fine, sweet slowness, his gun barrel angled down, but sensing, seeing, their pistols in their holsters instead of their hands, knowing he had the drop on them, and the sheriff speaking now, at first in a mumbled voice and then sharply, commandingly, as the look flickered and passed: "Drop it, Wes."

He raised the barrel slightly. The sheriff lifted his foot off TJ, who squirmed away, his hands still cuffed behind his back.

"Now, hold on, Wes," the sheriff said calmly. "Let's stop and think about this a minute." But Wesley was already thinking, *Wouldn't that beat all? In all this time, loading and watching them through the window, I couldn't have forgot to check it, could I?* He slipped his hand down the gun stock and switched off the safety latch. "Let's stop and think a minute," the sheriff was saying, "before somebody gets hurt. Let's work something out here."

But Wesley's mind wouldn't slow down now, racing at once back and ahead, feeling that pain in his foot again the moment before he heard the sheriff's black sedan rumbling up the drive, the rusted point of the nail standing up just waiting for him and the pain nothing like he would expect, just a dull ache and a shiver, so that he left his broom and bucket and went right over to the window, waiting, seeing the black sedan ripple in the noon heat as it slowly approached. And planning now, figuring what he ought to do because he knew why they were there. Figuring: you've lost, Wes, you can't buy any more time than what you've already got. It was just like Miss Childs had warned him before he rode past her on his mare outside of the hardware store, and they were claiming he'd insulted her or made some kind of insolent remark, and so out of this dirty lie the excuse they were needing would grow, and that would be enough, that would do the trick where plant jobs, bills of sale, well water, had been unable to succeed. That was a money-back guarantee. And did Miss Childs see it now? Did she understand? Wesley felt something in him lock shut. His mind was racing ahead now, starting to calculate, making plans as if by its own separate will. He found himself repeating: all right, all right, then. As he watched the sheriff and his deputy walk away, leaning and spitting, toward his cottage, he was not even sure when the thought came to him and sent him outside in a state of calm understanding, the thought that maybe never pronounced itself but which caused him to bend in through the open door and release the handbrake to keep the white men boxed in, unable to flee. As if he had to do this, first, before he could convince himself of what he would have to do next. And he wondered what part of this was God's will, what part the white men's and what part his own? He decided to use the split oak tree as a barricade. TJ could guide Cora through the woods until they got safe into town. Maybe get the two of them a pair of one-way tickets . . . but to where? And then what? And what was he planning for himself? He didn't know. But he saw it clearly: I've been running all my life, dodging this . . . well, I saw it coming, and I'm not moving out of the way again.

"That ain't him—" the deputy said, his voice a little high.

"Shut your mouth," the sheriff said.

"I'm telling you," the deputy said.

"Wes, you know better than to go and pull a gun on us."

"Let go," Wesley said to the deputy.

With a start, as if realizing for the first time that he held Cora's arm twisted in a wrestling grip, the deputy released her and took a step back. At the same time the sheriff began to talk quiet and easy like a grandfather, while Wesley watched his sister slide carefully alongside the porch, out of the way. He wasn't even listening to the sheriff but only watched, waiting for the sign that would tell him what to do, while the voice talked on, saying: "The way I see it, we always got along, didn't we? You never made trouble before that I know of. I think the judge'll take that into consideration. What do you say?" And Wesley thinking, *Didn't I already try? Didn't I? Was there anything I didn't do, that could have kept us from standing here?* And he thought how shameful it was, that it took handcuffs and a twisted arm to make him feel that razor against his cheek, that old friendly pressure urging him to sit down.

"Let's quit foolin now," said the sheriff.

Squinting in the light, he rested his thick hands on his hips.

"Let's all go down to the courthouse and clear this mess up."

Wesley eyed him distantly.

"You'll get a fair chance, Wes. I know you ain't guilty."

Guilty, he wanted to laugh. The bitterness and the sadness swept all through him and his knees shook a little as if they wanted him to sit.

"It was this'n—" the deputy said, pointing.

"Shut up."

Montgomery threw him a look to freeze the dead. That was the sign; Wesley saw it pass between them. With a sweet slowness, the sheriff insisted: "Come on, Wes. What do you say?" Speaking pleasantly, unhurried, while his left hand, clutching at his hip, swung up in a rapid, steady arc. At the same time his stomach peeled open, screaming, like an open mouth, and it took a long time for the sound of the gunshot, for the smell of charred powder and for the recoil Wesley never felt, for the sheriff to look down at himself, cradling his stomach, while he stepped backward and carefully squatted in the grass and Wesley swung to meet the deputy's pistol. But the crack of the gunshot had spooked it from his hand and the stunned blue eyes were looking on with a mixture of curiosity and horror while the sheriff struggled to keep the bright blood and the pale, viscid gleam he didn't want to believe from spilling into his lap. And already Wesley was laying plans, his mind racing ahead: set that barricade outside the front and back, to keep the doorways clear. TJ and Cora can take what they can carry. If they follow the woods alongside the river that would be better than the roads. He was so quickly engrossed by his thoughts that he didn't hear his name the first time it was called and only turned when TJ, almost screeching, hollered: "Wes!" They turned and watched the deputy fleeing headlong over the rolling lawn, through the gauze of sun that warped his image as he ran back toward the main house. Well, he sure wasn't boxed in like Wesley figured. But then it would cost him a spell of panic before he saw enough to follow the tire tracks downhill, where the sheriff's car was waiting for him, nestled all nice and comfortable on that patch of crabgrass. So there was time yet. Lots of time. "Wes," TJ was saying, his eyes wide. "Jesus, Wes." He made a swinging gesture with his hands.

"All right." Wesley nodded. He looked down at the deputy's pistol, which lay in the grass where he'd dropped it, shiny and black as the ratsnake Cora brought out of the main house in spring. Just a few yards away the sheriff was squatting, spilling blood into his lap, making wild swimming motions as if he were trying to cup it back inside where it belonged. "Stop it," Wesley said. His knees felt like bags of sand, shaking loose. But the dying man looked at him blandly, with no expression whatever. A foam the color of tobacco juice began dribbling from his lips. "The pistol," Cora said. She took a few steps into the yard and picked it up and, moving carefully behind the sheriff, held it out for Wesley to take. He stood looking at it for a while as if confronted by a strange new tool he'd never worked before. "All right," he said, and then to TJ: "Think you can help me drag him down the hill?"

Toward dawn Wesley dreamed that the river overflowed again, just like the flood last spring, and he walked slowly along the bank surveying the damage and looking for Cora in the rain. The current was stagnant, dark, barely rippling like the water of a pond. He dipped his foot in the water's edge and saw a cloud rise, slow and gaseous, drifting from the murky bottom. Around him drops of water trickled from hickory leaves while long, greenish puddles covered the ground like open sores. Afraid for Cora, though he didn't know why, he stepped gingerly around the puddles, leaving footprints. He was hearing his grandmother's voice again, speaking in a language he didn't understand, repeating something over and over. While he tried to make sense of it a humid breeze, smelling of washed-up fish, blew off the river. Stumbling from the bank, he landed knee-deep in the muck and, looking up, saw the old fisherman and automobile scavenger crossing the water in his weighed-down skiff. Still a long way off, he lifted one arm in a mischievous wave. And suddenly his grandmother's voice grew clear, as if she were speaking for the fisherman in her low, repetitive tone: You ain't fooling me, Wes. Not for a minute.

He watched the fisherman row closer over the currentless water, like a cloud crossing the sky.

He was running, running heedlessly, breaking through underbrush and jumping headstones, his eyes throbbing with fear, tripping and falling and shooting back up again, thrashing like a man pursued by hounds. He carried everything—a change of clothes, a few wadded-up dollar bills—rolled in a potato sack. No time for anything else. He followed the path halfway down, then cut across an open field which looked like the kind of place where a bull might roam. But it was empty, the long grass burned the color of straw. At the far end of the field he snagged his pants leg on a barbed-wire fence and had to pause for a moment to rip himself free. Then he ducked into the treeline and stood catching his breath. The sweat was pouring down his face in rivulets, in streams, as if he slept in the throes of fever. And he felt as if he were dreaming the sort of awful dream that wells up on the sickbed, twisting with violent colors and sensations. Then a scream broke the silence and he froze, trembling. But it wasn't the sheriff. It wasn't the hole in his stomach like a gaping mouth. Looking down on the road, he saw a stray dog rooting in the brush, barking. He started running again, threading his way along the treeline but keeping the road in sight, as if that narrow patch of yellow dirt was a line thrown out to save him. He couldn't bear even to look away from it: it was the way back to town. Back to the railroad station.

Crouching and peering in all directions, he zigzagged in and out of property lines and traced the edges of barren fields. It was no good running out of control, causing dogs to yammer; he slowed to a weary jog. Under the trees the noontime air was stagnant, suffocating. The potato sack, slung over his shoulder, felt scratchy and cumbersome as the sheriff's legs.

After a while he came upon a creeping stream and flopped down on his stomach, swallowing the tepid water in gulps. Then he turned over and closed his eyes, letting the sun and shade flash alternately over his face. He couldn't seem to get the sheriff out of his mind, the way he sat there in the grass looking confused, lost, like he was simple, even while Wesley searched his pockets for the handcuff keys. How he took the sheriff's legs, leaving Wesley the armpits, but soon enough they decided he was too heavy, so they each grabbed a foot and dragged him down the path on his back, leaving his head to bump against stones and roots as they went. By the time they reached the bottom of the hill he was covered with burrs and dirt. He looked like a corpse exhumed after days underground. "Jesus," he said, "ah, Jesus."

He was no sooner on his feet again than he heard a pair of childlike voices ring out. Looking through the trees, he spied two little blond-haired boys coming up the streambank with fishing rods swaying in their hands. They seemed to be playing a kind of vicious game as they went along, singing:

The devil's a liar and a conjure man too,
you don't look out, he'll conjure you.

Snatching up his potato sack, he sloshed through the water and tried to slip back into the woods, but one of the boys hollered, "Hey you!"

He stopped dead. His arms flopped down.

"What you think you're doing?"

A silly smile scrawled over his face as the boys closed in.

"You see them signs yonder?"

He looked down at them, grinning.

"Well, can you read or can't you?"

"No suh," said TJ.

"Well, them signs say NO TRESPASSING." The blond kid grafted a furious, exasperated look onto his face. He gripped his fishing rod like a switch.

"Sorry. I'll get movin now."

"Hold on a minute."

He stood still again, waiting for it to pass.

"Who said you could go?"

"Nobody."

"Don't you think you better ask polite?"

The other boy, the quiet one, smiled with admiration.

"You want me to get my pa?"

"No suh."

"Then speak up quick."

Grinning, he said: "All right if I get movin?"

The boy stood for a moment, considering.

"Don't let me catch you here again."

"No suh."

"Hey! Come back here!"

But it was too late, he was already running and the woods were tilting, fencing him in, as he broke through brambles and spiderwebs and kicked sharp knobs of shale with the toe of his shoe. After a while the aggrieved baying of the boys evaporated at his back. He passed a live oak standing with its crown wide-flung and weighted in the heat and he thought of Wesley gathering the chopped oak branches and split pieces of trunk from his woodpile, arranging them in a low, makeshift fence against the porch stairs. Meantime the sun beat down, boiling, on his neck. He remembered seeing Wesley through the cottage window and saying, "What? what?" He hurried onto the porch and stared at him in confusion and disbelief. "What the hell are you doing?" But Wesley ignored him, working away at his fence. That was when he realized: he's cracked his brain. Poor old Wes. Did it happen some days ago, or just now when the sheriff screamed? He ran back inside, searching for Cora, but she was gone. *I don't want no part of this mess,* he thought. While he filled his potato sack a whiskeylike fluid came up in his throat, so hot and sharp he bent over and gagged. Outside he found Cora crossing the yard, a bucket swaying slightly in her hands, sloshing threads of bright overspill from the rim. Behind her blank expression he detected that gleam of quiet fury and determination in her eyes, that look against which all pleas for reason would fail, and his most dire demands would meet with her mocking laugh. Fifty years of serving, without pause or rest, or ever having time for a family of her own, and she carried it in her blood and bones and in the bitter memory which grew and soured in her heart. Like a line of hundreds upon hundreds of buckets she would have to carry until the day she left them all behind. And TJ understood, he saw it clearly: *She ain't coming with me, she says no,* and there was no use fighting it. She was dragging her last bucket from that well.

Dazed and out of breath, he saw a curve in the road break the line of trees ahead of him. He would have to cross over. But first he had to rest a minute. He sat on the crest of a weedy ditch and put his head in his hands. It didn't make any sense. And when he thought of Cora back there with her crazy brother, building that ridiculous fence, he wanted to turn back. Drag her out of there by force. But what could he do? His eyeballs were throbbing and his feet hurt. If he wasn't careful, those white boys would find him again.

Looking up he saw the sky was a beautiful blue. Like colored glass. A few faint streaks of midday haze hung dissolving in the vicious glare. And he told himself: You can't afford to think about anything but that track under your legs, you've got to make your mind like that sky, clear and bright and even vicious, yes, if it means staying alive and free. He stood and looked up and down the dirt road. He would slit those boys' throats with his shaving razor or break their heads open with a rock. He had to get away. He had to get free.

He broke through a tangle of thorny brush and had only just started down the sharp slope of the ditch when he heard a rumble of car engines coming up fast behind the curve in the road. He scrambled back up the slope and crouched in a patch of poison ivy, where he watched as a bright red pickup came reeling round the bend, crowded with pale youths shouting and clinging to the sides, while a line of beat-up cars followed close behind, the faces of the drivers glazed and dead. He grated his teeth and prepared for the worst, for the screech of brakes and the voice yelling out, "There, boys!" But the cars whooshed by, leaving a cloud of torpid dust suspended in the air. Standing, he waited and listened. He looked down at the bed of shiny three-pointed leaflets clutching his legs. Then he started across the road.

When he was under cover of the trees again he thought how strange it was, how in the end life only repeated itself, and here he was again, just like that night so many years ago when he and Wes slipped through the woods in Appalachian darkness, running for the train. As he hurried on he kept to the edge of the road, trying not to think about Wes now, or Cora for that matter, barricaded in their cottage behind that makeshift fence. He had to keep his mind clear. But it kept coming back to him: the sharp smoky autumn air, the sudden horrible clinging of a spiderweb to his arm, and Wes beside him, breathing hard, arguing in his soft annoying tone of voice that they ought to head in this or that direction, though he didn't know, he couldn't know, for he'd never hitched a railcar by moonlight before, that much was obvious. Which he knew for certain when he heard the startled groan and, turning, saw Wes limping behind him as the train ran by, stooping to pull the scrap of two-by-four from the punctured sole of his foot. And when it was too late they watched the last car drift away into the darkness like a dream, the steel and smoke and the lights and the rush all fading, until there was nothing but the occasional lost cry of the whistle. They started walking right away; there was no use standing around saying what if. And he remembered how Wes leaned against him, using his shoulder for a crutch. That was a long time ago.

Soon he was hearing the drone of an engine again. He lay flattened in a grove of locust trees while the first police car, colored with gray road dust, whipped recklessly past. Then he was up and running, crossing the road into denser trees and heading uphill, feeling as though his legs were made of straw.

At the top of the hill he saw his luck had run out. Ahead the thickets gave way to open fields on both sides of the road. In one of the fields the lank figure of a farmer tramped uselessly through withered cornstalks. Watching the man with hatred, he fell onto a mossy patch of ground. It was no good. If he left the road he would get lost and end up miles away from where he wanted to be. But he couldn't continue the way he was going either. Not by daylight. For a while he lay resting and thinking. Finally, he came to the conclusion that he would have to find somewhere to hide until dark. It would be a quarter moon, not much to see by, and then he'd cross the fields in safety.

But the far-off yowl of a dog made him sit up straight.

Hounds, he thought, what if they have hounds?

He began crawling down the hillslope on his hands and knees, unable to stand and run, and afraid the farmer would spy him among the trees. When he reached the bottom, however, he discovered a small corn crib alongside the field where the farmer was dumping salvageable grain. It was a simple wood-planked box with a lid opening from the top. For a long time he lay under a thorn bush, breathing dust and waiting for the farmer to go away. When at last the man grew tired of counting his losses and wandered off in the direction of the house, TJ sprang up and crossed the short distance to the crib, where he leapt in without a moment wasted, shutting the lid over his head.

All afternoon he lay cramped and curled in the darkness, his head wedged into a corner of the crib. His only light and air came through cracks where the planks had warped apart. Meantime the sun beat down. He rolled the potato sack into a pillow and tried to get comfortable enough to rest. But it was stifling hot. The air inside was close, dusty, dry as a kiln. He felt as if he were breathing grain. He put his mouth up against the widest crack he could find. Sweating, he twisted in agony. The moment he began to relax, to reflect that he couldn't hear the dogs after all, his whole body would jerk abruptly and his hands sharply slap at his sides. A tickle ran over his skin—chiggers or spiders, he didn't know what.

Unspeakable hours later, he crept out under a black evening sky.

When he came out, his legs were covered with tiny welts. Half poison ivy, half bites. He was racked with thirst. It was so unbearable, he crept instinctively toward the farmer's house and searched around back until he located the well. Then, madly, he drew up a bucket. The shrill creaking of the crank filled the entire yard. When the bucket was up, he drank with desperation. Had anyone appeared he was prepared to die for that drink. But nobody came. He looked around. He waited and listened. The house appeared deserted.

A strange thought occurred to him. Walking over to the shadowed rear of the house, he peered in through a window. Inside he saw a well-kept kitchen, plain and orderly, the lights left on.

Slowly he circled the house, looking in on a series of empty rooms. He saw a chair pushed back from a table, as though someone had been interrupted in the middle of reading. A glass of what looked like beer stood half-filled on the table beside an open book. He went back to the kitchen door and, his heart pounding, tried the door handle. It opened. Turning, he spat up in the grass, briefly and violently. Then he slipped inside.

He came out with half a loaf of bread and four apples in his sack.

After walking a mile or so, he sat down and ate his supper. Twice a car passed on the road, its lights groping like hands in the darkness. He lay flat under the trees until it was gone. Then he sat again, resting and making plans. He had his railroad uniform, a couple of wadded-up dollars, and two apples for the next day. He would get there now, he was all right. He knew the train schedule by heart. Friday nights there was a northbound heading out just past eleven. It was the last departure till morning. But he would make it. He scratched his legs absently as he considered times and distances. He had a friend in Cleveland, and a woman in Chicago. Maybe he would pay a visit. He'd come back to Zion thinking it was time to settle down, but that was done now. You couldn't ever stop moving. The minute you stopped you were done.

He got up and started walking again, but every step he felt his heart faltering, his plans fading into remembrance. The past was alive tonight. An hour later he arrived at the outskirts of town and headed directly for the station. He discarded his pants—torn and filthy—in an alley, and changed into his porter's clothes. Around him the warehouses and the gas pumps huddled together on narrow, jagged streets, like abandoned tenements awaiting the wrecking crew. In the distance he could see the low brick station house and the long line of a resting train. It was one of the old 2-8-8-2s nicknamed "Chesapeakes" after the C&O line. He reached the station without encountering a single person, black or white. But once he arrived on the platform, he only stood watching, like a vagrant. Two ladies were stepping off the train in smart dresses, with bags in hand, while the ticket collector chatted under the lamp with a man in a feathered hat. He stood off behind a post where no one would see him. He watched. A few minutes went by. The ticket collector chortled at a joke.

"Hey, mister."

Like a shadow, an elderly black man sidled up behind him. He had dark, hollow cheeks and solicitous eyes wedged in deep under the brow; his dress was a pair of greasy overalls and a striped railroad cap with a crumpled brim.

"Mister."

"Yeah."

"Got a smoke?"

"Sorry."

The old man noticed his porter's uniform.

"That your train there?"

"Yeah."

"Say, I recollect you. You come through pretty regular."

"It's been a while."

"Jeffeson, right?"

He fixed the old man a hideous grin.

"That's right."

"I got a thing for names. Just ask my wife, she'll tell you."

"I'd better hurry up. Train's about to leave."

"She ain't going nowhere."

He stared at the old man, uncomprehending.

"What?" he said.

"Cracked a piston valve or something, I don't know what all. Didn't you see them people getting off? They ain't getting out of here till morning."

The train engine hissed. A shuddering of steel and steam. For a moment he stood looking confused, as if stranded in a foreign country. Then without speaking, he turned and headed slowly out toward the far end of the platform.

“Hey,” the old man called, “sure you ain’t got a smoke?”

He held up a limp hand in parting.

“You all right, Jeffeson?”

He said nothing in response.

“Wait a minute . . .” The old man came shuffling up from behind, eyeing him with a curious leer. “You got someplace to stay?”

“Yeah,” he said vaguely. A part of him wanted mordantly to laugh. He felt outmaneuvered by the simplest and most obvious stratagem.

“ ’Cause if you need it, my wife and I, we keep a nice room . . .”

He said nothing.

“Won’t cost you but a couple dollars . . .”

“No, thanks.”

“Look. I’m saying you don’t want to get caught outside tonight—”

Without responding he jumped off the railroad platform onto the dark gravel lot, unable to conceal his repugnance. He felt the hostility of the entire human race directed into a fine point located just between his eyes, as if some malevolent hunter had him dead to rights. The old man was just one among many obstacles intended to assist the hunter and his hounds. Even the inanimate train itself was a conspirator. And as he moved along the back streets, a flattened shadow clinging to brick walls and sliding over dusty walks, he thought of all the chief conspirators who had made his life so inhospitable: the aunts and uncles who preached an endless stream of Jesus and Education, the bosses who swaggered and spit on his shoe, even his friends among the railroad crew, whose hands searched out his bag at night, grabbing whatever they could. Once in his youth he’d made the mistake of believing in something, in those incestuous and backbiting political circles which advocate and advertise for an earthly paradise, as if that was something you could display on a billboard or sell from the back of a truck.

During those years he felt a sense of his own importance as an attender of secret meetings and a proselytizer for the faith, as a man the police would have possibly marked for surveillance had he ever remained in one place long enough for them to get wind of his activities, and who even tried to convert Cora as they loved and fought in their two-room shack. But over time the glamour wore off. The film flickering before his eyes seemed to fade away, rendering his political associates in smug and mundane colors, or else revealing wide-eyed fanatics like those following Garvey's ships out to sea. Ever since withdrawing his association he'd made it his business to believe only in the essential and hostile nature of his relation to the world.

He followed a winding, deserted road which led down toward the river. He planned on crossing a bridge to take him outside of town, then finding a place to pass the night. He dreaded the loneliness of the woods, but when he glanced over his shoulder the Blue Ridge had a stamped iron look, and the town, rising on its foothill, all the appearance of a sleeping enemy camp. It was better to keep to the outskirts, to the low places where whites didn't live. Soon the breath of the river reached him and he saw the stagnant, oily mass glittering under the moon. Warehouses and scrap lots marked by tall wire fences lined the bank. A squalid collection of houses stood here and there, dispersed among the hollows, their windows mostly dark. He wondered what the residents were doing inside, whether they slept in ignorance or followed that age-old instinct to bar the doors from fear. Without wanting to he was thinking about Wesley and Cora, wondering if they were arrested or dead, while a familiar voice nagged him out of the memory of a strange man sitting patiently on the perimeter of their political meetings, and never speaking, only listening and crossing his legs the one over the other, his hands neatly folded in his lap. One day he had suddenly cleared his throat and announced that the only worthwhile action was the impulsive, unchoreographed, and violent act of resistance. When asked why, the man flashed a faint, superior grin and said: It spreads like the pox. But TJ recalled hearing a few years later how that strange man's impulsive act of resistance was to leave his brains splattered on a motel wall. He wondered why Wesley didn't sell their land when the first offer came. Why he dragged the trouble out, believing that he could make it go away. Didn't he know any better? Cora too. Was their resistance—the political ideal of that madman crossing legs in the shadow of his memory—any different from a squalid suicide in a motel?

He followed the road as it turned along the sibilant riverside, down toward the iron bridge that crossed away out of town. Even by night the heat was oppressive; stopping next to a boathouse lot he took off his porter's shirt and, stuffing it in his sack, went on in his undershirt. You had to keep moving. You couldn't ever stop. He had no illusions anymore about the world he was living in, the world run by whites. An offhand, transparent excuse was all they required to begin piling up the kindling at your feet, and in fact they began doing that on the day you were born. When at last he arrived at the bridge he stood and waited a while before crossing. A fear of being caught halfway, arrested by headlights, left him paralyzed. The iron span of the bridge appeared to fence him in, its rising girders like the bars of a cell. But in the end there was nothing he could do, and gathering his courage and his breath, listening carefully for the sound of car engines, he dashed over the bridge in a sprint and collapsed on the other side in a pile of discarded rubber tires.

For a while he lay there among the garbage, panting, and he was overcome by a terrible sense of uselessness and regret. He didn't understand. Even after Wesley turned the first offer down there was still a chance to sell. Once the county more or less purchased the entire estate from that nephew down in Florida, they were left with nothing to stand on. Some old deed to the cottage, which the widow scrawled out on her deathbed? That wouldn't ever have a chance to hold up, because the whites in town weren't going to let it get that far. And Wesley knew it. He felt certain in his heart that he knew it. But then . . . what if it was like Cora said, and the county never intended to go through with the purchase, but only to drive them off? If she was right, it would be weeks, months, later before they learned they were getting nothing. But was that worse than facing down an angry mob? He clenched his teeth in frustration, turning among the rubber tires in a nightmare of the ghastly, inconceivable cruelties faithfully depicted in newspaper photographs of right and proudly grinning citizens gathered round the smoking wreck of a once-human body, or passed down in stories told by aunts and grandmothers of incidents remembered from times when, hard as it was to believe, life was even worse.

Some time later he got up and staggered a mile or so uphill, until he came to the edge of a dried-up field where a pair of grain silos, connected by tilting shafts, shared the silhouetted distance with an angular barn. In the darkness the structures appeared crude and ragged, like buildings in wartime newsreels. Thirsty and worn out, he slipped between the wire fence and crossed over the field until he stood in the shadow of the barn, looking up. Even by moonlight he could make out a wasps' nest hanging from the eaves. The outer walls appeared in poor condition, riddled with cracks and gaps, and he decided the place was likely abandoned. All the better. He found an old trough set to one side that offered a pool of warm, sour water, infested by mosquitoes. But he was grateful for anything. For the first time that day, he was beginning to feel safe.

When he was finished drinking he stood and looked over the broad double door of the barn before pulling cautiously on the rusted handle. The door swung open with ease. He stepped inside. While the door was open he had a look at the interior: a raw, umbrageous gloom, like the inside of a cave. No animals could be seen, not even a mouse skittered in the empty stalls, although a surprising scent of hide and manure still clung to the air, like memory, and beds of hay rose up here and there that once cows in their imperturbable reveries must have chewed.

He took another step over the bar of pale moonlight falling

from the doorway. In the far corners of the barn, webbed in gloom, he saw scraps of junk, trinkets left by a farmer who only had so much space in his moving truck.

Suddenly a light flashed on.

He reared back and felt the blood rush to his head and heard his own sharp gasp rip the silence. Out of the back of the barn an oil lamp rose and loomed forward, propelled by a large, crouching shadow.

"Shut that door," said a hissing voice.

He stood perfectly still.

"I said shut it goddammit—"

The lamp rushed forward and shafts of dim light jumped off the floor and clapboard walls, while the figure grunted and cursed, concealed behind the shining flame. Extending from a large, apelike hand, the metal blade of some crude farm implement winked under the sphere of light.

"Okay," he said, closing the broad door with a painful creak.

"Now latch it."

He did as he was told. All feeling was gone from his legs and he realized as he slipped the bolt into place that he might collapse in a heap, unable to stand.

"All right." The figure seemed to relax a bit. His voice was dry, harsh, and tinged with a profound disgust at the unavoidable difficulties of life. "Now come on over here," he said, hissing a string of half-suppressed curses.

TJ put one foot slowly in front of the other, as if walking a tightrope wire, until he stood in the middle of the barn. "That's close enough," said the man. He set his lamp down on the hay-strewn floor and, squatting on his haunches, glared up through the ring of light. A huge bloodless white man. Nearby on the floor of an empty stall the light revealed a half-eaten carcass of a chicken.

"What in hell d'you think you're doing?"

TJ stammered. The man's face was masked by a black growth of beard, like lichens covering a stone.

"Speak so I can understand."
"Nothing."
"Nothing," the man repeated with disgust.
"Just looking for somewhere to sleep."
"That right?"
He nodded cautiously.
"You some kind of tramp?"
He began to say he was sorry for busting in but the man cut him off.
"What you got there in that bag?"
Squatting, he glared up at TJ while wordlessly he lowered the potato sack from his shoulder and dropped it next to the lamp. No sooner had it struck the floor than the man pounced, spilling out its meager contents. "Apples," he said with distaste, but began immediately to devour them. TJ watched in amazement. He noticed the broad-striped black-and-white pants the man was wearing (he wore no shirt at all) and it began to dawn on him that for the last several days he'd been hearing rumors about a fugitive hiding outside of town.

While he watched dumbstruck, with a perverse fascination, the man snatched up his porter's shirt and rammed his thick arms into the sleeves. "Goddamn skinny, ain't you?" he said bitterly, attempting to close the shirt over his chest. Finally he gave up and left it hanging open.

"You can take it," TJ said. "I don't need it no more."

The other looked at him with amusement. Then his face altered and the humor vanished as quickly as it had appeared.

"You come through town, didn't you?"
"Well, yeah."
"Crossed that bridge yonder?"
TJ nodded.
"Who you runnin from?"
TJ stammered again.
"What's that?" the man growled.

"Never said I was running."

"Don't lie to me, boy."

An idea occurred to TJ. "The police," he allowed. He waited to see what effect this would have. But the man only spat a chewed apple core from his mouth. "Cigarettes," he said greedily. He raised the lid from the lamp and, touching a white stick to the flame, began directly to smoke.

"You know what I hear?" he said. He put the lamp down and looked up keenly, with an expression poised between curiosity and disgust.

TJ stared at him blankly.

"I hear some old boy killed that Sheriff Montgomery."

There was a long moment of silence.

"That true?"

TJ nodded slowly.

The man looked at him for a while, as if considering the weight of his word. Then he blurted out: "I would of liked a shot at him myself, and now I find some old boy's gone and done it for me. How about that?"

TJ said nothing.

"I been out here, just keepin myself alive. It seems like forever. You think that's an easy trick? Some days I was eatin bark off the trees."

TJ watched him fearfully.

"Now you come here and tell me how some old boy went and killed Montgomery and how there's cops crawlin all over the place and you say you're runnin away, so how am I supposed to figure it?"

"I didn't kill no one."

The man glared at him. "One thing I know: they gonna pin it on me just like they done every other killin in the state."

"I didn't—I can prove it."

"Yeah?"

"I know who shot him. I saw it happen."

The man's eyes sharpened to glistening slits. Clamping hold of TJ's wrist, he pulled him down, crouching, into the ring of lamplight.

"You saw Montgomery take the bullet?"

TJ nodded. Instinctively, he rushed to relate the story as if feeding a hungry wolf; altering the details slightly as he went, he emphasized the sheriff's foolishness, turning his death into a farce. But the fugitive only squatted, listening intently. "That all?" he finally said, after TJ explained how they dragged the sheriff's body down the hill. He looked away, disgusted.

"I was just in the wrong place," TJ said, "at the wrong time."

"Shut up."

TJ crouched perfectly still.

"That ain't no real satisfaction."

He nodded commiseratingly.

Suddenly the man's mood seemed to change and he glared at TJ with an evil-minded irony. "You know what they done with your friend? Huh?"

TJ shook his head. "I spent the day in a corn crib."

The man broke into a spasmodic fit of laughter.

"Get up," he said, suddenly standing.

TJ obeyed.

"Take off your pants."

"What?"

"Take them off," he said, brandishing the rusted blade.

For the second time that night, TJ felt like vomiting. "Wait," he said, holding up one hand, and then he was clutching his head, gasping for air on the floor, while the big man grunted and cursed, tugging at his legs. TJ went limp, allowing his pants to slide off, leaving his legs bare as jimsonweeds. He lay miserably lost in the throbbing of his head and only semiaware of the figure cursing and straining to fit into his pants. Finally, in a fit of rage, he flung them back in TJ's face, saying, "Goddamn skinny's what it is."

Then he gathered up the potato sack, filling it with what few things they had between them. "You know what I bet?" he said, scratching around in the gloom of the barn. "I bet your friend's just a heap of ashes by now. They carvin the ears off his face."

TJ groaned.

"Wish I was there myself: I'd like to get me a souvenir."

He gasped for air.

"Too bad you run off. You might of seen a rare sight." The man laughed again, a spasmodic fit like a death rattle. He walked over and lifted the lamp high, so that his black beard and his bright, disgusted eyes gleamed. "Go on and tell 'em about findin me here. It don't make no damn difference."

"I swear I won't tell—"

"They ain't never gonna hunt me down."

TJ felt that sense of confusion when a dream betrays its logic and the mind of the sleeper begins consciously to doubt. But the man bent down, looming over him. The pit of TJ's stomach fell away.

"Don't let me catch you again, understand?"

The big man grinned, then in one jarring motion he hurled the oil lamp onto the floor. There was a smash and jangle of glass; the barn went pitch-black. TJ heard his own startled cry as he rolled away, scrambling for a safe corner, feeling his hands pass over the slimy carcass of the chicken while his lungs filled with the dry, mucid dust of the straw. He gasped, afraid to cough. A certainty of imminent, painful death ran through him with the prescience of a nightmare. It was one of his deepest and most galling fears, that such terror and pain as he imagined might be only a shadow, an approximation of the real thing. But instead the barn door creaked open and he glimpsed the crude figure of the fugitive slipping into the moonlight, into the night outside—a moment's flash of the simian torso and shadowed hand gripping his potato sack—before the door clapped shut and pitch-darkness covered him again.

12

Not the thing but the idea of the thing. The street as she rushed out from the bland shadow of the government office shocked her with its caustic glare, its whirl of dust devils blooming and collapsing in the air, caking the brick sidewalks and parked automobiles, before she realized that the majority of the automobiles were in motion, backing out from the police station lot and pausing as they turned around in the road, then jerking forward in the same spirit of uniformity in which they had arrived. The cars gunned their engines and sped past her and around the corner, heading en masse toward the state road. She nearly tripped on the marble stairs, nearly dropped the briefcase which she did not altogether have a reason for carrying other than the small comfort it gave her, the feeling of some modicum of control. And then the sound: it came up through the bottoms of her feet and up through her bones and only lastly entered her ears—the recognizable throttles of Fords and Lincolns and Chevrolets. She put her free hand over her mouth and creased her eyes, hurrying in the direction of the bank while the few remaining cars whisked away down the road, their chrome tails winking.

She began hearing the snap of her shoe heels on the sidewalk bricks and realized the last of the mob was gone. From the doorways and windows surrounding the square a few owlish faces watched her openly and without interest. The excitement was over and they were disappointed. But she was only half aware of the people, the streets she was leaving behind, the railroad overpass that loomed and fell away, until she arrived at the corner where the bank stood unremarkably, its blinds drawn to keep out the daylight, and she was through the glass door and crossing the lobby in its cool and echoing quiet while her mind rushed ahead. With a shocked expression the teller coughed into her fist and said, "Why, Elsa," as if the sight of the manager's daughter was something out of the ordinary, and Elsa, walking right by without returning the spurious pleasantry, made her way down the hallway to her father's office door. She went in without knocking and found him on the telephone. He motioned her into a chair while he continued to talk, glancing helplessly at a clock on the wall. "Listen, I have to go," he was saying to the hook-shaped receiver. "Well, I know—but listen, can I call you back?" He hung up with a tired sigh. "Elsa, I know what you're going to say—" But she was already talking over top of him.

"The keys, have you got the keys?"

He paused strangely before answering. "You mean to the car?"

"Yes, the car."

"Well," he said, "sure—"

And she was telling him how she needed him to drive her at once to the Wesleys'—no, the Peers' estate which the Wesleys apparently felt and believed was their birthright—because now that the mob was riled there was no time for waiting round and the sheriff—

"Sheriff Montgomery," her father interrupted. "I know, I've heard."

And then she was telling him that what everybody had heard was a lot of bull and it would have been better for someone to come and ask her instead of believing whatever gossip the deputy felt like spreading around and worse, contributing, blowing it all into some kind of tawdry melodrama just so they could play the part of the heroes, galloping to the rescue in their automobiles.

"So you see, I have to find Montgomery before those idiots get their hands on him, before they even get a chance to convince or threaten him—"

"Threaten the sheriff?"

"You know they'll do it. A mob like that: it's always the lowest and dirtiest that take the lead and everyone will follow, everyone will go along."

"Yes, I expect you're right. Elsa, my head's been splitting all morning." He reached halfheartedly for a bottle of aspirin standing on a phone book at the end of the desk. Elsa snatched it up and passed it to him. "I realize these last few months I've been so preoccupied with"—he waved his free hand as if to indicate the room, the building, the inimical strip of sky glaring through his window—"this, I haven't taken time to listen or explain. What a waste."

She asked what he meant.

"It could have been better spent—the bank's in bad shape anyway."

"Dad . . ." But her words dissolved in shock at his stolidity. He was sitting there as if perplexed by a mathematics formula. As if the afternoon lay before him without urgent purpose or need, without the hundreds of individual minutes lining up in which a decision must be made. Meantime, he fooled with the aspirin bottle, apparently unable to pry open the lid, while she looked on in stifled horror. Finally the lid made a sharp popping sound. He extracted a pair of chalk-white pills and swallowed them without water. "When you lose money and you can't stop from losing it, how much worse can it get? Elsa, listen . . ." But he only sat there looking hard and hopeless like a child confessing some misdemeanor to his parents.

Elsa said, "What, dad? What is it?"

"Montgomery's dead," her father said.

Elsa tried the word. She had to try it once and then to her father's matter-of-fact answering nod say it again out loud because otherwise it wouldn't be real, it would be an unfleshed and impossible idea, whereas the simple voicing of the word gave shape and life or at least some shadow of shape and life to what her instincts, her feelings, were fully prepared to disbelieve.

"Dead," she said.

"Killed," her father said, "ambushed, murdered. At least that's what everyone's saying. I'm sorry, but then naturally nobody told you."

"It can't be true."

He looked at her hopelessly.

"And no explanation?"

"There's got to be an explanation for common murder?"

"I'm telling you Wesley's not that kind of man."

"All right," her father said, "I'll tell you what I know: Montgomery and that deputy Dodds went out there to arrest him. They had a warrant, and they tried presenting it to the sister but she lied and said he wasn't home. So apparently they decided to arrest *her*. That deputy was just putting the cuffs on her when Wesley came out of the house with a shotgun and some stranger at his side—they're saying it's this fugitive that Montgomery let get away—and Wesley told Montgomery and the deputy they were trespassing. They argued, as you'd expect, and in the middle of it Wesley just raised the shotgun and fired. The deputy ran back to get help—he says he was outgunned. They just went out there to retrieve the body."

"That's his story?" Elsa said. And then she was telling him again what a shameless gossip this deputy was and how surely he was only lying to make himself come out the better. But even as she argued she felt her own doubt, her memory of guns stored in the corner of Wesley's closet; and worse, she sensed an inexorable logic at work under the surface of her thoughts. Her father looked down at the papers strewn on his desk. "That's not the point," he said, "as you're well aware."

"Yes," she said, "but we're wasting time. Have you got your keys?"

"In my pocket," he said, and standing, held out one hand as if to give pause. "And I guess you already know I'm against it, and I'll go along only because I can see you'll go ahead without me. But I hope you understand there's nothing you can do for a man like that: when he picked up that shotgun he gave up being a man and went back to the animals, no matter how you choose to look at it." And Elsa was ushering him out of the office and saying, "Yes, yes," as you would to placate a dull-witted and obstinate child. Then they were through the hallway and she was half pushing him into the now-deserted lobby where he paused and said in a whisper that she would have to wait a moment while he gave notice that he was leaving early, and then she stood there appalled as he seemed to take his time speaking to the teller and answering trite questions about what she was to do at closing time.

By the time she succeeded in getting him outside a numb fatalism was beginning to settle in. She had lost already—what? twenty minutes? half an hour?—to the mob, which would probably need only a slight head start over common sense and the law, and then the law itself was in question now that Wesley had gone and shot the one man in the entire county who could have with a single word or glance sent them all back to their homes and jobs complaining bitterly until the next election, when they would file out and unanimously elect him into office again. And now that he was dead, and all self-restraint gone with him, who would keep control? Perhaps they'll beat it out of town, she told herself, as they climbed into her father's car and swung out onto the avenue, the engine cautiously and slowly whirring. Just maybe they'll have the good sense and means to disappear while the main house is being sacked, looted, stripped, and the cottage soaked with gasoline.

And the side of the road filing slowly by, the parade of dry weeds and honeysuckle and oak trees and dogwoods, the yellow and orange colors in the land, good tenable land that ought to look a shade better than a Midwest dust bowl, and the white farmhouses with their tilting roofs and drainpipes running down the corners and their porches open to the air, and the people standing in their yards doing chores or shooting bull and those holed up inside all of them subject to the same brittleness and decay: Elsa watched closely as they wheeled past in slow motion, time for every detail to account for itself, to be weighed and judged in the scale of her memory—the chickens scratching on a gravel drive, the caterpillar tents hanging like webbed tumors in the branches, the dog yammering and twice leaping at its fence. Time for the corn husks to dry a little more, for the river to shrink another inch down the bank. Plenty of time for her to reflect on the worst that might happen: she had read the newspaper reports that occasionally appeared in the *Progress*, knew as everyone throughout the county knew the various stages of a lynching like the parts of a mass: the crime and arrest, then the mob, perhaps no more than a dozen of them willing, far outnumbered by the crowd of onlookers and well-wishers flocking and descending from literally miles around, so that often the railroads would offer special rates to and from the town in question for the usually brief duration of the waiting, then followed by the ritual negotiation and giving up of the prisoner and, progressing quickly now, what everyone had come running to see—the rope cinched to his neck and the torches lighting his clothes, transforming him into a living torch, and the triumphant satisfaction of his howls until, all at once, the prisoner stiffened and the show was over too quickly. Not that the public ritual was through. They would wait by the body while it glowed and shriveled, until what had been a man an hour before resembled a mummy unearthed after thousands of years, and now the cameras came out for the picture-taking, the mob all smiles and composure, standing with the blackened corpse framed in the foreground, waiting patiently for it to cool. And lastly the sacrament: shoving and crowding round with their pocketknives flicked open for the keepsake and hacking, sawing at a finger, a jawbone, or an ear . . . And strangely, as she dwelled on the horror, a perverse sense of calm overcame her. The knot in her stomach seemed to loosen and unwind.

She looked out the window at the fields of sulking grass edging the state road. They were almost at the point where the junkyard rooster and the road sign 2 MI. ZION marked the nameless dirt road where they would turn.

Her father made a dry coughing sound in his throat.

"Montgomery was a friend, you know."

"I know," Elsa said.

"Did I ever tell you the story about that investment we saved from the crash?"

"He mentioned it. Last March, I believe."

"I never told you before?"

"No, you never did."

"Well, that was a heck of a trick we pulled off." He looked down the road nostalgically, and to her unresponsive silence said: "I expect you just forgot. Sometimes I remember stories my father told me that didn't seem to matter or make any sense, especially when I was young, and I'd nod and pretend I was listening and not think about it again for thirty years. And suddenly one day, out of nowhere, there it would be, playing in my ears as though I were just hearing it for the first time. Now Sheriff Montgomery, there was a man who couldn't spare a nickel at the time. Horse races. Did you know he was much of a gambler? I never saw the attraction of it myself, although Sweeny tells me it has a way of getting in your blood."

"Sweeny again."

"He was good enough to give the news about Sheriff Montgomery."

She looked at him as if from a distance.

"You mean—all this—Sweeny said what the deputy said . . ."

"What do you expect, Elsa? Dead men don't talk."

"What a dull cliché."

"Why don't I turn around and take you home—" But in the same moment Elsa was shouting for him to stop and actually reaching out to grab hold of the steering wheel as if she might by merely touching it compel the car to slow down and at the same time craning her neck to see what had appeared suddenly in the rearview mirror, flickering like a shadow in the corner of her eye. Her father hit the brakes, the car jerked and bounced, throwing up a broad swath of dust, and she was out, leaving the car door swinging on its hinge and raising a hand to shade the fiercely beating sun. And she was right: she'd glimpsed him springing across the road like a deer after he must have waited, crouching in the tangle of brush, for them to pass. At a quarter mile's distance she caught his dark, lanky outline disappearing into the woods and then, a minute or two later, reemerging to scuttle up the hillside like a stick figure racing over a patchwork quilt, heading toward the far treeline which stood impassive and seamless as an ivy-coated wall.

"Who was that?" her father called. He was standing beside the car door with one hand on the rolled-down window.

"Nobody," Elsa said, and she turned back relieved, even smiling a little as one who knows a secret nobody else has guessed. Because if the stranger, fugitive, whoever he was, had managed thus far to elude and outwit the mob, then it was possible that Wesley and Cora had also escaped. Yet even as she indulged in such hopes the absurdity of it all nagged at her, the idea of two fifty-year-olds outrunning townsmen with dogs and guns in a part of the county where few Negroes lived. "Come on," she said to her father, rounding the car again and sitting, waiting, "it's a left there at the road sign."

Three older men were leaning against the parked cars, observing with detached interest the movements of the self-appointed deputies up the hillside.

"They ought to come at it from the other side."

"Ought to check for windows first."

Frowning, they traded cigarettes and chewing gum.

"Did anyone catch the Steeplechase?"

"I was there, sure."

"And it was Forty Winks, wasn't it?"

"Ghost Dancer by a neck."

"That filly?"

"She's quick as lightning out the gate."

"You think that's a surprise? I read about the race up in Saratoga and would you believe some no-name horse called Esposa won the prize? Has anyone ever heard of Esposa? And with Count Arthur running second."

A loud flat crack made them pause and look up the hill, where the deputies were quickly crouching and flattening themselves behind various tree trunks and headstones. At the same time a balloon of steel-blue smoke drifted over one of the two front-facing cottage windows, dissolving as it floated straight up in the stillborn air. The men could make out the crack where the gun had fit through and the sill on which it had been leveled.

"Get down," someone shouted.

And another voice with indignation: "They're shooting back!"

At the bottom of the hill the three older men laughed. "Sounds like a shotgun." The others nodded. "What I would do is sneak a couple of fellas around the back." A cloud of yellowing dust was showing away down the road.

"How many you figure's holed up in there?"

"A couple."

"No more than three by their own story."

"Enough to cover all sides?"

"There's probably no window on the stove end."

"Nah."

"Two could do it."

"Sure thing. I had a buddy in the army that said two can defend a foxhole against twenty if both sides are equally armed."

A second report crackled from somewhere in the graveyard and the older men looked speculatively toward the cottage, which showed no perceivable sign of damage. Meantime the approaching car came into view.

"Here's reinforcements," one of them quipped.

"Police?"

The squad car came on slowly, reluctantly, pausing beside the dozen or so cars and pickup trucks haphazardly parked along the roadside or close against the gate, while the officer appeared to look them over. Finally he drove up to the burned and wrinkled watchful faces sneering with casual disdain like socialites at a private party. He put his elbow out the window and left his car engine running. " 'Afternoon," he said, a polite, quiet voice. "How you gentlemen doing?" They coolly nodded. "There any law officers present here?" They shook their heads in tandem. "I see. How many are you?"

"Twenty, twenty-five."

"You laid hands on the suspect?"

"No sir. It looks like a standoff."

"Well. Guess I'd better have a look." He shut off his engine and with great effort stepped out of the car. He stood over six feet tall, trim and hooknosed, with a dark shadow of a beard. "How long you all been at it?" he said.

"No more than half an hour."

"Anyone hurt?"

"Nah."

"Well, they got about five minutes till the rest of the officers arrive."

They were moving up the hill on their bellies like children

playing war, fearful and careful to keep behind cover and therefore confined to the strip of woods directly facing the cottage and the graveyard set a little to the left. To move around either side would mean crossing the open lawn and exposing oneself to fire or else circling farther out of the way than any of them were prepared to go.

"Here comes the brigade," the officer said.

Far down the road they could see the long tendrils of dust snaking up over the roadside scrub, revealing a caravan nearly the size of the original mob's. Soon the roar of the engines and then the squad cars themselves became apparent and discernible through the noise and haze of sun and the townsmen on the hill looked down with a mixture of dismay and relief.

"What you think's taking so long?"

"They just feeling each other out. Kind of like that German and Joe Louis."

"Sounds like that was a good fight."

"Joe Louis standing there in the ring, jabbing and dancing around, expecting to win easy, till that German lays into him. Boom-boom."

"I read about it in the paper."

"It sure was a surprise."

"Louis starts swinging wild. And that German moves in, quick and powerful, takes him to the ropes. And Louis just staggering something pitiful."

"Nobody more surprised than him."

"I would of paid cash money to see it."

"Boom-boom."

"And Louis falls."

"Ring the bell. Fight's over."

The long line of squad cars came careering and braking round the bend in a flurry of horns and headlights, nearly driving one another into a ditch as they wheeled in and parked haphazardly among the empty cars and trucks lining the cemetery gate. And already the officers were getting out, gesturing and shouting orders to the gunmen on the hill. Elsa watched from the rear of the caravan that had overtaken and all but knocked them off the road; her father had pulled over and waited for them to go by. "This is crazy," he said, "somebody's going to get killed." They waited in silence for the last of the squad cars before he would pull out again, compulsively squinting and glancing in his rearview mirror. He drove even slower now, maddeningly slow, crawling along and braking for every bump and rut as if consciously meaning to prolong the torture, his white-knuckled hands firmly gripping the wheel and the sweat breaking out on his neck and running down the bridge of his nose until Elsa worried that he would faint. And she felt that insidious sense of calm coming over her again, telling her there was nothing left to be done. Yet all the while she knew, she understood very clearly: *if only to clear your own name . . .* and she remembered the advice Oscar Wedge had given her earlier that day, Wedge who must not have known the extent to which his client was in danger or else . . . *don't accuse that deputy of anything worse than spitting in the grass.*

And she understood that she would never know the truth, that truth among her countrymen was itself something mutable and artificial, to be shaped to the task at hand, and in fact she could arrange for one of several versions of the truth and choose according to her whim, according to her advantage or even spite. The façade of what she said would be speciously upheld and preserved for the general public good, and in her own mind she was not even certain any longer what she would do. If she altered the deputy's story in a way that distanced Wesley from the crime, she might yet remove the taint from her name, whereas if she contradicted him outright she contradicted and thereby accused the entire community . . . and where would that get her? But there was a bleaker possibility still. Now that Wesley had gone and made himself a murderer there was the chance she was not even relevant, that she'd become disposable, the mere insult that precedes and is eclipsed by the duel. As she brooded upon such thoughts, passing seamlessly and abstractedly through her mind like the leaf shadows flickering over the windshield, they rounded a bend in the road and, keeping their distance from the mob, arrived at the scene of the crime.

By then the mob was loosely netted about the hilltop, semi-organized and drawing in close as they dared, the outraged townsmen with hunting rifles rigged to their shoulders and the officers in their gray and blue uniforms. She could just make out the Wesleys' cottage through the clustered trees and the constantly fluctuating groups of gunmen; the cottage appeared very calm and quiet, indifferent-looking, impossible to believe it could be the source or object of so much violent activity. "I have to go—" Elsa said, and the moment the car stopped she was pushing open the door, still in motion, when her father reached out and grabbed her hand, saying, "Just a minute, I want to get something straight." He sat there unrelenting and immovable in his seat while a vertical bar of shadow snaked over his face and down the front of his shirt. They both looked out the window in surprise; a thin reef of clouds appearing from nowhere serenely crossed the sky, as if dredged from the nearby river. "Before you go making trouble," her father said sternly, "I hope you realize that whatever the reason your Wesley had for shooting Montgomery, this is the price he's got to pay. He knew it beforehand. It's no secret. Every child raised within a hundred miles of here knows."

"Dad—" she said. But he clamped her hand so tight her knuckles began to ache. "Elsa, I want you to understand. You and I may not applaud it, we may wish it were otherwise, but there has to be a way—a mechanism for punishing the crime . . ."

Again she sensed the logic at work under the surface. Why had she rushed out here anyway? For Wesley's sake? As though by simply appearing in the flesh she might counteract this story that already had its own malignant reality? The logic seemed to answer her by subtraction, a paring back of alternatives toward a single possibility. She protested half to her father, half to this other whispering voice: "Even though he never spoke a cross word to me, much less slandered and scandalized me like these others, this deputy, your friend Sweeny have done."

"That's right," he said, "even though they all put the shotgun in his hands, loaded and cocked it for him and pulled the trigger for him too."

"Yes, I understand perfectly—" And she pushed her way through the half-open door, feeling the palpable weight of the heat on the back of her neck. As her foot touched the crackling dirt the entire landscape went into motion as though she'd stepped off a carousel at a bustling fairground. The little hillside appeared blasted by sunlight, overrun with revelers and gawkers and thrillseekers scrambling about here and there in a struggle to carry out the officers' orders—they were shouting "Spread out, you bunch of jackasses!"—while the officers themselves split into pairs: a few of them ambling down the road at a methodical, unhurried pace, a few more fanning up through the graves to stand and gesture with their gun barrels. And the tall officer speaking with three older men by the cemetery gate himself moving closer because she'd fixed on him and was bearing down fast, saying, "Excuse me, officer," in a voice buried under the clamor, until he turned and stared at her in bemusement and shock. "Afternoon, miss."

But she was already insisting: "Did they get away?"

He continued looking at her bemusedly, speculatively, with a touch of mannered reserve. "You must be the young lady in question," he said. The older men looked on in horror. Meantime the officer was wiping his forehead with a handkerchief and telling her not to worry, the suspects weren't going anywhere. He smiled through his shadow of a beard. "If you look up at that cottage there you can see for yourself they're shut in pretty tight."

"Then," she said, groping, "are you the one in charge?"

"In charge," the officer laughed.

Just then from the back of the cottage a mute flat pop reported and echoed down the hillside and after it a spattering, festive sound of firecrackers, followed by the steel-blue cloud ballooning over the cottage roof where it hung blandly drifting as if exhaled from the woodstove pipe. "Maybe you better step back across the road, miss." The officer motioned vaguely with his handkerchief. "It might take a while yet to flush them out."

And her father, furious, calling: "Elsa, get over here."

"A strange business," the officer said. The older men watched her wordlessly like stricken paralytics. "I guess we all know that Wesley good enough. But there's three or four in there to put up such a fight. I never saw anything like it. Never figured him for the type, you know, the troublemaker. It's nothing against him personally, but the law's the law." And then he looked at her politely, chidingly, as if pleading a reasonable case. "Why don't you go over where your father's waiting for you? We'll nab them soon enough all right and there's nothing you can do to help us."

Even as he prattled unhurriedly another car was arriving and unloading its assembly of gunmen and bystanders, a few women and boys, running to ally with the crowd on the hill or else standing in their work clothes at the edge of the road and waving fans at their faces, like puppets stitched together from various odds and ends, blobs of candle wax, wood splinters, and scrap metal, moving with a kind of inchoate unity and sense of purpose, with the primal darkness of a ritual dance.

"I saw the fugitive," she said with surprising calm, "on the road, running in the direction of town. I know his face . . ." But the officer's eyes strayed back over the hillside; he was not going to be the one to disillusion her. "Everybody knows"—and looking squarely at the officer, the last of her vanity choked and obliterated by a single face-saving lie—"he swore to kill Montgomery for putting him in jail."

When at last she turned and left them alone the three older men watched her go silently and with embarrassed displeasure through the dust-fogged afternoon light coloring the road. What this generation was coming to they didn't know. It was a hopeless case. Finally one of them remarked that the officer was right and the law was the law.

"That's God's truth," another said.

"You can't fight the law."

"No sir."

"Looks like a standoff to me."

"That Wesley ought to give himself up."

"He always struck me a little biggety."

The fisherman rowed closer and closer in his timeworn skiff, his oartips dimpling the motionless river, while Wesley in the muck to his knees felt the panicky nag of something he ought to remember, some reason why he'd gone searching for Cora along the flooded bank. He couldn't place it. But for some reason he was smelling a sharp, acrid odor unlike the scent of washed-up fish, and it put him in mind of the woodstove. Then his grandmother's voice was returning, only different, high and strained, and by the time he recognized the voice was Cora's he was sitting up in his chair by the shot-out windowpanes beyond which the mob huddled secretly among the dawn shadows, an invisible presence in the bushes and trees, and the crackling, the scratching sound in the rafters was mixing with that acrid odor he smelled from the riverbank which only now could he place—it was smoke—and he was hearing Cora calling as if from a distance—"William!"—before he realized he'd dozed off . . . could it have been more than a minute? But long enough for somebody to sneak up, to hurl that flaming bottle of gasoline, or whatever it was. Yet it seemed to him still . . . strange . . . he could see the old fisherman rowing, and even as he lifted the shotgun, groping his way toward the door through thickening billows while Cora, halfway across the room, hollered "Don't you go out there, William!"—he sensed the skiff slipping silent over the water and the old man singing in his rough scavenger's voice as he came on, a song like the bitter tiding of eternity.